I0761347

The Dawn-Builder, originally published in 1910, was John G. Neihardt's first novel. At the center of it is a one-eyed, peg-legged man named Waters. He comes to Fort Calhoun, Nebraska Territory, in 1862 and drinks himself into a hole when he isn't setting type on the town's newspaper. Because his thirst is metaphysical as well as alcoholic, he only temporarily loses sight of the possibility of happiness, of building his own dawn. Like all memorable characters, Waters can't be contained on the page. Isolated by his physical ugliness, marked by loneliness not yet deadened by silence, compromised by his own excessive energy, he reaches out to a young woman who is farther outside society than he is and to a kindly widow and her son. *The Dawn-Builder* is reminiscent of Twain in its frontier humor, of Poe in its bizarre adventures, and of Dickens in its casting of some busybodies who belong to the Needle Club. Its return to print will be welcomed by John G. Neihardt's many admirers.

The Dawn-Builder

by

John G. Neihardt

University of Nebraska Press
Lincoln and London

Manufactured in the United States of America
First Landmark Edition printing: 1991

Library of Congress Cataloging-in-Publication Data
Neihardt, John Gneisenau, 1881–1973.
The dawn builder / by John G. Neihardt.
p. cm.
ISBN 0-8032-3330-2 (cl)
I. Title.
PS3527.E35D38 1991
813'.52—dc20
90-21279 CIP

Originally published in 1910 by Mitchell Kennerly, New York.
Reprinted by arrangement with the John G. Neihardt Trust

CONTENTS

PART ONE

THE FIRST NOTCH

PART TWO

THE ISLAND

PART THREE

THE BIG WORLD

PART FOUR

TOWARD THE SUMMER

THE DAWN-BUILDER

PART ONE

THE FIRST NOTCH

I

The Coming of Mr. Waters

To St. Louis, June 3, '62

James Simpson, Esq.,
Editor *Trumpet,*
Fort Calhoun, N. T.

Dear Jim:

The man who will hand you this note goes by the name of Mr. Waters, which will, as I firmly believe from reputation and appearance, prove to be a misnomer. I commend him to you for three reasons: first, because of his wooden leg; second, because of his blind eye; third, because he says he is a printer. I think it was a printer you asked me to send to you. I found him down at the river landing, busy in maintaining a prone attitude, and industriously sunning himself. Mr. Simpson, I take pleasure in introducing to you Mr. Waters.

Yours, etc.,

J. C.

Mr. James Simpson, editor and proprietor of the Fort Calhoun *Trumpet,* read this introductory note with conflicting emotions. He scowled and smiled alternately. The sight of the familiar scrawl of his friend, exciting, as it did, memories of old time friendship, could not quite overcome the irritation caused by the light manner in which the serious predicament of Mr. Simpson seemed to have been treated.

In all the long line of the followers of Gutenberg, Mr. Simpson felt distinguished as the only Job of the profession. During the issuance of six weekly editions of the *Trumpet,* he had employed half as many printers. Each had come, contracted the war fever, and gone—swallowed up by the great angry cloud in the East. As a result, the erstwhile strident *Trumpet* had degenerated rapidly to the station of a child's whistle—a thing of faintness and caprice.

It was for this reason that Mr. Simpson had despatched an appealing letter to his friend in St. Louis, asking that he send not simply a printer, but a printer with unique qualifications. "Send me a printer," he had written, "who is physically disabled for military service in some insuperable manner."

Mr. Simpson looked up from the note of introduction with a scowl hanging heavily from his brow, and fixed a pair of narrowed and bitterly scrutinizing eyes upon the face of Mr. Waters. He saw a man near thirty-five years of age, of medium height, with a pair of broad shoulders, drooped with habits of slouchiness, from which a threadbare coat hung like a visible joke. His head was large, shaped for intelligence, and covered with a heavy tangled growth of yellow hair, that gave every indication of curls, should it ever be encouraged with a washing. The sun-faded ends of his locks nestled affectionately about his ears. His face was shaped for expressions of kindness, but its many lines of past emotions made it bewildering.

The man had but one eye. A pitiful growth of short, sandy hair straggled down his cheeks, and flared up into the semblance of a dying flame where the scrubby moustache gathered in bristles above a sensitive mouth, quivering at the corners, and with lips dried and parched as with long use of stimulants.

As the critical and somewhat disapproving gaze of the editor travelled down from the crown of the man's head, across the shabby face, tanned throat, ragged shirt, buttonless coat, and trousers drawn askew by defective suspenders, he discovered for the first time that the description of his friend was not wanting with regard to the one leg, the left, which was supplied from the knee with a battered iron-shod wooden stump, now nervously beating time on the floor to some careless tune in its owner's head.

When Mr. Simpson's eyes had completed the downward tour of inspection, they began the return trip toward the man's face, re-noting the appearance of the applicant with the least expression of doubt, that rapidly changed as the visual ascent continued, and finally softened into a quiet twinkle of mirth as they reached the level of the man's anxious eye.

"Ever set any type in your life?"

"Quite a considerable," replied Mr. Waters.

"All right," said the editor, "I'll try you."

Mr. Simpson, being a man of much dignity and few words, took a sheet of copy from the hook, handed it to the new type-setter, and motioned him toward an empty stool that sat before the rickety cases, at which a bare-footed, freckle-faced, frowsel-headed boy of about twelve years, laboriously clicked type into a stick with many painful gyrations of mouth and much wriggling of toes, nervous with enormous responsibility.

As Waters stumped toward the cases, the boy rested the unfinished stick upon his case and stared curiously into the single eye of the newly hired.

For a moment expressions of doubt chased themselves among the freckles of the boy's face, then the man's eye twinkled kindly, and he smiled. The smile was a halo that spread and glorified his face.

Immediately the boy responded with an honest, mouth-stretching grin, accompanied by a simpering elongation of the eyes that gave his face the bland expression of a peaceful cat, dreaming in the sun. Still smiling, Waters climbed upon the stool, poked his wooden leg through the rounds, and with the dexterity of one who is happy with the consciousness of friendship, ran his eye down the copy of a pompous war editorial, and the room was filled with the antiphony of clicking type.

II

THE CRIME OF THE ZODIAC

During the second week of Waters' employment, Mr. Simpson announced that he would be away several days, stating that business necessitated a trip to Omaha City, a distance of some twenty-five miles down the Missouri River. The deportment of the new foreman during the previous week had been so satisfactory that the editor felt safe in leaving him in charge of the *Trumpet*.

For some time after the departure of Mr. Simpson on a southbound packet, Waters and the boy sat silently at their cases. Finally laying down his stick, Waters turned his monocular gaze upon the boy.

"What'd you say your name was?"

"Henry Sprangs."

"Would you mind bein' called *Specks?*"

"Huh uh," replied the boy, shaking his head negatively and simpering with good-nature.

"Well," said the foreman, "when I first lay my eye onto you, I says 'That chap ought to be named Specks.' No harm meant, you know."

With a spasmodic industry, partly caused by sudden bashfulness, the two fell violently to sticking type-metal. Suddenly the man again laid down his stick.

"Well, you see," he said, with a comic seriousness in his eye, "I said this way, 'mebbe Specks and me could be cronies.' How'd you like bein' my crony—huh?"

"I'd like it awfully, Mr. Waters."

"Then it's cronies we be—cronies for——" and he extended a big dirty paw to the boy, who took it bashfully—— "cronies for a thous—and—years—and—a—day!"

Waters nervously fumbled in a side pocket of his coat, pulled out a pipe and a pouch of tobacco and fell to smoking desperately.

"You see," he began between puffs, "they hain't many folks that's real true cronies; mighty few of 'em, Specks; mighty few of 'em. This here pipe has been about my only crony for quite a spell. Sometimes I git awfully lonesome, Specks, and then I need a crony."

The least suggestion of a film dimmed the eye of Waters and was reproduced sympathetically in the eyes of the boy.

"You see," he continued, "when a feller gets tired of hisself, w'y then he needs another feller what ain't tired of hisself, to tell him he ain't all bad, less'n he fergits—fergits what his mother used to tell him; to be a good boy, and all that sort of thing, you know. It's durned easy to be bad when you ain't got no crony."

"But you're good always—hain't you, Mr. Waters?" said the boy wonderingly.

"When I ain't lonesome—sometimes, Specks; but then——" and he sighed—"I'm middlin' lonesome most of the time."

"W'y, is your pa and your ma both of 'em dead?" inquired the boy inferentially.

Waters smiled. But this time it was simply the stretching of a parched mouth without the halo.

" 'Tain't that," he said, and fell to work with exaggerated industry.

"And you see," again began the foreman droningly, timing his words with the click of the type, "I could tell you a lot of true yarns about pirates and buried treasures, and how I lost my looker and how I got this wooden kicker; and say, I know where there's a buried treasure!"

"Huh!" The boy's body stiffened into an exclamation point.

"Yessiree, think I'm a-spinnin' you a yarn? Would a feller lie to his crony?"

"Where is it?" cried the boy, converting a half stickful into hopeless pi in his excitement.

"Clost by, Specks, but I hain't ready to show you yet."

The boy fell nervously to throwing in the pied type and Waters puffed his pipe and worked many minutes in silence.

Suddenly the foreman blew a long breath that whirred drily through his lips like a gusty hot-wind wheezing up parched gulches in August.

In an awesome whisper he announced his condition.

"I'm—dry!"

Specks looked at his crony in wonderment and pointed to the water pail, but the foreman shook his head hopelessly.

"Water! When I was just a little squallin' feller," he said, "the old folks called me Waters; never could stand the name nor the thing since. I can recollect that I took to drinkin' milk to onct; drank that till I got so big I was ashamed of myself. But no, siree, I couldn't never get used to water! W'y, Specks—*water!* Do you know what water is made out of? W'y, *oxgyn* and *hydrigin!* Them's both of 'em rank poisons to my system!"

He slapped his hands upon the region of his stomach.

"Reckon you've heard tell of Sahary, hain't you? Well, Specks, this here *is* Sahary!"

Specks dropped his lower jaw in astonishment at the startling geography of Mr. Waters.

"Yes, sir!" continued Waters; "this here is worse'n Sahary. It's somethin' that hain't in the g'ographies, Specks. It's h—e—double—l! Did you ever see clay so dry of an August that it cracked like a sore lip? Well, that there clay was all soaked with wet 'longside of my stomach! I'm *dry,* and things can't never be no wetter till there's moist're; and it takes money to make moist're. Say, Specks, you hain't got some dimes concealed about you?"

It happened that Specks had, and he readily loaned them to his crony, who immediately started for the door. After some time he returned, grinning pleasantly. He threw himself into a chair and produced a large flask of whiskey. He pulled the cork, and placing the flask to his lips, took a long deliberate pull at the liquor.

"It's been pretty danged cloudy fer some time, Specks," he said; "but it's goin' to rain a spell now, Specks, and by and by the sun's goin' to come out."

He took another pull at the liquor and his smile got back its halo.

"I can feel the verd're a-growin' all over my arid trac's," he announced, with a sigh and an expression of supreme comfort. "The birds is beginnin' to twitter in my head."

He put his mouth down over the neck of the flask a third time, and it showered quite heavily for a minute. Then the sun came out.

"Say, Specks," he went on garrulously, now completely oblivious of his work, "don't you know, I love my dear old stomach! Never deny her nothin' whatever. Me and her has been cronies and ached fer emptiness lots of times when we hadn't nothin' else particular to be about. When I die op'lent or rich or somethin', goin' to will everything I got to my stomach. Good in me—eh?"

"Say," he continued amid hiccoughing, "I was borned thirsty; borned that-a-way. Yes, sir. 'Tain't my fault, howsomever. It's the Zodiac's!"

"The *what's?*" gasped Specks in awe at the marvellous verbosity of his crony.

"W'y, the *Zodiac's!*" reiterated Waters sharply. "You hunt me up an almanax, and I'll explain it to you. Yes, that's one a-hangin' on the wall there. Now, Specks, you give me your undivisible intention, as the schoolma'am says; your derisible extension; you know what I mean. Well, do you see that ring around that feller that's got the horr'ble rip into his belly? Well, that there is nothin' more nor less than the Zodiac! Learnin' is sweet—hain't it?"

Mr. Waters' smile was extravagant.

"Well," he continued with the air of a pedagogue, "do you see them there crawdads and lions and tarantellers and billy goats and things pasted onto the ring around that feller with the ripped stomach? Them, Specks, *them* is the signs of the Zodiac!"

At this critical point in the astrological education of Specks, Waters smiled a broad and maudlin smile by way of deepening the impression.

"Yes, sir, Specks, them's the signs of the Zodiac! Now every feller what gets borned has got to be borned in one of them there signs. Understand? If he refuses," continued Waters with impressive deliberation, "if he refuses to be borned under one of them there signs, w'y then he gets the beautiful priv'lege of bein' borned into this here kind and pleasant world snatched from him afore he gets a mouth to squall with about it.

"Now I was borned in this here sign where the feller 'thout no shirt on is a-pourin' out the liquor. They call that feller Aq'ar'us, which means in the Irish tongue, *him that dispenses liquors!* Now perhaps there hain't no happenin' in a man's life that he'd ought to be so careful about as bein' borned. First, he'd ought to pick hisself a good ma; second, he'd ought to aim to get into a rich fambly; third, he'd ought to have some kind of a pa; and fourth, Specks, *fourth,* he'd ought to wait till he can get the right sign. *There* was the mistake of my c'reer! Hang it, Specks, I'd ought to knowed better than bein' borned under that there sign!"

Waters produced a vacuum in the flask in his efforts to drink the last drop. He removed his mouth with a report like that of a distant gun.

"Yes, sir, Specks," he continued with a weary inflection in his voice, "bein' borned was bad enough, but bein' borned under them conditions was abs'-lutely ru'nous! Seemed like I knowed I was bein' borned under a thirsty sign, 'cause the first thing I knowed after I come to, I was a-bellerin' my little lungs out fer a drink. Hain't never got enough to drink yet. Got to be thirsty till they drop me into the bitter hole and kick the clods into my mouth."

At the last weary word, Waters ran down like a neglected clock. His jaw dropped; his eye winked convulsively and then closed with a nervous lid. He leaned limply back in his chair and began to snore.

Specks was frightened; not for himself, but for his crony. He felt a lump in his throat at the thought of Mr. Simpson discharging the foreman. He tried to arouse the heavy sleeper.

"G'off!" muttered Waters, blubbering something with twitching lips, that doubtless would have been masterly swearing, had the lips been sober enough.

Specks sat dejectedly on the floor and rocked his head in his hands. Suddenly he was seized with a strong resolution. Perhaps Mr. Simpson would return next day. By that time there should be at least two galleys of type set. Specks resolved to set the type himself.

With much tugging, he dragged his slumbering crony into a back room, placed a bundle of papers under his head, then went to his stool and fell to work with desperate energy. All day he worked. At times tears came into his eyes and he snivelled softly. For what if Mr. Waters, his first real crony, should go away?

Specks was the only child of the widow, Mrs. Sprangs, whose husband had gone West with the great tide of goldseekers in the early fifties, leaving her in the little Missouri River town, to which he hoped to return in a few years, rich enough to make his wife and little son happy. But as no word had been received since his going, Mrs. Sprangs, little by little, lost hope and accepted widowhood with inward grief and outward resignation. For years she had supported herself and her boy by washing clothes.

Perhaps it was his own life that made the heart of the boy respond to the lonesomeness of Mr. Waters.

At supper Specks was nervous and preoccupied. His tongue, which generally ran at too rapid a rate for his tired mother's comfort, was strangely still. But when his mother, fearing for his health, questioned him closely, Specks ran off into an elaborate rhapsody concerning cronies and buried treasure, through which the name of Mr. Waters ran like a recurring melody.

After supper, Specks again startled his mother by washing his feet promptly at eight o'clock and going to bed without a struggle. This was unheard of, and Mrs. Sprangs fell to sleep that night unusually happy at the prospect of raising a boy with habits of such promising regularity. She felt a warm place in her heart for this Mr. Waters. He must be a very good man, she thought, to exercise so commendable an influence over her son.

But Specks did not fall to sleep. He sat upon the edge of his bed, listening with strained ears to the breathing of his mother. When the breathing at last came with the depth and regularity of heavy slumber, he crept stealthily out of the house and ran at the top of his speed to the office of the *Trumpet.*

Carefully covering the windows that no one might see his light, he lit a battered brass lamp hanging above the cases. Being assured of the well-being of his crony by the sound of heavy breathing from the back room, Specks began setting type with nervous energy.

In the dead of the night he was aroused from his stupor-like attention to his work by a groan from the back room.

"Don't be too plagued hard onto me." It was the voice of Waters, tossing in drunken slumber. "Don't want to be a bad feller, Specks." The voice became fuddled. "You'd ought to know I've been lonesome. Give me a chance." After another period of unintelligible muttering, the voice of Waters came faintly again. "If nobody cared, wouldn't you be like me?" The sleeper turned heavily and began to snore again.

At four o'clock in the morning, Specks placed the last necessary stickful of type in the galleys. Then taking the lamp, he tiptoed into the back room. Waters lay on his back. His face was hardly recognizable as the one that had borne the smile with the halo. It was marked as with years of suffering and mental anguish, and under the twitching eyelids tears sparkled in the lamplight.

III

The Cutting of the Notch

"Say, Specks," said Waters on the Saturday afternoon following his entanglement with the Zodiac, "let's you and me take a boat and go up the river to-morrow. Mebbe I could spin a few yarns about when I was the cap'n of a sailin' vessel and how I lost my eye and my leg; and say, mebbe I could show you somethin' nice about handlin' a boat."

Specks was delighted.

"And then we'd hunt for the buried treasure!" he cried excitedly. Then his countenance darkened. "Don't know as ma would let me go, though. Mebbe if you'd ask her, she'd let me."

"*Me?*"

There was the faintest hint of sadness in the voice of Waters.

The boy's eyes dilated in wonderment. "W'y, my ma is awful good, Mr. Waters," he said; "—and pretty," he added irrelevantly.

"Does she know I hain't got only one eye?"

The boy nodded affirmatively.

"*And* a wooden leg?"

Another nod.

"*And* ragged clothes?"

A third nod.

"Then I'll ask her, Specks."

They worked for some time in silence.

"Say," said Specks, suddenly turning upon Waters, "*grin* when you ask her—like you do at me!"

So it happened that evening as Mrs. Sprangs was wearily putting the fag end of a large washing through the rinse, that Specks, with face beaming premature conciliation, appeared upon the scene, half leading, half dragging by the hand, a ragged and reluctant visitor, who bashfully supervised the noisy evolutions of his iron-shod leg with a downcast eye.

Mrs. Sprangs, a woman in the early thirties, of medium height and rather substantial build, with a winsome motherliness glowing through the many lines of care that seamed her face, raised her head from the washtub and looked at the visitor with a sudden catching of the breath. For a breathless moment her dripping hands hung motionless above the tub.

Waters, venturing a glance upward in the awkward silence, saw the expression of the woman's face and dropped his eye nervously, while his lips twitched as with a bitterness of heart.

"Say, ma, this is him!" Specks cried with a forced joyfulness. Then drawing closer to his crony, he gave the man a friendly dig in the ribs. "*Grin!*" he prompted in a stage whisper.

Waters, like a man who does his duty, raised his eye and spread his lips in a vain attempt to simulate good nature.

"This is Mr. Waters?" said Mrs. Sprangs, hurriedly wiping her hands upon her apron, and extending the first dried to Mr. Waters, who took it limply. "The boy has been talking of nothing else, Mr. Waters. I'm glad you came. Won't you stay for supper? I've got some meat on boiling, and it won't be long."

The voice of Mrs. Sprangs was soft and sincere, and as Waters listened, the skeleton smile took on its halo. Specks, more delighted at the ultimate success of his crony's smile than at the prospect of eating supper together, danced about the place on one foot.

"Goody! You're going to stay, you're going to stay! Take off your hat, Mr. Waters! You're going to stay!"

Grasping the battered headpiece of his crony he politely threw it into a corner and followed it with his own.

During the preparation for supper, Waters administered a shock to his nervous system by carefully washing his face and combing his hair. Then he sat down and wistfully watched the rapid movements of Mrs. Sprangs, vibrating between stove and table. Lulled by the domestic clanking of knives and forks and plates, he closed his eye and dreamed sweetly after his manner. He tried to imagine this place as his home, Specks as his boy, and Mrs. Sprangs——

He did not permit himself to dream further, but opened his eye and looked carelessly out of the window. A strange sweet music throbbed in his blood. The barren stretch of prairie upon which he gazed abstractedly, was touched with the last sunlight that seemed to go into his blood and glorify him.

At supper Waters ate much and spoke little, while the tongue of Mrs. Sprangs ran on pleasantly. Waters listened and heard nothing but music, setting his own indefinite meaning to the sound.

The mother readily permitted the boy to go with his crony next day; and at the insistence of Specks, Waters stayed all night with his crony, that they might get an earlier start.

"I'll put up a lunch for you," said Mrs. Sprangs; "I want the boy to have a good time, because he works so hard, when at his age he ought to be playing, Mr. Waters. And he's a mighty big help to his mother. Times have been hard since Sprangs went away and never came back," she said pensively.

A strange mixed feeling of anger and joy shook Mr. Waters, and emboldened him to ask: "He's dead—Mr. Sprangs?"

Mrs. Sprangs shook her head sadly. "We've give him up."

That night Specks talked himself to sleep about

sailing vessels and their captains, and buried treasure, to all of which Mr. Waters answered only in monosyllables. When at last the boy slept, his dreams were full of an heroic man with flowing yellow locks, who did impossible things, with his eye glaring like a bull's-eye lantern, and his iron-shod wooden leg making small thunder as he ramped about in a confusion of storm and mutiny and shipwreck.

But the thoughts of the other may be said to have been commonplace. He was contemplating the advisability of buying a can of varnish for his wooden leg.

The next morning, the two cronies, reaching the river at sunrise, with a dinner basket, a shovel and a pick (the latter brought at the insistence of Specks), pushed off in a small boat, and Waters with the ease of a skilful oarsman pushed up stream, keeping near the shore where the current was light. He was even more garrulous than was his wont. His face shone with an inner sunlight. He timed the long pull at the oars with the wild air of an old sea-song.

"Guess you never hunted treasure afore," he remarked affably. "Guess mebbe you're wonderin' how I come to know about this buried treasure. Well, Specks, Mr. Waters he helped to bury this one hisself."

Specks opened his eyes wide in surprise.

"Ten years ago," Waters went on, as he pulled

leisurely at the oars, "I was carpenter on the steamboat *Saucy Heels,* runnin' between St. Louis and Fort Benton. One Spring we started up the river with a cargo of whiskey. Keg after keg of it, boy—keg after keg! Think of it! When the niggers was a-loadin' it at St. Louis, mebbe I didn't get dry! There was enough liquor in that boat to drown a boatload of good swimmers all to onc't. All the way up the river I dreamt about swimmin' in seas of the stuff. It was a fine moonlight night when we got to a place about five miles above here. I was out onto the deck a-pacin' up and down, when all of a suddent she stopped with a chug, shiverin' all over like a man does when you shove a long knife blade into him. You're too young to know about that, though. She'd struck a snag, and you could feel her a-settlin' fast. Everybody comes runnin' on deck, but we couldn't save her. Had to lower the boats and get away.

"Well, Specks, when we was pullin' away, the boat settled down until only the stacks was showin'. I pretty nigh bawled when I thought of all that good liquor down there at the bottom and me naturally such a thirsty feller.

"I says to myself like this: 'Mr. Waters, you get the bearin's of that treasure, and some time or other, mebbe you'll be glad you did.' That's what I says; 'cause you see, I knowed that she'd sink in the sand and get buried up, and 'twasn't likely nobody'd try to raise her them days.

"Them days the channel was clost into the Nebrasky side, and the Saucy went down in the channel within a hundred feet of a high bluff that looked something like an Injun's head from down the river, and it had a big bowlder a-stickin' out of it for a nose."

At that moment the boy raised his eyes from the animated face of Mr. Waters and looked up the river. There, about two miles across the expanse of yellow water, was the Indian Head bluff, nose and all. Specks gave a shout of triumph. Waters smiled, but did not turn around.

"As I was sayin'," continued Waters, "while we was a-pullin' away in the moonlight, I got to thinkin' about all that good liquor into the *Saucy Heels'* belly, and I says to myself 'I'd like to be buried like her with a bellyful like her'n, 'cause it *was* good liquor.'

"That night the crew made camp on shore. Along about three o'clock when they was all a-sleepin', I sneaks away, and takin' one of the smallest boats, I takes up the river, keepin' clost to the bluffs. About sunrise I hides in the brush till afternoon. Then I drops down the river, and when I was sure the crew had gone on down the river back to Kanesville, I pulls out to where the boat went down, and ties up to the smoke-stacks. Then I marks the spot.

"I looked up the river and down the river for landmarks. Up the river was a bluff with a sharp point at the top of it and a big tree growin' out of one side of it. Down the river there was another bluff, not so high as the first, and shaped about like a loaf of bread. I drawed a line from the bluff with a tree on it to the bluff that looked like a loaf of bread. I drawed another line from the Injun Head bluff down to my feet, and that last just about struck the other line square."

At the last word Mr. Waters' face suddenly darkened. He began to whistle softly under his moustache, but this time it was not the rollicking sailor's air, but a low, soft, caressing sequence of notes, like an old-fashioned love-song. That which he did next was utterly incomprehensible to Specks. Instead of pushing violently on toward the buried treasure, as the boy would have done, Waters turned the prow of the boat toward the shore, and pushed into a quiet cove over which a large cottonwood cast an inviting shade.

"Let's rest," he said, momentarily breaking the soft thread of the whistled air. Then he pulled the boat on shore, and finding a grassy knoll under the shade, he threw himself upon his back, and for many minutes there was no sound but the lapping of the water on the sand and the drone of a faintly whistled melody.

"Sun's warm," he remarked at length, with a seeming irrelevance that exasperated Specks. "Air's soft!" And the melody began again. "Like to lay onto my back and breathe—jest breathe."

After lighting his pipe he spoke again softly, like

a man in a dream. "Say, boy," he said, puffing violently like an engine taking a difficult grade; "you've got a nice ma—damned nice ma!"

A meadow-lark filled the embarrassed silence with its clear notes. Waters lazily watched the smoke from his pipe ascending in graceful spirals.

"Hain't never goin' to drink no more, Specks," he announced. " 'Tain't no use drinkin' liquor, when it ain't what a feller's been thirsty for always."

Several hours passed, during which Waters spoke little except to answer the questions of the impatient Specks.

"I'm hungry," exclaimed Specks, when he had at last run short of questions and had failed to arouse his crony. Together the two went down to the boat to get the lunch. "You git dinner, and I'll be there d'rectly, Specks," said Waters.

When the meal had been spread, Specks, having repeatedly called without answer, went in search of his crony. Waters was leaning over the side of the boat and gazing at his reflection in the water.

At the sound of the boy's approach, he raised his head.

"Say, Specks," he asked, "could you notice my bad eye *much,* pervidin' you liked me some?"

After dinner, Waters was again provokingly silent, except once when he raised himself upon his elbow and with a rapt expression upon his face, said with a voice like a low cry of supplication: "They hain't no shadders no place! Did you hear that medder lark? I want to believe what he says!"

Then he took a jack-knife out of his pocket and with infinite care cut a deep notch in the upper end of his wooden leg. "Once for every time I'm happy," he explained; and Specks was mystified.

As the two cronies drifted down stream toward home that afternoon, Waters said very little. In fact, this is all he said: "Specks, I guess I'll quit cussin'!"

IV

The Treasure

Upon the following Monday morning the foreman of the *Trumpet* astonished Mr. Simpson and Specks by appearing at the office with a carefully sandpapered and varnished wooden leg; furthermore, the ragged portions of his clothes had been patched with almost feminine deftness. In addition to this the straggling whiskers had been shaved, his ears cleansed, and the erstwhile unkempt hair had been washed and combed, and now glistened with golden curls.

Mr. Simpson, being a man of strong opinions and few words, looked long and critically over his glasses, and finally expressed his surprise laconically: "I'll be cussed!"

Waters simply smiled at this criticism, and all that week was as sunny as his locks of gold.

On the following Saturday evening, he invited himself to accompany Specks home, to the great delight of the boy.

"You see," he said, whistling softly in the midst of a broken sentence, "I want to talk business"—

more whistling—"with your"—ever so softly—"ma."

Mrs. Sprangs, influenced by the praise of his crony, that Specks sang in ecstatic crescendo from day to day, received Waters with a frank cordiality that put a sudden crimson in his weather-beaten and recently shaven cheek.

An invitation to supper was readily accepted by Waters. Throughout the meal, he was entertainingly loquacious. He drew endlessly upon his checkered past for tales partly credible; and his droll and jovial manner drew from his toil-worn hostess more laughter than she had known "since Sprangs left," as she avowed with a sudden drooping of spirits.

At the name of Sprangs the face of the guest darkened perceptibly, as a sunny sky darkens with the passing of a cloud.

When the dishes had been removed, the party of three withdrew to the "front" room. Waters had grown strangely silent. He fumbled his fingers, twiddled his thumbs, coughed and finally broke the silence: "Keer 'f I smoke?" Mrs. Sprangs liked the smell of smoke. "Sprangs used to smoke of evenings," she explained.

Waters lit his pipe and puffed furiously, hiding his troubled face in a gray cloud. When the cloud cleared, he raised a faint and embarrassed voice.

"Well, you see, Mrs. Sprangs—" He could get no further, and proceeded only when he had again clouded his face with smoke, speaking through the cloud. "You see, me and Specks here is cronies. We like each other pretty dam— that is, we think a lot of one 'nother. I says, mebbe you'd oughtn't work so hard. Not as I'd be meddlin', but—" He blew out a great cloud of smoke to hide his confusion—"but—well, I want to give the boy a little money now and then—so's he won't need to work so dam—, so awful hard, that is."

Frightened with his own words, he endeavored to retrieve the disaster. "Looks like it might rain soon!" Feeling foolish, he built a blue fog about his head and blushed in it. When he at length ventured to emerge from his cloud, Mrs. Sprangs was slowly shaking her head.

"It's awfully kind of you, Mr. Waters; you're awfully good to speak of it. But it wouldn't be right, Mr. Waters; it wouldn't be just right."

"Well, I was just a-thinkin', that's all, you know—just a-thinkin', that's all."

Waters spoke as though the matter were of small moment to him. Then he switched the conversation disconnectedly to the weather, as though that were of infinitely greater consequence.

"It *does* look like rain; I see a big bank of clouds in the East as we come up."

In fact the sky had been clear all day.

There was a heavy silence for some moments, during which Waters gave undue attention to his pipe stem, which had mysteriously refused to draw. During the few moments of silence, the man's brain was feverishly active. His face lightened; he thought he had run upon a scheme whereby Mrs. Sprangs would receive aid at his hands. There was the sunken cargo of fine liquors. He knew where it had lain hidden these ten years. He and the boy would discover it together, and he would set up a saloon and sell it. Half the profits would thus rightfully belong to Specks. If Mrs. Sprangs refused to allow Specks to be half owner of the saloon, why then he would buy Specks' interest and pay in monthly instalments. Yet his heart sickened at the thought of the temptation that would thus come to him. It was for this reason that he had suddenly decided to forego further search for the treasure on the previous Sunday, to the great mystification of Specks.

But now it was different. He would discover it—he and Specks. He would not drink—not a drop. And maybe—maybe—who could tell?—in the Spring when the ice went down the river and the robins came and the meadow-larks were singing—well, wouldn't he have plenty of money? Maybe then—when the hills were getting back their green, maybe——

Waters blushed and began to talk in an agitation which seemed wholly unwarranted.

"Can Specks and me go up the river again tomorrow?"

Mrs. Sprangs readily consented. So early the next morning the two cronies put off from the Calhoun landing in a rowboat, equipped with spades, picks and a lantern. There was nothing leisurely about the manner of Waters. He rolled his sleeves above the elbows, braced his legs, and pulled up the stream with a long powerful stroke.

By way of enlivening the conversation, which Waters allowed to lag, Specks made a number of enthusiastic remarks concerning the quality of his crony's rowing.

"Learned it when I was sailin' the sea," he announced with an air of pride. "When I was your age, I was a-stickin' type like you; but I didn't keep at it. Never kept at nothin'; run away to sea; and I was the cap'n of a sailin' vessel onc't," he continued, grunting with his long strokes. "Yes, sir, Specks, *cap'n!* That's how I lost my leg and my looker, you know."

"How?" queried Specks.

"Piruts!" explained Waters laconically.

It was at least the seventh explanation of the calamity, and Specks, in the whole-heartedness of his chumship, did his best to believe them all at once. The required mental effort, however, produced silence.

An hour before noon the two cronies had pulled in to the shore over which towered the Indian Head bluff. The river, which had formerly flowed almost at the foot of the bluff, was now three-quarters of a mile distant from it, having left a flat bottom of sand covered with a heavy growth of willow brush.

The size of the willows indicated that the ever capricious Missouri had swerved from its old channel within a year or two after the sinking of the *Saucy Heels*.

Waters carefully examined the landscape and readily located the other two bluffs; one down stream from the Indian Head, shaped like a loaf of bread; the other, up stream, marked conspicuously at its summit with an unusually large scrub oak standing alone against the sky.

Having placed himself on a line between the two smaller bluffs, Waters, followed by Specks, walked rapidly on among the willows, until he came to that point where a line drawn from the Indian Head's summit to his feet made a right angle with the imaginary line upon which he stood.

"This is about the place, Specks," he said thoughtfully.

Then the two fell to cutting away the willows. The sand being moist was easily piled up. After several hours of hard labor, Waters struck something with his pick.

"There she is!" he cried, and the two fell madly to clearing away the sand, disclosing a level surface, covered with rusty sheet metal.

"It's the hurricane deck of the *Saucy Heels!*" declared Waters; and after a few hollow-sounding strokes from the pick, the rotten wood gave way. Soon Waters cut a hole large enough to admit a body.

Lighting the lantern, he lowered it into the hole, and the two, lying down, gazed into the darkness. A gust of foul air almost stifled them. They saw indistinctly in the ghostly glow of the flickering lantern flame, the interior of a steamboat's cabin. The walls were covered with mold and slime. As Specks gazed, he shivered with dread. The glow of the lantern availed but to cast a sickly illumination in the putrid air, and the deserted aspect of the room, with its scant furniture still in order as though nothing had happened, was like a sick man's memory of a melancholy dream.

"It's the old place," muttered Waters musingly; "the old place."

Then, with a sudden movement, he slung the lantern bail over one arm, threw his legs into the hole, and letting himself down at arm's length, dropped.

The sound of his iron-shod wooden leg, striking upon the damp boards of the floor, was sepulchral. It suggested the impatient grave-digger, kicking an unusually large clod onto the rough-box.

Specks lay upon his stomach, stricken motionless with the dread mystery of the place. He heard the dull whine of rusty hinges; then the sound of coughing, and the iron-shod leg stumping on into another room. The lantern glow was swallowed in the heavy darkness. Fainter, fainter, the reverberating sound of coughing and the stumping of the wooden leg came up to him. Then these were swallowed up as though drunken in by the impenetrable darkness, and there was no sound but the occasional drip of water, echoing dismally in the cavernous night of the place.

"Mr. Waters, oh, Mr. Waters!" Specks' voice rumbled down the darkness, like the sound of a distant explosion; then the awful silence, pierced by the drip-drop of the water.

As Specks listened, he fancied he heard a faint answer, yet he was not sure. It might have been the far cry of a belated echo. A great fear seized him. Had his crony met with an accident in the gruesome place? He thought of going to the aid of his crony, and shivered. No, he would wait awhile; and anyway, he had no lantern. Half an hour passed. It seemed a week. Specks waited, his ears strained in the heavy silence, and his eyes strained in the heavy darkness. An hour passed.

Suddenly he heard a hoarse muffled song; it came up from the hollow earth as though the dead were singing with their mouths half full of grave dust.

> All to the tune of the booming sail,
> The shriek of the blowing sp-r-ay,
> The devil he waltzed up over the rail
> And led the ship as-tr-ay;
> Tra-le-la-le-la-le-O
> Tra-le-la-le-lay!
>
> Oh, I was the cap'n of the ship,
> And I was a merry so-ul;

The fishes stripped my skeleton,
The devil got my so-ul;
With a tra-le-la-le-la-le-O
And a tra-le-la-le-lay!

And it's what if the tides go in and out,
And what if the old world gro-ans,
I sing in the emerald halls of the sea,
And jig with my rattling bo-nes;
With a tra-le-la-le-la-le-O
And a tra-le-la-le-lay.
Oh-ho,
Tra-la-lay!

The song reverberated through the damp chambers, until it seemed a hundred wheezing throats, dry with grave rot, took up the nonsensical refrain. As Specks peered into the darkness and heard the song, he shivered as one whom a nightmare holds speechless.

"With an oh-ho,
Tra-le-la-le-lay."

The song suddenly ceased, as though a great sea wind had blown it out of the mouth of the singer. There grew up from the black depths a sound as of a number of men quarrelling. There were cursings and blows—all muffled as sounds in a dream.

Could it be possible, Specks thought, that there really were such things as ghosts, and that Mr.

Waters was quarrelling over the treasure with those who had followed the river years before?

Specks suddenly remembered the words of Waters: "They hain't many folks what's real true cronies." Was he a real true crony if he left Mr. Waters in possible danger now? No, he would go in search of his crony!

He gathered a bunch of long slough grass, and twisted it into torches. With these under his arm, he jumped down into the boat's cabin, rolling over and over on the slimy floor. When he arose, he stood transfixed and shivering with fear for several moments. Then he took a match from his pocket, and lit a torch. The flaring light made him bolder. He tried to whistle; it wouldn't come.

"Mr. Waters! Oh, Mr. Waters!" he cried, as he pushed through the half open door of the room.

> "With an oh-ho,
> Tra-le-la-le-lay."

Only the wild fragment of a refrain came for answer. Specks found himself in a room in which rotting ropes and rusty chains were piled. There was a stairway leading down into the darkness ahead of him.

> "Tra-le-la-le-la-le-lay,
> Tra-le-la-le-oh!
> With an oh-ho,
> Tra-le-la-le-lay!"

The song came up the stairs. Specks pushed on and started down the steps, that yielded with an oozing sound under his feet. When he was half way down, a step gave way, and he tumbled to the bottom, landing in ooze and slime and total darkness, the torch having been extinguished in the fall. Specks struck another match, and found his torches. He lit one, and proceeded in the direction of the song, which was louder now. He came to another half open door and another flight of stairs, which he descended. Now for the first time, having become accustomed to the darkness, Specks noticed the foulness of the air; it almost stifled him. The torch burned with an impoverished light that filled the shadows with ghosts. Gasping, he held the torch high above his head and pushed on toward the wild song, sometimes rising to a shout and sometimes dwindling to an eerie croon.

He suddenly found himself standing in another doorway, through which he could see a long room, stacked full of kegs, row on row up to the ceiling. The song came out from among the kegs, and Specks hurried toward it, half recognizing, as he thought, the voice of his crony.

"Oh the devil and me
Went out to sea
With a tra——"

As though the singer had been taken overboard

by the wash of a tremendous sea, the song ceased abruptly.

"Stand back there!"

The sharp words, hurled through the shadows in the coarse gutturals of anger, chilled Specks like a gust of cold wind. At a distance of about twenty feet from him he saw Waters, leaning against the kegs. The lantern, with a smashed globe, lay near. He had unbuckled his wooden leg, and now grasped it by the smaller end. The dim light falling upon his face illumined a most terrible countenance. His eye was dilated with the darkness, which had been shattered by the boy's torch, and he blinked wildly in the unaccustomed light. He was haggard, and the light deepened the lines in his face. His hat had fallen off, and his long ruffled hair hung in tangles about his forehead and ears. A keg in one of the tiers near by was dripping from a shattered bung. This explained matters to Specks. Waters and the Zodiac had gotten tangled again.

"Stand back there! Hain't I the cap'n of this here ship?"

Waters swung his wooden leg furiously about his head, the swinging straps at the knee whistling strangely in the stuffy place. He let the missile fly at the boy's head. Specks ducked, and the wooden leg struck his torch, extinguishing it. As the darkness shut in about him, he shrieked and dropped upon his stomach. He lay as close as possible to the slimy floor and shivered.

"Oh, Mr. Waters!" he whimpered softly, hoping to soothe his crony. "Oh, Mr. Waters, I'm your crony—don't you know?"

The shock of the returning darkness and the shriek had sobered Waters partially. "Oh, boy, boy—did I kill you? Yell again! You ain't dead?"

"N-o-o!" whimpered Specks.

Waters crawled on his hands and knees through the darkness, till he reached the body of Specks, stretched face downward on the slimy floor, but very much alive and quivering with fright. He put his arms tenderly about his crony, and they both wept hysterically for awhile.

Waters fumbled in his pocket for a match, hopped over to the globeless lantern and lit it. Then Specks recovered the wooden leg and helped buckle it on. Waters was now fairly sober, but trembling nervously.

"Look, Specks!" he said, pointing to the kegs, piled tier on tier to the ceiling, "thousands of dollars, Specks, thousands of dollars!"

The prospect of sudden wealth destroyed all fear for Specks. He immediately began planning means for carrying a small cargo down to Calhoun. Although Waters was weakened with his recent intoxication, the two managed to get five kegs of the liquor to the room in the upper cabin which they had first entered. They stood several kegs on end, and Waters was thus enabled to reach the hole in the roof, and draw himself up. Then, with the use of a rusty chain, found in the next room, the kegs were hoisted through the hole.

Having covered the opening carefully with willows and sand, that the place might not be discovered should any one pass that way, which was quite improbable in that early day, the two cronies loaded the boat with the liquor and started down the river.

As they floated down the stream in the cloudless starry night, the two organized the firm of Waters & Co., Liquor Dealers, and Waters announced that he would run the business, with Specks as silent partner.

Then the conversation languished. The senior member of the new liquor firm was wrestling with his conscience. For half an hour he was endeavoring to reason away a persistent shame over his recent entanglement with the Zodiac.

That which he said, when at last he broke the silence, was incomprehensible to Specks, but no doubt it meant much to Waters: "Specks, you have always got to figger on a feller havin' guts!"

V

Waters & Co., Liquor Dealers

When Waters came to the printing office on the following Monday morning, he made an announcement that fairly knocked the wind out of the *Trumpet.* It did not blow for three weeks. The foreman tendered his resignation to Mr. Simpson, and insisted that the same should take effect at once. He spoke his piece with his hat in his hand and triumph in his eye. The speech in which he explained that he was forced to take this sudden step through an unforeseen stroke of good fortune, had cost him several sleepless hours the night before, when he had drawn on his memory of the pompous war editorials he had set up, that his resignation might be couched in terms befitting the dignity of the senior member of the firm of Waters & Co.

Mr. Simpson built a blue fog of profanity about himself, and said things in it somewhat derogatory of the general character of Luck. When the first burst of wrath had allowed the blue fog to clear away, the foreman had departed, and the sound of his retreating iron-shod leg came in faintly at the door.

That day, there was a new topic under discussion at the grocery store. For weeks past, no new bad man had been reported, no Indian "skeer" had been scattered by the freighters, and the wisdom of the loungers had been lavished upon the unsuspecting leaders of the great war. But upon this particular day the war was shamefully neglected.

"They's somethin' mysteerus to it!" said the grocery man to his audience; "somethin' mysteerus!"

"Who? What?" inquired a newly arrived delegate.

"Why, ain't you heerd? That one-eyed, wooden-legged printer and the speckled youngster of the widder's is building a saloon down by the river!"

"A saloon?"

"A saloon!"

"And Waters has throwed up his job!"

"Throwed it up?"

"Throwed it up!"

"Somethin' mysteerus about it!"

"Looks that away!"

"Where'll they git the liquor?"

The grocer smiled a superior smile for answer.

"That Waters is a strange feller!"

"Folks hes it that he was onc't a pirut!"

"A pirut?"

"A pirut!"

"What's the boy a-helpin' him for?"

"Hain't you heerd?"

Most of the audience shook its head negatively.

"Hain't Mrs. Sprangs a widder?"

The collective mouth of the audience stretched itself into a knowing grin.

"Sweet onto one 'nother!"

The collective mouth of the audience laughed.

"Leastwise, that's what folks is sayin'."

"But the liquor?"

"Mysteerus."

That afternoon there was not a prune nor a pipeful of tobacco sold at the grocery store. The social centre of Calhoun had moved down to the river, and the shack, which Waters and Specks were building, was that social centre. While Waters sawed and hammered, Specks was engaged with a cottonwood board and a can of paint, with which he was elaborating a sign, which, when completed, read as follows:

Berried Trashure Buffit
Waters & Compny

The onlookers gasped with wonder as the sign developed.

"Buried Treasure?"

"Buried Treasure!"

"Ah!"

"Oh!"

"But the liquor?"

"Mysteerus!"

"Looks like a pirut!"

"Who knows? Mebbe that's why he's got only one leg and one eye!"

"But the liquor?"

"Mysteerus!"

When the two cronies had finished their work for the day, the crowd followed them up the street, keeping at a distance compatible with piratical possibilities. That night the convention at the grocery store did not adjourn until the lamp burned out. The convention, unconventionally, came to a conclusion: That Waters was an ex-pirate; that Waters and Mrs. Sprangs were sweet "onto one 'nother," and that the liquor problem was utterly mysterious.

But the sensation of the week reached its climax on the morning of the second day, when the buried treasure buffet opened for business with five kegs of liquor in stock.

An habitual lounger, arriving late at the grocery store, out of breath and wiping his moustache, dropped the news in among the loungers, dozing in the morning heat, as a small boy drops his stone into a slumbering frog pond, and with like effect.

"Huh!"

"Just come from there!"

"Where'd they get it?"

"Dunno."

"Good liquor?"

"Slips down like goosegrease!"

One lounger got up from the counter where he had been reclining, and sauntered out into the street. The gossip went on.

"Buried!"

"Buried?"

"Buried Treasure!"

A second lounger dropped silently out of the conference. Then a third and a fourth, until the grocer, finding himself alone, got up, stretched himself, yawned, and after carefully locking his front door, hurried toward the indisputable social centre.

When he entered the shack, which was the "Buried Treasure Buffet," he found the place crowded. Waters, behind the cottonwood bar, was beating rapid bass with his iron-shod foot to the tenor of the silver which he raked into the till. His one eye had more than the brilliance of the ordinary two. His hair was carefully combed. His tanned neck was imprisoned in a high white collar, and his face glistened with triumph—assisted by a recent shave.

A bare-footed boy gazed in at the door with a light on his face that made his tan and freckles transparent. He was engaged in hopping about on either foot, and making fantastic motions to attract the busy eye of Waters. When for a moment he was successful, he winked a wise wink as of one who means to say: "We know!"

"Where'd you get it?" inquired a customer, bracing himself to hold his place at the bar, and wiping his mouth luxuriously.

"Where in thunder *did* you get it? Gimme 'nother!"

"Well, now," began Waters, drawling with an air

that savored of mystery and wisdom; "has any of you fellers ever heard of magic?" Then he hurried to fill another bunch of glasses at a dripping tap.

"Magic?"

"Uh huh," answered Waters, and he accompanied his laconic reply with a movement of the hands like a prestidigitator. Everybody looked at everybody.

"Well, mebbe you're lyin' and mebbe you hain't—gimme 'nother!"

By sundown, Fort Calhoun was on its sea-legs. The night was like a night of celebration. Everybody seemed to be out on the street making noises. The very dogs caught the spirit of the hour and howled up and down the town.

Late in the night, the senior member of the firm of Waters & Co. closed and barred the door of the Buffet; then he counted his money. The result almost staggered him. This sudden success gave him a wild desire to celebrate the events of the day.

He took a glass from the bar, placed it under the tap, and ran it full. Tremblingly he put it to his lips that burned to receive the draught. A mist passed before him. In the mist was the vision of a little weather-beaten house. Then the vision faded and was replaced by a neat "front" room with a trim, plump woman sitting in it. The face of the woman was patient and kind. And lying upon his stomach at the feet of the woman was a boy with a tanned and freckled face.

The mist passed, and Waters was staring upon the glass of brown liquor. A light went over the face of the man. He dropped the glass to the floor, and ground it into fragments under his foot.

VI

The Cry of the Lonesome

The Summer grew old and the fame of the Buried Treasure grew big in the land. It reached even so far as Omaha City. Steamboats, that ordinarily plied in contempt past the little port of Calhoun, began to put in for a few hours to accommodate passengers who were lured by the mystery of this excellent liquor to be had of Waters & Co. Freighters, cowboys, settlers, came many miles as pilgrims to test the magic of this Western Lourdes. So heavy was the liquor trade that Waters & Co. made regular nocturnal trips twice a week to the sunken cargo, and the wonder of the thing grew into an almost superstitious awe, when an exhausted supply of the evening was replaced in the morning.

As the Summer passed, the character of Waters became grave. He drank no more, and the careless manner which characterized him on his first appearance in Calhoun, passed away. He joked no more with Specks; he told no more tales of mutiny and shipwreck. One fixed idea swayed him. He, who had wandered all his life among men, companionless and lonesome, was about to hear a kind voice of companionship, feel the touch of a warm hand in the darkness. In the stillness of the years he had waited, and his ears were busy fashioning the long-awaited voice. In the darkness of the world he had walked, and his dream toiled to build prodigious dawns in the heavy darkness.

During the first week of his business career, Waters formulated the plan of his life. He would wait until his share of the earnings of the firm should reach a thousand dollars; and then—well, then, he would build his dawn; he would hear the voice, he would feel the hand.

Every Saturday evening he had given his crony half the earnings of the trade, insisting that this was merely a weekly instalment of the purchase price of Specks' half interest in the discovery.

Mrs. Sprangs had ceased to take in washing, and consequently the gossips of the village worked overtime.

One Sunday morning in early September, Waters arose early and after carefully cleaning his varnished wooden leg, dressed himself in a new suit. When he appeared on the main street of the village a sensation was the result. Waters in a new suit was a paradox. But he was blind to the eyes riveted upon him, deaf to the babble of loungers about him. The night before he had counted the thousandth dollar, and that day he would build his dawn.

He walked rapidly up the street, and as he walked,

a faint light grew in his soul, as when the first spark of the dawn glows with the breath of the morning. When he had come in sight of the little weather-beaten cottage, about which his dreams had thrown a halo, he stopped suddenly, and stood, nervously beating time in the sand with his wooden leg to some tune in his head. At length, he wheeled slowly about and retraced his steps.

The spark sank into the grayness of ashes.

After walking slowly to the other end of the town, he turned as if by sudden inspiration, and walked rapidly up the street again, past the wondering loungers, whom he neither saw nor heard.

"Airin' his new duds!" was the unanimous verdict.

When Waters again reached the spot where he had stopped before, he stopped again, started nervously, stopped, pushed the sand about with his foot, and again turned, slowly walking down the street, his head drooped, his lips moving with unspoken words. All that day he was not seen again. Had the loungers witnessed the manner in which he spent that day, public sentiment might have hinted at insanity.

He sat upon a heap of sand near the river, at intervals tossing pebbles with infinite care into the muddy stream. "If I hit that bubble," he would mutter to himself, "she will; if I miss, she won't. She will—she won't—she will—she won't." The words ran persistently in his head like the fragments of a half-forgotten song.

For hours he sat with his elbows upon his knees, and his face resting in his hands, gazing into the muddy water. At length he was aroused by an unusually large cluster of bubbles, floating into the area of his vision. He grasped a stone at his feet and hurled it powerfully at the floating bubbles, as though he were striking at an imaginary foe. The missile went wide of the mark. Shaken with sudden and mysterious anger, Waters leaped to his feet and stalked toward the town. That evening, in the late twilight, a stumping figure hurried through the dark back streets of the village toward the house of the widow. Unfalteringly it approached a window, from which a shaft of light fell, cutting a space of kindness from the deepening gloom.

It was Waters. He stood in the shadow and looked within wistfully, as one hungry might look through the windows of a banquet hall. Mrs. Sprangs sat near the table reading. Her face had lost some of its weariness, and Waters felt a great joy. Near the woman sat Specks, also reading. The scene was like a draught of wine to the man without. It was a far gaze from the heights of Pisgah.

Waters approached the door, and lifted his hand in act to knock; faltered, then slowly removed his hand. As he did so, his gaze fell upon his wooden leg, smitten with the shaft of light from the window.

His heart sank; a cloud went across his dawn. Slowly turning, he walked away, and did not look back until he was out of the village with the open prairie about him.

The first peep of the rising moon silvered the hilltops. Waters walked in a dream of bitterness. " 'Tain't no use," he muttered, " 'tain't no use. She'd be ashamed of my kicker and my bad eye. 'Tain't no varnish that can varnish me!" After walking some time in silence he suddenly found himself upon a bluff, overlooking the far stretches of the Missouri, its turbid waters transmuted into silver with the moon which had now cleared the horizon. Before him, the river lay a glinting lake, that narrowed with distance into a thread of tarnished silver, extending into the mist.

As he gazed, the far cry of a pack of coyotes in the shadows of the hills shivered icily through the air, as though the cold and lonesome light had grown vocal. It was a cry of kinship to Waters. The instinct of the lonesome wild animal in a strange jungle seized him. Involuntarily he raised his face to the sky, and answered the plaint of the coyotes with a long loud cry that was less than half human. The echoes came back faintly from the bluffs and the heavy silence of the night returned.

As Waters gazed into the broad translucent night, a feeling of reverence shook him, as a wind shakes a scrub oak clinging to a barren bluff. The bitterness of the man's heart died out. He extended his arms into the silvered night and hurled his voice outward into the empty spaces.

"Le' me be happy!" he cried.

But for the faint echoes of his own voice, the night seemed to contain only the cold glow of the moon. Involuntarily Waters knelt and hid his face upon his knees. He remained thus for some time. Then he leaped to his feet as though a hand had touched him. Hope had returned, and there was a small rift in the cloud that hung across his dawn.

Was it that he had heard or felt God?

Perhaps. Yet it was this thought that ran like a merry lilt in his brain: *"I will send to St. Louis for a cork kicker!"*

VII

The Cork Leg

During the next week, a southbound packet put in at Calhoun. While drawing a glass of "Buried Treasure" for the captain, Waters opened a conversation. He stated that he was interested in cork legs. The conversation ended satisfactorily by Waters appointing the captain agent for the purchase of a cork leg in St. Louis, and by placing an adequate sum in the hands of the captain, including purchase price and a liberal commission.

"I'll send her up by the first boat north," said the captain.

When the boat pulled out into the stream, Waters stood on the landing, watching wistfully. He waited until the sound of the exhaust grew fainter and fainter, and died down a bend of the river. Then he gazed abstractedly across the stretch of yellow water, watching the trail of smoke slowly fade into the blue sky.

That day was the beginning of a new and strange restlessness for Waters. Often he caught himself leaning idly across the bar while thirsty customers waited. Mentally he was viewing himself upon two legs that had real shoes at the ends of them.

Would the sun persist in sticking in the sky when it should have set hours before? Would the nights never pass? And why did the dawns lie so lazily in the east when they should have been burning the zenith or racing down the decline of the evening? Often, half unconsciously, Waters would wander down to the landing and gaze down stream, straining his eyes to catch the first far hint of smoke from a steamboat's funnels. Every sound startled him; he was constantly listening for the rumble of a steamboat's whistle. His senses of sight and hearing became abnormal. They monopolized his brain with torrents of false messages. He hardly felt or tasted or smelled; he only heard and saw—heard steamboat whistles, saw the smoke of packets.

For weeks he lived in such suspense, the slave of the two usurping senses. In vain he strained his ears for the far rumble of the whistle; in vain he gazed for the thin trails of smoke in the south.

But one day, near the last of October, the cloud appeared and the whistle sounded. Waters was ecstatic. He threw his hat in the air and shouted until he was hoarse. Then he laughed until he was sad, and tears came. The grocery store joked that night over the supposed drunkenness of Waters.

It was late evening when the boat pulled in to the landing. Waters was the first to put his foot on the gang-plank. The question which he put to the captain, and the manner in which he put it, convinced the crowd of listeners as to the temulent condition of the senior member of the firm of Waters & Co.

"*Where's my leg?*"

The captain remarked with a superior smile that he'd burn eternally if he knew; it surely was not fastened to *him!*

Waters slinked out of the crowd of merrymakers, who were preparing for a dance on board the "last boat up." The first and last boats of a season were events in the life of every little river town, and were received as such. This boat was on its way to the north, where it would winter.

The promised dawn of Waters died out like a flame unfed. He walked slowly up to the buffet, entered and turned the lock behind him. Without lighting the lamp, he went behind the bar, took a glass and sat down by a tapped keg of liquor. He ran the glass full and drank it at a swallow. This was followed by a half dozen others.

" 'Tain't no use," he muttered feebly, like a sick man; " 'tain't no damned use."

The distant sound of the fiddle and the shuffle of dancing feet were heard dimly from the boat.

"This here world was made for wolves at first," he mumbled, but half audibly, for the kegs and the bar began to whirl in a giddy dance. Everything was dancing. The people were dancing on the boat; the very darkness was dancing about him.

"Made for wolves," he reiterated with a dizzy swing in his voice; "but they chased all the damned wolves out and things has been awk'ard ever since!"

He grasped impotently at the whirling darkness. It wouldn't stand still, but spit impudently at him, derisively at him, with lurid sparks.

Life is a hunt for happiness. The game is scarce and the hunters are many. They who miss the game, grumble because they have not found it. Men go a-hunting for happiness as they would go a-hunting for jack-rabbits, seeking it by its tracks. A few learn that happiness grows out, not in. Waters had thrown all his hopes of happiness upon the attainment of a piece of cork.

As he gazed into the dizzy darkness, it seemed that a brilliant light grew out of the shadow, and in the centre of the light, as in an aureole, the face of Mrs. Sprangs. The light from the face smote him like a fist in anger, and he fell backward upon his elbows, trembling.

As he stared, the brilliance faded into a melancholy gray, out of which a huge cork leg, as though fastened to a ponderous but invisible body, stalked toward him. Impotent with terror, he heard the dull pounding of the approaching foot. On came the Leg. It stepped upon his toes, strode up his leg, over his body, which at every step was racked with dull twinges. It stepped upon his throat and choked him. Its weight crushed him to the floor, and with a dull thud it planted its ponderous foot over his eye. His brain ached with the weight. And then he saw no more, felt no more, until the gray of the dawn aroused him.

VIII

The Epic Cry

Winter had shut in about Fort Calhoun—the lonesome, bitter Winter. There is nothing, perhaps, at once more majestic and hopeless than a prairie Winter when the country is new. In the Summer there is something so generous, even prodigal, about the prairie. It gives its best lavishly. It is big-hearted and kindly careless. It is a benevolent giant, clothed with vast blue spaces, shaken with sudden anger, subdued with sudden pity. It is this that makes the Winter terrible: the great heart fails—a Titan's despair.

From a window of the Buried Treasure Buffet, Waters had watched the failing of the mighty heart. He had gazed upon the hills that daily became more seared with the first frosts. He had gazed upon the river, from the time the first ice began running until the stream was choked from bank to bank.

He saw all this, and he became akin to the great silent prairie, because his heart was bitter with a despair that was as an echo of the great white Despair without.

Little by little he had drifted back to the old bitter consolation, back to the Zodiac with its one unfortunate sign. He drank much, said bitter things about the world, and constantly accused Aquarius. He had not visited at the home of Specks since early in the Fall. Whenever he found the face of Mrs. Sprangs growing up in his head when he closed his eye, he invariably aroused himself, and had another drink.

Even the cork leg, which would come with the first steamer in the Spring—surely it would come—but what the deuce was the difference?—even the leg had become a doubtful good. To be sure, in his dreams it preached to him a winsome gospel of happiness; but when he awoke Waters sneered it aside for a lying prophet. Then he drank more than he wanted, said bitter things about the world, and constantly quarrelled with the Zodiac. Who does not, secretly at least, quarrel with some Aquarius?

One morning in early February, Waters sat looking up the stretches of the river to the north, where the landscape hourly grew dimmer with the increasing scurry of fine dry snow, driven by a light southeast wind.

As he sat gazing, the door of the shack opened, admitting Specks and a bluster of snow.

"Hello, Specks!" cried Waters, attempting to be jovial. "Goin' to blizzard, think?"

"Ma's sick!"

"Huh?"

"Ma's sick!" repeated the boy breathlessly, and with an appeal in his eye. "She's about to die!"

"Huh? Sick!" Waters leaped up, shaken with a strange mixed passion, including shame, pity, affection, sorrow.

"About to die!" The words were so many heavy blows. As by a miracle, the long rejected gospel of the cork leg became convincing. The lying prophet was vindicated. The Summer with the teaching of the meadow-larks came back again. "About to die!" The little weather-beaten cottage grew up very plainly before Waters. The face of a woman blossomed out of the mist that passed before him. Why did it seem so very near, just as it was about to pass away?

"Did the doctor say so?"

"There's no doctor nearer than Omaha City," Specks answered; "and nobody'll go, because the road's so bad; and she'll die, Mr. Waters!"

Waters breathed heavily.

"Maybe she's dying now!" exclaimed Specks nervously, as he dashed wildly out of the door and disappeared in the spindrift of snow. Waters stood motionless, staring out upon the white stretch of river and bluff and prairie, like a man in a dream. He hardly thought; he was dazed.

Suddenly something out of the great white spaces went into his blood and shook him like a strong wind. It was the spirit of magnificent Defiance, the spirit that sleeps in all Sublimity, in the immensity of the ocean, the vastness of the prairie, the magnitude of mountains. He heard the Cry of the Epic.

The wind was whipping into the northwest. With the fine snow that lay upon the ground, this meant much to one who knew the prairie. Waters wrapt himself carefully, drew on a pair of heavy mittens, placed a bottle of liquor in his pocket, and went out into the storm, locking the door of the shack behind him. He had decided to walk to Omaha City. He would get there by midnight—if the wind—if the wind—

The northwest boomed with a sudden wild gust, and swept the half articulate words from his lips. It was a challenge. Waters heard and understood. He would battle with giants that day—great white pitiless giants, huge, volatile, writhing, biting, hissing, stinging giants.

A man is very small in a quiet prairie. He dwindles to a speck when it is in anger. Waters turned his back to the storm without a thought of giving up the undertaking. The long-endured bitterness of heart had taught him the abandonment of self, and the Cry had expanded him, filled him with the defiant joy of the fighter.

He felt no fear of that which he knew to be before him. The contemplation of the possible odds thrilled him.

The light snow scurried in long snake-like streamers past him and hissed about his feet. *Boom!* The northwest had burst into a hurricane! It was the ultimatum of the Elements to the enemy—a man with one eye and a wooden leg.

The enemy tottered, floundered for a moment in the snow, blinded with the sudden fury of the attack, then set his teeth and trudged into the seething gray twilight of the storm. A strange, one-sided battle had begun. It was the violence of the Infinite sustained by the defiant Finite. Titan blows fell upon the pigmy.

Yet there was no eye to look into the narrow zone of battle, hemmed with the writhing, sibilant snow maze that conjured late evening under the noon.

It is easy to imagine the many elemental phenomena as being merely the human passions projected upon a larger canvas. A cyclone is sudden anger, a south wind is feminine tenderness, rainfall is grief, the Spring sunshine is love. Madness is the conglomeration of all passions. A blizzard is the madness of the air. It has the blind fury of anger, the hiss of hate, the shout of joy, the dusk of melancholy, the shiver of fear, the cold sting of jealousy; and when its force is spent, it wraps its victims in a shroud of white, which may be an act of love—a savage love.

A blizzard transforms. What it touches it leaves grotesque. It annihilates the boundary line of light and darkness. In its breath the night becomes merely a deepening of shadow upon the dim twilight of the day.

"Have to keep to the river," muttered Waters; "—to the river—to the river—to the river." The words went on running in his head. He trudged and floundered on for some time—perhaps hours; he did not know. In a blizzard, even the sense of time is lost.

Suddenly he was conscious of a stinging sensation on the left side of his face. He had been walking with his *left* side to the wind; whereas, the wind blew *down* the river.

"Back to the wind—back to the wind—back to the—oh!" He had struck his head against a tree. "A tree! I must be in the bottom east of the river," he thought confusedly. He tried to think clearly about the matter; but nothing would come clearly. He was dazed. His thoughts whirled dizzily, even as the snow.

"Oh, yes," he muttered, as if with sudden inspiration; "back to the wind—back to the wind—back to the wind." And he trudged off, stepping in time to the drone of his addled brain.

After he had walked for hours and hours, as it seemed to him, still keeping step to the drone of his head, he again ran against a tree. The shock aroused him. He fumbled about the trunk and with a sinking of the heart, he thought he recognized the same tree that he had struck before. Breathless, he leaned against the tree and tried to think.

Oh, yes—the liquor! It was the liquor he had

been looking for all the time. Strange that he had not thought of the liquor! He drank a great draught, and the delirium passed.

For the first time he noted that it was night. He must have been walking five hours; and where was he? "I'm lost—lost—lost," he muttered, stalking rapidly down the wind into the mad night. "Lost—lost—lost." He kept time to the terrible words.

Suddenly the writhing darkness ahead of him was illumined with a soft light, and in it grew the old vision—the weather-beaten cottage, the cheery sitting room—the woman's face. Ah, the woman's face! Yes, it was that he was looking for. Surely it was that, and not the liquor at all. Not the liquor!

As the light and vision were swirled away into the dizzy darkness, reality came upon Waters as a shout to one who is asleep. He was going after the doctor to Omaha City—the doctor for Mrs. Sprangs. Again the buffeting of the storm maddened him. A great anger shook him. With his teeth set, and his back to the great wind, he strode into the storm. The rage of a fighter in the face of overwhelming odds was in his heart. He swore and struck at the storm with his clenched fists. He wished that the wind might materialize into a wild beast, that he might die with his teeth set in its neck.

But a blizzard is an anger without intelligence, a bodiless foe, an enemy without nerves. It knows not its strength for attack, and feels no blow of defence. It is irresistible and invulnerable.

Waters began to stumble and fall frequently. Once he fell upon his face and was half persuaded to lie still. The wind's shout, however, would not let him sleep. "*The doctor—the doctor!*" it shouted and roared and shrieked, until he arose with difficulty and pushed on into the storm. Once his heart leaped with the joy of sudden hope. He saw specks of fire before him. Surely they were the lights of Omaha City. He dashed on wildly, but the specks of fire were sucked away into the vortex of the night.

Waters wanted to lie down and sleep. But the wind was so noisy with its shouting. Why would not the wind let him sleep? All about him were beds of down—warm pleasant beds; but the wind went on shouting about the doctor. And he strode on.

Despair crept icily through his veins. There is a terrible strength and power for endurance in desperation. Hope avails to goad the limbs only until that moment when the limbs become feeble; then it vanishes, and despair fights defeat. More heroes are the product of the probability of failure than of the possibility of success. It is the difference between the narcotic and the stimulant.

A time came when even the sense of despair left Waters. He felt nothing. He was simply a thought blown about the darkness on a pitiless wind; and that thought was about the doctor. He laughed hysterically when, in his delirium, he saw the streets of Omaha City, up which he walked right to a door that had a doctor's name upon the plate. He put out his fist and knocked feebly. Then a sense of ease came over him. He lay down in front of the door and swooned deliciously into sleep.

The wind shouted no more; it was quiet that he might sleep.

Early the next morning, after the departure of Waters for Omaha City, a man living upon the outskirts of Calhoun, ventured out into the storm to go to the grocery store. As he pushed through the still blinding flurries, he stumbled against the body of a man. It was Waters. Bewildered by the storm, he had travelled all afternoon and most of the night within a short radius of the town, and had fallen with exhaustion almost where he had started. His discoverer, with the aid of a neighbor, carried him to the grocery store.

"Think you can go right off, doc?" said Waters, when at last he awoke from the lethargy of the cold. He looked up from the counter upon which he lay, and was surprised that he did not see the doctor's door with the name upon it.

"Come now, Mr. Waters, don't be a goin' off that away," said the grocer soothingly. "We all knows how a feller gits when he's—well, *that a way!*"

"How?" Waters asked peevishly.

"Well, now, Mr. Waters," continued the grocer, in the wheedling tone one uses to a sick child, "well now, you see, mebbe you've been the least mite subject to spirits; that is, mebbe you've been drinking. You see, we found you out in the street under a snow bank, but you hain't hurt much; snow pertected you. You'll come round."

"What 's that?" cried Waters; "drunk? Can a man walk to Omaha City in one night and git drunk, too? Who brung me here? I just laid down by the doctor's door to sleep. Awful tired. Just laid down to sleep, and here's all you fellers grinnin' at me. What's it mean?"

The grin widened, and one produced a half-emptied liquor flask. "This your'n?" said he.

Waters mumbled something about it being his flask, and that he had taken a drink by the tree. "Couldn't have got there without it," he muttered. "Never would've found myself without it."

"B'lieve he's gettin' 'em!" whispered a lounger rather audibly to the grocer.

"Snakes," returned the grocer with a positive nod.

"You fellers is all damned fools!" cried Waters. "Le' me up!" And to the surprise of all, the lately resuscitated arose and tottered out the front door.

When he arrived at the Buried Treasure Buffet, he took a drink, lit a fire, and discovered that his hands were aching, and that several of his fingers and toes were numb. "Must have laid out somewhere," he mused. "Funny—danged funny! Where'd they find me? Mebbe I was just drunk.

But no, I can remember starting fair and square enough, just after Specks was here. Can't remember drinkin' any more after that."

Waters' head was dull, and he ached as a result of the exposure. Was he to believe himself, or the loungers at the store? Had he really fought with the storm? Or was it only the nightmare of a drunken sleep. He lit his pipe with difficulty and tried to smoke. But the smoke didn't agree with him. "B'lieve I'm sick," he said. He felt stunned. He lay down upon a couch near the stove, and an hour later was awakened from a feverish doze by the entrance of Specks.

"Ma's almost well!" Specks announced joyously. "She's glad now we didn't send for the doctor."

Waters looked in a peculiar, dazed way at the boy.

"You sick, Mr. Waters?" he asked, his spirits falling as he drew near the couch.

"Caught a little cold, Specks—just a little cold like." He took the boy's hand in his. "Did Waters ever lie to you that you knowed of, Specks?" he said slowly. The boy's head shook a violent negative. "Well, yesterday, after you was here, I went to Omaha City after doc. Bad storm, Specks; never see the like. It was hell froze! But I got there, Specks, and I told doc. Didn't he come?"

A shadow of embarrassment went over the face of the boy and he looked down his nose.

"How'd I get back, Specks? Tell me that! How'd I get back?"

"You're sick, Mr. Waters," said Specks; "don't you think you'd ought to sleep?"

Waters with eye strangely dimmed stared long at the boy, and then said feebly: "A feller won't lie to his crony, Specks." He closed his eye and went off into a restless sleep.

Waters was sick two weeks, and Specks took faithful care of his crony. But the epic cry—it had dwindled into village gossip.

IX

The First Boat

If you ever knew how to whistle a merry tune, it is hard to avoid remembering it when the ice breaks up and booms down swollen channels, and when the first thunder shakes the sky and the mixed scent of rain and new grass is everywhere.

Waters startled himself one sunny Spring morning by whistling a gay tune. It was the first of the kind since the last boat came up in the Fall. Later on in the day, as he waited for custom behind the bar, he suddenly made a discovery. The whistled tune had changed into the air of an old love song which he had whistled the preceding Summer, when the blue sky was very near, and the meadow-larks said tender things.

The human heart is a garden marvellously fertile. The weeds of bitterness grow there, but at certain seasons a smile or an old tune or a kind word will make the weed plot flare with the bloom of Summer. The softly whistled air spread a flame of bloom in the heart of Waters. He began to calculate how long it would be before the river would be open, and how long after that it would be before the first steamer would land at Calhoun with his cork leg; and how long after that it would be before he could learn to use it well enough to make a call on Mrs. Sprangs, and how long after that until——

And at this point he took up the broken thread of his whistled air with undue diligence.

Again he began to spend a great deal of time sweeping the Southern horizon for a trail of smoke, and straining his ears for the first far whistle of a northbound packet.

The Spring was far into May when the boat arrived. Among the things which were put off at the landing was a long, round package addressed to Mr. Waters, Mgr. Waters & Co., Fort Calhoun, N. T. Waters pounced upon the package and hurried to the Buffet, locking himself in. Then he untied the bundle and his sunrise began again with a great streamer of light! It was his cork leg.

He slowly unbuckled his wooden leg, removed it, gazed upon it, then leaned it against the wall. "Good-bye, old feller," he said; "don't think I'm castin' you off in my prosperity. But you see, Stumpy, a feller's got to progress on'ard and up'ard. You've been a good leg to me, if you *was* always hombly. And then—mebbe I'll come back to you—mebbe I'll come back."

The one notch carved near the upper end of the old leg seemed to Waters to assume the intelligence of a reproachful eye. "Mebbe I'll come back," he muttered again; then he began carefully to fit on the cork leg.

When the night had fallen, he went down to the river and indulged in the most abandoned capers, walking, galloping, running, jumping—by way of practice, preliminary to his public appearance upon the morrow. The result of the practice was so satisfactory that he decided upon the next Sunday for the completion of his sunrise, which had lingered so long.

During the whole week Waters was the talk of the village again, and the effect of the new sensation was felt at the Buffet in increased daily receipts.

Upon the following Sunday morning, dressed in his best, Waters went out with the intention of going at once to the home of Mrs. Sprangs. At noon he returned to the Buffet, no nearer to his object than in the morning. All afternoon he endeavored to drive himself to the door of the weather-beaten cottage, but returned, dejected, to his shack in the evening. Then he spent several hours in examining his face in a hand mirror, wondering if there were any glass eyes in St. Louis.

When he fell asleep he did not rest, but busily all the night chased recalcitrant glass eyes that would not remain in place, but rolled away provokingly—always a little out of reach—always just a little out of reach.

X

The Second Boat

One evening in early June there was an unusual attendance at the grocery store convention. A steamboat had arrived from the South that afternoon, and everybody was talking at once.

"They say he brought back nothin' but his hide and some old clothes!"

"Who?"

"Hain't you heard?"

"W'y, Bill Sprangs, the widder's husband!"

"He's been gone nigh onto ten years—been prospectin' out West!"

"Thought he was dead!"

"So'd the widder!"

"What'll Waters do now?"

"Dunno."

The talk went on far into the night. That night Waters did not go to bed. By the light of a candle he sat bent over a sheet of writing paper. Several hours elapsed before he folded the paper and placed it in an envelope; yet this was all he wrote:

"My dear crony: I'm going to take to the river again. Be good to yourself and do what you are a mind with the treasure. It's your'n. So is all the money I've got. It's hid under the big rock that you know about. Going up to Fort Benton with the next boat out of the City. Be back next Spring, mebbe.

"Waters.

"P. S.—This was wrote at midnight."

After sealing and addressing the envelope, he, went out and dropped the letter in the box of the grocery store post office. Then he returned to the Buffet.

He placed a large flask of whiskey in his pocket, put his old wooden leg under his arm, and blowing out the light, he went out and locked the door.

When he had reached the river landing he looked carefully about him, and finding himself alone in the silent star-lit night, sat down upon a coil of rope and unbuckled his new cork limb. Then he sighed, fitted his old wooden leg, with its one notch, to the accustomed stump, and buckled it tight.

He then did that which would have been incomprehensible to an observer, if there had been any. He grasped the cork leg by the foot, whirled it rapidly about his head until it whirred dismally in the silence and flung it far out into the stream.

He watched it floating in the muddy swirl until it was lost in the shadows. Then he stumped away southward into the night.

PART TWO

THE ISLAND

I

The Roustabout

The freight packet *Emilie,* of St. Louis, bound for Fort Benton, had touched at Omaha about the middle of June. Waters had gone aboard as general roustabout. During the run to Sioux City he had spoken little, obeying the brutal commands of the mate with the hangdog air of a man whom Fate has recently lifted out of happiness by the scruff of the neck.

At first he had been merely stunned—a derelict, drifting, as of old, into the suck of the convenient event. Then, in accordance with his temperamental tendency, having awakened dazedly amidst a new chaos, he began to lay out, tentatively, his new cosmos. He thought of the gold fields of the Northwest; but wealth had little lure for him now. He thought of returning to the sea by the next boat down. This looking backward only increased the heartache.

Finally he discovered, with a twinge of conscience which steadily grew less, that only one business, so far as he could ascertain, had any charms for him—the business of being very drunk. Accordingly, when the *Emilie* touched at Sioux City, Mr. Waters became the proprietor of a large and flourishing jag; and when the boat sailed, he was in possession of a goodly sinking fund in the form of a jug of whiskey.

Roustabouts were scarce on the upper river in those days; and Waters was simply tumbled into his bunk with a good prospect for docked wages. However, Mr. Waters had no intention of allowing the new business to run him. He intended to run the business.

Emerging from the first wild plunge into the new undertaking, he found his business at a low ebb, and at once dipped into the sinking fund. Forthwith, things began to happen on board the boat. Mr. Waters annexed the *Emilie,* and decided to convert the same into a pleasure craft. For a day he was allowed to enjoy his suddenly acquired wealth. All on board had, at some time or other, experienced the transient munificence of the well-liquored; and Waters was used for purposes of entertainment.

But when he intruded wantonly into the sacred precincts of the captain's authority, that autocrat of wounded dignity ordered the drunken roustabout to be bound and put to bed, and the sinking fund to be confiscated. Waters refused to abdicate, and delivered his ultimatum to the rebellious captain, which stated plainly to what particular locality the outraged officer might take himself. Having declared war, he backed up against the wheel house, unbuckled his wooden leg and stood ready for battle. This was late in the evening. The *Emilie* had already made two hundred and fifty miles above Sioux City, and would sail all night, as the high waters of the June rise made the channel safe.

The bell had jangled, and all hands had tumbled aft to enforce the order. But darkness fell, and still the order was not enforced. No one cared for a broken head. A parley ensued; but the Thing in the shadow of the wheel house would listen to no overtures of peace.

"You fellers can't put Waters off with a steam-nigger, you can't, you——" And then the voice in the shadow of the wheel house went off into elaborate profanity, that had the strange shivery effect of a rattlesnake's burr.

At this moment a tall, burly roustabout came up and pushed his way roughly through the faltering bunch. "Bring on your lanterns, and let me get at the damned rooster! I'll kick him into the river!" The men advanced behind the impetuous roustabout, who made for the shadow of the wheel house. As the winking lanterns of the crew drew up in a semicircle about the place the light fell upon an incarnate Terror. Mr. Waters leaned against the wheel house; his unkempt hair straggled in a tangle about his forehead and ears, his face was pinched with mental anguish and drunkenness. The dim light deepened the lines that told a hieroglyphic tale of bitterness. His one eye glared, and the empty socket was inflamed. His parched and cracked lower lip hung nervously in a savage leer. His left hand sprawled against the wheel house to support him upon his one leg, and his wooden limb was wielded menacingly as a war-club.

The big man, at the sight of the face, fell back, and the semicircle of winking lanterns slowly widened. Waters laughed, and the joyless sound lingered in the heavy night like a menace.

At midnight the few who remained on deck, keeping watch over the man in the shadow of the wheel house, heard the clatter of a dropped club, the sound of a falling body. They approached the shadow and saw Waters lying face downward in a heap. He was snoring heavily, with an occasional spasmodic catching of the breath.

A few minutes later the landing bell sounded, the engines slowed down until the boat hovered motionless in the current. All hands turned out on deck to learn what was going on. "What's up?" queried an engineer, thrusting his head out of the engine room.

"Putting the one-legged roustabout off," said the mate; "we're just passing Old Man's Island—that's it—that black blotch over there. Guess it'll sober him some, talking to the inhabitants!" And for some reason the mate and the engineer and all who stood near joined in a hearty chuckle.

At the sound of the bell the engine increased speed; the boat swung about and headed for a long narrow strip of dusk, lying to the west of the channel. Its powerful reflectors, cutting a swath of light through the darkness, bored a luminous tunnel into the gloom of the wooded shore. The boat pulled slowly up to the bank. The gang-plank fell upon the sand and a pair of deck-hands crossed it, bearing by the shoulders and legs the limp slumbering body of Waters.

They dropped the sleeping man upon the sand and placed his detached wooden leg beside him.

"Here, you rousters!" bawled the captain, "come a running there—take this grub and jug of liquor and lay it beside him. I guess he'll feel in need of stimulants before he gets acquainted. I'd like to see them when they come together," he added to the mate.

The liquor and victuals were placed near Waters, then the plank was raised, and the *Emilie* pulled out into the current.

As the boat groaned again with the effort of getting away, a sharp report came from the island, and something chugged into the side of the cabin.

"Hey there!" cried the mate; "the old man doesn't like visitors! Swing that light onto the shore!"

The yellow arm of light swung about and touched

the island again. Suddenly, as the projected circle of day flitted across the shore, the apparition of a gaunt, bewhiskered old man, holding a smoking rifle in his hands, sprang out of the night, as if thrown upon a canvas, and as suddenly disappeared into the dark again. When the arm of light retraced the spot where the apparition had appeared, there was nothing to be seen but the drunken roustabout lying in a heap upon the shore, and behind him the heavy timber.

Again the arm of light swung about, felt far ahead for the channel, grew dimmer and dimmer, faded into an indistinct glow, and the noise of the toiling engine came like the muffled wheeze of an asthmatic sleeper. Then this was swallowed up, and there was no light, and only the sound of the river's lapping and the snore of Waters.

In his dreams, Waters battled with terrors. Now he was struggling with storm-driven floods that overwhelmed him; now he held crowds at bay; now he clutched at the throat of some man whose face was hidden. He could hear the wheezing breath, the rattle in the man's throat, and always at this juncture the face became visible, and it was the face of the man who came unexpectedly out of the West. Then suddenly these things faded. A dazzling light smote athwart his dream, through which, it seemed, he caught a transitory gleam of kindly features—the faces of Mrs. Sprangs and his mother curiously mixed.

Then with a shock like that of a trumpet's blast to the ear, a great light fell upon his face. He opened his eye directly in the horizontal glare of the morning sun that burned the summits of the distant bluffs and girded the river with a band of flame. A shuffle of feet near by in the sand attracted him. Wearily he raised himself upon his elbow, and turned his head in the direction of the sound. Immediately he closed his eye. The thing which he had gazed upon dazzled him, still drowsy with the clinging debauch. It was, or seemed to be, a young woman.

In the supersensitive condition of his nerves, Waters received a vivid picture. The young woman was of middle height, slender and gracefully formed. A loose robe was hung carelessly from her shoulders, somewhat after the manner of the ancient Greeks. This, of course, Waters did not know; he had merely caught a picture of something that seemed to him to be overpoweringly, impossibly beautiful. The sun-bronzed shapely arms, extended in surprise, lifted the drapery of her shoulders. The body beneath seemed transparent in the dawn, formed of mist and sunlight.

Her face, frail and nobly formed, bore that wan light of inquiring innocence which a lover of Grecian lore would place upon the face of a nymph startled by a sleeping satyr. Her hair was red-gold, and the sunlight smote it into a flame that burned to her waist and clung about her lithe figure like a halo.

Her feet and ankles, bare and wet with dew, sparkled in the light like the feet of an immortal.

When Waters again ventured to open his eye with the uncertain fear of a drunkard in a delirium, the figure had vanished. He raised himself to a sitting posture and tried to think.

"I guess I'm gettin' 'em," he mused with a bitter mirth. "Improvement on snakes though!" Then he discovered his wooden leg, buckled it on, and tottered toward the spot where the vision had disappeared.

He thought he could distinguish the marks of dainty toes in the sand. He got upon his knee for closer inspection, but his poor head buzzed and whirled with the exertion, and he decided with the irrelevance of intoxication that he ought to sleep some more. Thereupon he fell on his face, and the daylight whirled dizzily until it went out like a candle in a draught.

During the swoon-like sleep that followed, Waters dreamed that he was being lifted and carried. It all seemed to be happening without any relation to time and space. He was only half conscious of being roughly handled without the desire or ability to interfere. Then even the sense of this passed.

II

Waters Wakes

Waters groaned and opened his eye. He saw nothing; the darkness was the darkness of the blind. "Hum-hum-hum—night again! Devil of a good sleep!" He yawned as he spoke, opening and closing his mouth wearily in a vain attempt to get the fuzz of dissipation off his tongue and the bitter taste of the morning after out of his mouth. Then he decided he would rub his eye. His hands would not move from his sides. With a second desperate effort he learned that his arms were held down by the wrists that ached with the violent effort to be free. Also his legs were bound. His head buzzed and swam dizzily. He listened intently, and noted a sound: *chug chug chug*. It suggested the hog-like grunt and puff of a steamer rooting up stream.

"Guess I'm on the *Emilie* yet," he muttered in bewilderment. "Got me tied down. Hey there! Le' me up!" A thousand metallic voices in the darkness answered *Me up—me up*. "Yes, le' me up—I say there!" *There—er—er,* said the voices.

After another violent struggle, Waters noted that

the *chug chug* as of a steamer's exhaust, was louder and faster. "Can't be I'm on the *Emilie*—that's my heart beatin' in my temples," mused Waters. "I'm inside of somethin' big and dark and damp and holler. Seems like I dreamed of bein' brung somewheres. *Ugh—ugh—ugh.*" He coughed violently in the damp air, and there came a mocking sound as of a thousand invisible dogs baying at the midnight.

"Bark, you idiots!" he yelled, the dying liquor in his head conjuring up all sorts of fantastic notions. The echoes died slowly and the heavy silence crept back into the damp and dark.

After another violent and prolonged effort, Waters lay quite still and tried to think. He wondered if he had not been thrown into some deep hole, or had he not left the boat, or——. Then suddenly the memory of the brilliant something he had seen burning in the horizontal sun, shot through his brain like a thin, keen ray of sunlight through a chink in a dark room.

"I wonder was it a woman?" mused Waters. "Never see nothin' like it. No more'n half dressed neither! Looked like her hair was burnin'."

Then slowly, falteringly, almost remorsefully, the dazed thoughts of Waters crept back into the years when his mother used to talk to him about angels that watched over him while he slept. Angels! Maybe it was an angel! He felt a sudden shame at having spoken lightly of the vision, so pure was the thought of that far away time. In his maudlin condition tears came easily and ran down his cheeks. When he would have brushed them away, the sense of being a prisoner came upon him stronger than before, for the liquor was dying under the new excitement. A cold perspiration came out upon his forehead. He saw things in the darkness and shivered.

"Help! Help!" he yelled. Panting, he lay still and stared dizzily into the darkness.

Presently a point of light appeared far away. It flickered and burned blue as though struggling mightily to support the weight of night that crushed about its small globular day. Waters blinked at the unaccustomed light and wondered. He closed his eye doubtfully. "I've sure got 'em!" he muttered; "Seein' and hearin' all sorts of things! Wisht I had a drink!"

A sound of bare feet approaching on the damp floor made him open his eye. The light had grown larger, and he could distinguish the head of a man in the circular glow, the trunk being hidden in the shadow.

"Seein' em' again!" he muttered with bitter mirth. "Man's head now, a-walkin' through the air 'thout no legs! Better'n snakes, though!"

The approaching head shook with violent coughing, and the light flickered in a trembling hand. Slowly the footsteps came near and the globe of light waxed larger and more brilliant, until it engulfed Waters. He closed his eye that ached with the paradox of light in this sepulchral somewhere.

At the sound of violent coughing near him Waters opened his eye and saw an old man standing in the centre of the zone of light cast by an upheld candle. His head was large, and to a student of mythology would have suggested Zeus. His forehead was massive and seamed with horizontal wrinkles. Bushy eyebrows, giving a sinister appearance, clustered above his deep-set eyes that shone with the unusual brilliance of erratic strength.

His gray hair hung in careless tangles about his head. His shoulders were broad and stooped, and about them was thrown a loose dark robe, leaving a sunken chest bare, hideous with shrunken muscles traced deeply with the shadows of the sputtering candle.

The man stood motionless for many minutes, save when he was shaken by violent coughing. His eyes were held upon Waters without a blink to break the wild glare of his gaze. Waters, lying helplessly upon his back, shivered. He caught himself remembering the ogres of nightmare that had stared down through closely drawn blankets upon him when he was a child. With a shudder he closed his eye. Suddenly his accustomed bitter weariness of life came upon him. He looked up at the old man before him and grinned.

"Well, you gray-whiskered old goat," he said, "I'm dry! Got any wet goods concealed about your pockets?" He forced a dry loud laugh that rang down the vaulted darkness.

"I came to kill you!" said the old man in a deep vibrant voice.

"That all?" queried Waters, with the bravado of exhausted nerves. And he laughed again loud and long.

For the first time across the face of the old man flashed a human expression. It was one of surprise that by degrees transformed the habitual malevolence of his features into something almost kindly. Suddenly the light in his face vanished, and the malevolence returned. He deliberately pulled a long-bladed knife from his garments.

Waters had reached that stage of nervous excitement in which fear vanishes. The bitterness of the past weeks and the dying of the liquor in his head had subdued the natural instinct to cherish life. When the old man stooped to place the blade at his throat, Waters grinned.

"Better whet it on your boot some—tough hide!" he remarked.

The old man's body was straightened in surprise. The knife dropped to the ground.

"You are not *afraid?*" he whispered, with a light as of recognition in his eyes.

"Me afeerd?" Waters laughed again. "Say, old man, you're only a dream—hain't you? Get away! I don't want to dream no more. Want to sleep."

The massive gray head fell upon the sunken chest

as in profound thought. Then slowly, sonorously, like the speaking of an oracle, the old man said:

"You are the man of whom I have been dreaming for years! You have come at last!"

III

The Physician of the Universe

When the old man had cut the cords that bound Waters, he took the candle from the ground where he had placed it. "Come," he said. Waters, feeling again the freedom of his limbs, stood still and tried to find himself.

"Shall I throttle this old goat?" he queried mentally, "and run? Where'll I run to? Wonder if I'm dreamin'!" He struck himself a blow on the point of the chin. "No, you ain't a-dreamin'," he muttered; "Waters, you ain't asleep. Wonder if there's any liquor in these parts!"

The candle of the retreating old man burned blue and grew smaller and more weird in the intervening darkness. "Guess he knows how he got in here," Waters mused; and he followed rapidly after the waning light. When he had overtaken the hobbling old man, he was breathless and bewildered. "Say, old man, for God's sake, am I awake?" he gasped.

"Living is a nightmare," replied the old man, wheezing with the damp and the rapid gait he had taken; "I alone in all the world am awake. Come, you, too, shall waken!" The words were spoken with the nonchalant precision of a catechism lesson.

"Somebody hain't right," muttered Waters, shaking his head in bewilderment; "somebody's got 'em! Is it him or me, me or him——" Suddenly the old man was swallowed with his candle in the darkness.

"Dad! Dad!" shouted Waters with a sudden access of tenderness in his childish terror. He rushed headlong into the darkness and soon came in sight of the old man again, stooping to pass through an aperture in the wall of the cavernous place. He stooped and followed, finding himself in a room with walls of rock that were visible in the wan twilight coming in through an opening at the further end. When his eye had at length become accustomed to the light, Waters became aware of a collection of books, stacked row upon row to the roof of the place. In one corner stood a table bearing papers, books and writing utensils. Before it was a block of wood serving for a chair. The old man motioned Waters to sit down upon the block of wood. Then with a kind, almost paternal, expression upon his stern features, he approached his wondering guest.

"Poor aching human Atom!" he began in a soft caressing voice; "you have suffered much, have you not? Felt great longings that whipped your poor blood into a fever. You have dreamed and thirsted for vast impossible oceans; and you have awakened with your tongue bitter and dry as dust. Is it not so?"

"Y-e-s, Dad," answered Waters in a weak voice. He was not so sure about the oceans in particular; but at that moment he was prodigiously dry. He half expected the old man to produce a demijohn from beneath his garments.

Oh, for a keg—two kegs—three kegs of the buried treasure!

Phew-oo-oo-oo! He blew a long dry breath through his parched lips. "Yes, yes, Dad," he said, and eyed the nooks of the place hopefully.

"Poor aching Atom!" monotonously continued the old man. "Poor aching Atom, driven in the pitiless dust storm of the universe!"

Phew-oo-oo-oo, went Waters a second time. The prospect was very arid.

"Listen!" whispered the old man, assuming an attitude of profound attention. "Can you not hear the crying of souls, pinched, goaded, burned, belabored with passion? Like desperate swimmers in a stream fierce with eddies, they fight with the pitiless swirl of the universe!"

Phew-oo-oo-oo, went Waters a third time, but with an optimistic upward inflection. The simile of the stream was much more promising than the previous dust storm.

"They are crying aloud for death!" said the old man. "The word is a mockery! It is the name of a nothing. Procreate! Beget other sentience! Incarnate more suffering! Let us have more voices to cry out the universal pang! Give the universe innumerable tongues! It has a fever to talk about!"

"Uh—huh," idiotically assented Waters, with a conciliatory inflection. He was somewhat frightened, and his thirst was not growing less. He wanted to awaken a responsive chord of comradeship in his strange companion. But during a moment's silence the eyes of the other glared in the half light of the place.

"Look at me! What do you see? You see a man like yourself, but shrunken with suffering!"

Waters was now staring with a fascinated gaze. Something strong and subtle in the old man held the bleared eye of Waters. He could not look away.

"Look again! What do you see? You see a Titanic Idea. *I—am—about—to be—God!*"

The last words were uttered in a low sibilant tone. A tremor passed over the body of Waters. His face paled; his breath came quicker and more labored.

"When I was a child, breathing the first painful breath of existence, a great revelation came to me in a vision. At first it only terrified me. I grew in wisdom, and the vision became a reality. I resolved to banish suffering. This I resolved to do for love of my fellows, who are blind and can not see the vision." The old man's voice was soft but penetrating. "They laughed at me. What did I care?

They drove me into the Wilderness. What do I care—I who am about to be God?"

The old man drew near to Waters and closed the staring eye with a soft touch of his fingers.

"You, too, shall see the vision. You are now lifted far above the earth. You can see it all—mountains, valleys, plains, hills, rivers, cities; you see it all. Look!" He spoke sharply, raising his voice to a commanding pitch.

A sensation of being lifted came over Waters. It seemed he looked downward from a great height.

A dim consciousness of the voice of the old man crept into the brain of Waters. As the voice continued, Waters *saw* what it said. He took the whole world in at a glance. From his great altitude men were very small. They were as innumerable ants toiling upon a hill; toiling to build that which crumbled under the toilers' touch. A seething mass of life, striving, fighting, killing, begetting, writhing in pain that led to greater pain. A howling, shrieking mass, living that it might suffer and die; dying that it might be born again. A mad grasping after nothing! It was all as though a wanton creator, vicious with lonesomeness, had incarnated a nightmare—something to satisfy the morbid itch of giant nerves!

The voice ceased. With a sickening sense of rapid falling, Waters opened his eye and found himself staring upon the old man.

"You have seen it," said the old man quietly. "Is it not terrible?"

"Y—e—s," replied Waters in a faint voice.

"Listen!" resumed the old man. "Twenty-five years ago I conceived a plan to annihilate all suffering. Never in the innumerable ages since the nebulous infinite fevered into consciousness has so colossal an idea as mine been conceived. Archimedes of old dreamed of a mighty lever. It remained to me—*me*—to supply the fulcrum for that lever. Listen! You shall hear it all. You shall feel the omnipotence of my sublime Idea. There is but one thing—Matter. It is eternal and infinite. It is Space. Matter is composed of molecules, each of which is attracted to the other, owing to a certain relative juxtaposition.

"This attraction is Life, Force, Soul, Spirit, which have been personified as Brahm, Ahriman, Wotan, Jove, Osiris, Jehovah, and all the fabled beings of the pantheon of Man."

"Uh huh," assented Waters in an appeasing manner, as of one who solicits mercy.

"Matter was originally an inert mass in the vast darkness. Action is therefore abnormal. Then, is not conscious life, which is a form of action, the Malady of Matter? The names of the gods are men's names for the infinite disease! Mythology is the Pathology of Space!"

Waters shuffled nervously but did not shift his gaze as the old man continued.

"Consciousness is one phase of the attraction between molecules, when a certain requisite relative position occurs. The most familiar instance of molecules in such relation each to each is the animal brain. It is not the only dwelling of consciousness. Throughout Space, attraction is identical. The Systems, with their planets corresponding to the brain's molecules, compose an infinite Brain that aches with a terrible Thought. The Universe tosses in a nightmare!"

The next sentence was spoken almost in a whisper.

"It is left to me to be the Physician of the Universe! Life of itself can not die," continued the old man; "it merely acts in another way. In order to stop the life of the smallest animalcule it would be necessary to check the innumerable systems!"

The old man ceased speaking for a moment. The light in his eyes blazed into a glare of triumph as he spoke the next sentence.

"It is that which we shall do!"

The daring words shivered down the dark vaults and died into a menacing whisper.

"Listen!" He hurled the word into the momentary silence. "Unity of vibration is life. Contrariety of attraction in the most infinitesimal part of the systems, would neutralize their charmed motion. It would be as a discord shattering a harmony. The sustaining motion being removed, the systems would collapse into Chaos—dark, cold, pulseless, painless! A shower of impotent dust! The dream of the ancient Greek shall be realized through me!

It shall be an avenging of the wrongs of Chance since pangless Eternity fevered into aching Time! And I shall be the Avenger—*I—I!*"

The voice grew into a muffled shout. A terrible ecstasy shook the frail frame of the old man. His face was transfigured with a sublime anger. Suddenly he paled. He reeled like a drunken man. The veins upon his forehead and neck swelled blue. His head dropped upon his sunken chest. And then the whole form collapsed into a writhing heap upon the ground.

Waters leaped to his feet and tried to shout. He could not make a sound. A cold tremor ran up his spine and chilled the base of his brain. His teeth chattered. Then he turned and dashed through the opening at the further end of the place, through which the kind light of day filtered dimly.

He reached the surface and found himself inside a log hut. Finding the door, he rushed against it with his shoulder. The wood yielded and he found himself in the open air. It was evening, with a red glow slanting downward from the West through a heavy growth of timber.

A path lay before him. He dashed wildly down it. He would leap into the river! He would leave this cursed island of nightmare! A love and longing for the great selfish world, which he had left, rushed back upon him.

Suddenly, as he ran, a wild and beautiful sound grew up in the evening stillness. It was not merely a shout; it was not as a song. Yet it was both far reaching and musical. As though the sound were a tangible barrier, Waters stopped and listened. Words floated in the sound.

Farewell, Friend of the red hair,
Friend of the glowing face, friend of the blaz-
ing hair!
Sleepy Friend, sleep not long in the under dark.
Listen, I sing you to sleep!
Through the long night I shall hunger for you.
Through the dreary dusk I shall dream of you.
I shall draw your glowing face upon the shadows,
Your flaming hair upon the darkness;
I shall thirst for your dawn-kiss,
Hunger for your morning caress!
Sleepy Friend, covering your face with a cloudy
arm,
Sleep not long!

The sound, sonorously soft, rose in a thrilling crescendo and died into lingering echoes. Waters listened breathlessly. Like a powerful intoxicant the sound soothed his shaken nerves. When it had ceased, he cautiously approached the place where it had died.

As he reached a little knoll, he stopped and stared in bewilderment. The path before him led to the basin of a large, clear spring, lined at the brink with mosses; and there, waist-deep in the water, was the exquisite figure of a young woman. Her skin glowed with the cool bath. Her body was slender but perfectly formed, and her limbs moved with the subtle grace that characterizes the movements of wild animals.

Waters pushed a branch aside and stepped forward. As he did so, the sharp crack of a twig startled the fair bather. Her arms, dripping with the cool water, were checked in air. Her head was thrown back in surprise and expectation. Suddenly the setting sun drove a shaft of light through a rift in the leaves, illuminating the region of the spring. The girl's wet body sparkled in the glare. Her heavy red-gold hair, tossed carelessly upon her shoulders and flowing down her back, glinted as a trailing gossamer cloud smitten by the last shaft of the day.

Waters buried his face in his hands and knelt in the path. His brain reeled. He was dizzy with the supernatural vision. It was as a madman's rehabilitation of some clinging Grecian legend. For many enchanted minutes Waters dared not look toward the spring. When at length he looked up, there was nothing before him but the pool of water, a faintly glinting splotch of silver, darkening slowly with the fall of night.

IV

The Compelling Dream

For many charmed minutes Waters remained motionless, staring fixedly upon the darkening pool. It seemed to him that he dare not stir. Something terrible in beauty was potential in the shadows deepening about him. He scarcely breathed. Was it a woman—this thing of air and sunlight? Was it a dream—this seeming incarnation of evening? Beauty is terrible to those unaccustomed to gaze upon it. The imperfect had gazed upon Perfection. Could this exalted something be a woman? The women of Waters' life had cooked and darned and scrubbed. Could this Something cook and darn and scrub? Waters was seized with a cynical doubt that broke the spell. He rubbed his hand across his face. It seemed that he had brushed something away. The pool had grown dark, except for the faint silver glint of an early star, looking downward through the leaves.

"Huh!" he ejaculated, getting unsteadily to his feet. "Beats the devil how liquor does stay by you these days, Waters! Seein' things! Every which kind of a thing! Blue blazes, Mr. Waters, do drag yourself together somehow! You're seein' with t'other eye. That eye always gets to seein' things t'other can't when liquor gets into you!

"Phew-oo-oo. Liquor! I'm drier'n air-slacked lime!"

Waters, shuddering with the memory of the old man, hurried on to the shore, and came upon the spot where he had been placed by the crew of the *Emilie*. To his great joy, he discovered the jug of liquor and the victuals which had been left beside him. He pounced upon the jug first.

"Guess I'll eat and drink first and swim somewheres afterwards. Say, old Stomach," he apostrophized with a sudden access of hilarity; "been pretty dusty down there, hain't it? I bet it has! Here comes a shower. Look out!" He tipped the jug to his lips and drank deeply, finishing with a snort of relief. "How you like the fall showers after the hot summer, huh?" he continued, addressing his digestive organ. "I see heavy clouds on the horizon. Guess it's goin' to rain some more—about four fingers, I guess." He tipped the jug a second time and drank until his face was purple. Then he fell to the victuals and ate ravenously. Meanwhile the last pale glow failed in the West, and the stars sprinkled cold fire on the river.

Waters, with a sudden inspiration, remembered that he ought to have a pipe and some tobacco about him. He found both, together with a small supply of matches. Then he lit his pipe. He sat comfortably with his arms upon his knees and stared out across the river. A thin white streamer of smoke wavered starward from his pipe.

"Now this is comfort—it *is* that!" mused he. "Hain't much comp'ny hereabouts tho'. But comp'ny hain't much use to a feller nohow. Puff—puff—puff. Feller's got to—puff—puff—puff—just about be his own comp'ny in this here world. Beats all how a little grub does change the complexion of things. Takes the freckles off'n the face of Nature. There's several blessin's in the world after all. Some of 'em's in barrels. Now there's liquor! S'prisin' what it'll do for you! I recollect drinkin' enough onc't to make me think I was emp'rer of the Chinese with the sun a-shinin' up at me! Great thing! Puff—puff—puff.

"Say," he continued with temulent incoherence: "Wonder, was it a woman! Wisht it was!" He was seized with a violent hiccoughing which marred his temporary optimism.

"If it was a woman, what'd you do with your bad eye and your wooden leg, Waters? Huh?" He uttered the interrogatory sound with a snarl of bitterness. "Huh? huh?" he repeated with insulting insistence, as if to taunt his own imperfections for being his.

His head began to swim. By contiguity of thought, the old pessimism which had accompanied so many of his past sprees, seized him. " 'Tain't no infernal use," he muttered; " 'tain't!" He dropped his head on his knees and fell into slumber.

It seemed that he had barely fallen asleep when he heard a voice close to his ear: *"Wake!"*

Waters raised his head and found that he had fallen upon his side. The East was red with early dawn. He blinked in the light and rubbed his eye. Then he sat up and looked about. The old man stood before him. His face was pale and there were deep blue circles under his lustreless eyes. His body trembled. The terrible nervous energy that had emanated from him the night before was lacking. Waters stared.

"Do not fear me," said the old man, in a weak, almost pitiful voice. "This morning I am powerless, even as yourself. I am so lonesome. Talk to me. Let me hear the voice of another who has suffered. Oh, it is terrible to be a man. Let us be friends. Let us cling desperately together." The words were uttered without force.

"Yes, Dad," said Waters; "Let's be friends. Hain't nobody cares for me. Be my Dad!"

"What do men call you?" asked the old man.

"They didn't hardly ever call me," replied Waters. "They didn't need me. My name's Waters."

"Waters," said the old man pensively; "I need you, I who carry a desert in my breast. You will indeed be waters to me."

They were silent for some time. The miracle of dawn was in development. The river before them glittered. There was birdsong above them. The old man broke the silence.

"I terrified you with what seemed vagaries to you. Vagaries? Look into my breast! Are not mirages natural to a desert?"

There was a second and a longer silence. Then the old man spoke again. "Waters, I have dreamed so long. I am like a rag-weed that has drooped and sulked and dreamed all through the heat of the Summer. To-day I feel the frost upon my head. I begin to love the sun. Can you laugh, Waters? When I was a boy, before this great dream came, I remember that I could laugh. I will try again." The old man made a pitiful grimace and cackled far down in his throat. "I can't laugh," he whispered with terror in his voice. "Waters, can you laugh? You look as though you could laugh. *Laugh!*"

"Don't feel like it, Dad."

"Laugh!" cried the old man, some of the former energy rushing into his eyes.

"I'll try, Dad." Waters delivered himself of a loud ha-ha that was far from merry.

"There!" cried the old man triumphantly. "Laugh again!"

"Mebbe if you'd tickle me in the ribs I could laugh better," said Waters naïvely.

The old man, with the seriousness of a surgeon

at a difficult operation, tickled Waters at the indicated place. Waters, seized with the ridiculousness of the situation, laughed merrily, loud and long.

The old man was ecstatic. "I would give my omnipotent Idea for the power of laughter," he said. Then the old shadows came back into his face. "No," he continued wearily; "I am driven by the Dream. I must dispel the nightmare of the Universe! I must be God!"

He leaped to his feet, his emaciated body vibrant with mad power. He stood for a moment trembling. Then he sat down again beside Waters.

"I must tell you of my great dream," he began. "You shall aid me. You shall be the lieutenant of a god! Think of that! Listen!" While gazing into the old man's eyes, Waters felt the strange sensation of loss of self-control that he had felt the day before.

"My name was Ambrose Ambrosen. Now I am a great dream fleshed. I need no name. I am unique in the Universe. I was born in Boston. My parents gave me unusual educational advantages. But school did little for me. It was the Dream! I was eighteen years old when the great plan was conceived. I remember I had been wandering in a dismal cloud for months, driven by a great despair. I remember one night I walked the floor of my room after midnight, my brain convulsed with inexplicable anguish. Suddenly, as I pondered the question of the banishment of universal suffering, a great light shot through my brain. It was day suddenly burning the zenith of midnight. The solution of the Dream had come! I had conceived the Titanic Idea. I would be, not the petty savior of a race; not even a creator. Selfishness creates. No, I would be the universal Annihilator! I would pull down the cosmic pillars about my head, and become an atom in a pangless shower of dust!

"I was absorbed in my great Dream. Ambrosen was no more. There was only a human form encasing an awful Idea.

"In my ecstasy I ventured to tell my Dream. My friends stared and then shunned me. They called me mad, because I saw clearly and with the perfect vision. I entered into a terrible isolation. I lost the power of laughter. I was without country, kin, companions. I toiled unceasingly with my great problem alone. With mathematics I bombarded the universe. Ah, it is sublime to be alone—*but it is terrible!*" The old man's voice fell from its excited pitch to an impressive whisper. His eyes were brilliant. Suddenly they grew soft. His voice arose again in a low musical tone.

"But one day, when I was near thirty, a human being crept into my isolation, as a subtle, clinging perfume creeps. It was a beautiful girl. Her hair was like a golden sunset. Her face was delicately formed as a dream face. She was slender and frail.

She believed in my dream. She did not believe because she understood, but because she loved the dreamer.

"At the death of my father I received a large fortune. What was money to me? Dust! I decided to use it as a means for complete isolation, the better to elaborate my plan. I bought a small river vessel at New Orleans, and loaded it with everything necessary for the accomplishment of my great task. I omitted nothing. I brought my books; also I brought goats, and many varieties of seeds, that the body might have food. How poor a thing is flesh to be a part of a god's conception!

"I bought a few negroes for a crew, ascended the Mississippi, thence up the Missouri into the Wilderness. I chose this island because it seemed to be adapted to my needs. Here I could nurture the mighty dream. That was twenty years ago. The boat and the crew are out yonder." The old man indicated the river's channel with a sweep of the arm. "Three years of ecstasy passed," he continued. "I thought I saw the success of my undertaking. But the girl wept at nights; and often in the mornings I would miss her at my side to find her gazing wistfully across the river into the sunrise; gazing with eyes that slowly lost their lustre, always into the East.

"I did not say, 'Let us go back'; we could not go back. And then—there was the Dream—always the

Dream. In the Spring of the third year she died giving birth to a girl."

At the mention of the girl, Waters started and would have spoken, but the old man continued dreamily: "Then for a time I was only a man, lonesome and broken-hearted. I forgot to dream. It seemed as though I were one who had dwelt in a spacious temple, magnificent with columns and mysterious with dim colonnades, tenanted by a spirit that filled the magnificence and was the life of the mystery. The spirit had left my temple. I became afraid of its vastness. I had never before been conscious of the possible terrors of silence and vastness. I hid my face, but I heard her speaking in the nightwind. I dared not look upon the dawn or the sunset, lest I should see her gloriously burning hair, out of reach, always out of reach.

"For a space all things were jumbled, and I was conscious only of a great ache thrust through the darkness about me like a blade. I do not know how long this continued. I only know that a small cry aroused me. It was the cry of the child, hungry and wishing to live. Then I lost for a time all my bitterness toward the scheme of things. I, who had dared to believe in nothing, setting my face toward infinite darkness and silence, grew to love the sunlight and the singing of birds; because I had unconsciously absorbed the spirit of the child. I vowed to teach the girl in such a way that she might grow flowerlike sunward. From the time that she learned to lisp, I read the poets to her. And when I had taught her to read, these became her companions—the poets and the sunlight and the birds."

As the old man spoke, his face had grown steadily more expressive of tenderness, until a something seraphic shone in his eyes.

"Dad," whispered Waters awesomely: "I seen her last night! She was a-burnin' on her head. I could see clean through her—only there wasn't nothin' on t'other side but sunlight! And I heard her sing, like the wind used to sing around the house of nights when I was a little feller. Was it her, Dad? Was it real?"

The old man sighed, and his eyes became lustreless.

"Nothing is real," he said wearily; "nothing but suffering. Come, let us go. To-morrow we shall begin the great task. Will you help me, Waters?"

Although Waters' conception of the task in hand was exceedingly vague, the memory of the brilliant something that had burned upward from the crystal pool helped him to answer almost joyfully: "Yes, Dad!"

They walked toward the interior of the island. After a long silence, the old man said: "I have been so weak to-day, Waters. What if even I be only a man?"

V

The Mystic Chord of Seven Strings

When the two, walking down a woodland path together, came in sight of the log house from which Waters had fled the evening before, he noted with wonder that a column of smoke ascended from the rude clay chimney. Also, the scent of something cooking gladdened his nostrils. Since leaving the shore the old man had lapsed into a deep study, walking along with his arms behind his back, his head bent forward, muttering unintelligibly to himself. Waters seized upon this opportunity to be affable.

"Who's a-cookin' for this layout, Dad?" he said pleasantly, hoping to arouse his companion to a comfortable familiarity.

The old man raised his head, and gazing blankly at Waters, as though he saw through and far beyond him, went on muttering to himself, but in a louder voice: "Seven, fourteen, twenty-one, twenty-eight, thirty-five, forty-two, forty-nine—seven times seven is forty-nine."

"Shouldn't wonder at all," answered Waters,

courageously endeavoring to fit into the scheme of things. "And eight times eight is sixty with four to carry. 'Rithmetic's interestin'. Who's manufacturin' the biscuits?"

The old man continued muttering to himself for a moment. Then with a start, as though he had just wakened, he said: "Oh, cook? Diana."

"Dinah, eh?" queried Waters. "Colored, eh? Make good cooks—them niggers!" But the old man had again lapsed into a deep study. As they drew nearer to the log house, the scent of cooking breakfast aroused the deep home instinct in Waters. He saw before him a most peaceful scene that wiped from his mind, capable of the most sanguine optimism on the least pretext, all memory of the horror he had so lately experienced. The log house stood in the centre of a vegetable garden that filled the clearing. It was of ample size, built substantially of heavy logs covered with moss, and its roof was almost entirely covered with wild cucumber vines, now laden with their snowy bloom. "Looks comfortable like," mused Waters; "beats me if it don't look like a woman was hoverin' about somewheres. Looks too homelike for a place 'thout a woman. Wonder if it's the one I seen!" His heart beat more rapidly at the thought. "No," he mused; "never seen a dream that could cook victuals!"

As they neared the open door, the sound of a voice carolling a wild sweet air, came out with the scent of cooking. Waters had never heard such singing except at the spring the evening before. It was to him more like the ecstatic rhapsody of a bird threaded by the dull minor of the wind, than the songs with which he was familiar. The voice suddenly fell from its ecstatic height into a croon and ceased.

Following the old man, who was still muttering to himself, he passed through the door. The first sight of the interior checked him. He stood and stared. He saw, kneeling before a fireplace in which something was cooking, the figure of a young woman. The glow of the wood embers in the fireplace smote upward on her face and hair. The loose sleeves of her odd garment were tucked up, displaying her arms bare to the shoulders and glowing with the firelight.

The sudden realization of what had seemed a dream to him thrilled Waters. "She's real!" he exclaimed. The young woman, at the sound of the voice, sprang up from the fireplace, and stood staring upon the figure in the doorway. Her delicate face, with its combined expressions of child and woman, warmed the heart of Waters. The warmth permeated his whole body, and grew into a softened light upon his disfigured face, as he smiled the haloed smile that had won the heart of his first crony. Immediately the puzzled expression died upon the girl's face. Her blue eyes softened as cold skies soften with morning. During the silence that had fallen, the old man had ceased muttering and now stood gazing upon the man and the girl. When he spoke, his voice was soft and lacked that nervous pitch which had heretofore characterized it.

"Daughter," said he, "this is the one of whom I have dreamed so long. He has come out of the world to help us. Waters, this is my daughter, Diana."

Again Waters and the girl exchanged smiles but neither spoke. The old man gave Waters a chair, and then sat down at the table, resting his chin upon his hands and gazing into distance. Waters steadily followed the girl about with his gaze, grinning pleasantly whenever he caught her eyes.

"Nice little thing," he thought. "Wonder if she's thinkin' of my bad eye and my wooden leg. Guess Dad won't need to tie me down no more."

During breakfast, Waters ate little, although he had been hungry a half hour before. It sufficed him to watch furtively this mysterious dream-girl eating like an ordinary being. He was still deep in wonder when Ambrosen arose from the table and requested Waters to follow him.

They passed out of the room, through another room, and into another that Waters recognized as the place from which he had fled the evening before, for he saw the entrance to the cavern sloping downward from the centre of the room.

The old man took a half dozen candles from a shelf, and having lit one, led the way into the subterranean library.

Waters shivered as he thought of the experience of the day before in this place. They stooped through the aperture into the dark cavern beyond. The old man walked on rapidly, holding his candle above his head. Waters stumped after, reluctant to follow, yet wishing to humor his companion.

"Say, Dad," he said, attempting to arouse a comfortable conversation, "you've got a nice little girl." The old man did not reply, but hurried on rapidly. "Wonder where we're sailin' for?" muttered Waters.

After walking rapidly for some time, the faint white glow of day crept in at a chink in the roof of the cavern. The old man stopped and lit the other candles which he carried. These he placed in crannies about the wall, and in the twilight Waters could distinguish piles of material ranged along the jagged walls; great rolls of wire, ranging in size from the E string of a violin to a small steel cable; tools of all descriptions; strips of steel, nails, bolts, chains. All these Waters could distinguish, with many other articles concerning the use of which he knew nothing.

"This your junk shop?" asked Waters, endeavoring once more to infuse a spirit of sanity into the situation.

The old man's eyes glowed in the half light, as a miser's might when counting his gold pieces.

"This is my treasure," he said excitedly. "It is of this that we shall build the colossal engine which shall accomplish my great purpose! See! Here it shall be built! Oh, you will say it is to be a very wonderful engine! You will tremble when I tell you of it! It will consist of seven harps, ranging from the size of a concert harp to one twenty feet in height. The first and smallest shall have forty-nine strings, the next forty-two, the next thirty-five, and so on, until the last shall have only seven, and they shall be the largest of all the strings in the graduated series. Will it not be a terrific engine?

"Oh, but I see you have not yet caught the intricate meaning of my words. The last group in the seven consists of seven strings. *Seven!* Ah, ha, ha, ha!" The old man laughed triumphantly. "You see I have discovered it—the great secret of the Mystic Seven! It is the sustaining number of the Universe! Since the Cosmos emerged from Chaos, with all the marvels of light and sound, this number has been dominant! *Seven!* How many colors exist in a ray of sunlight? Count them! Violet, indigo, blue, green, yellow, orange and red—ah, ha! Seven!"

The glory of childish triumph illumined the haggard eyes.

"And again—in all the realm of sound with its infinite variety of combinations, how many notes can you count—notes of which all sounds are but combinations? Again I ask you to count: c, d, e, f, g, a, b. The final c of the octave is simply the former c pitched higher. How many? *Seven!* Ah, 'ha, ha, ha!"

The old man's eyebrows were drawn upward in ecstasy from the eyes that glared brilliantly.

"Not only in the physical Universe, but in the history of Man the Mystic Number has been powerful. It seems that some faint conception of the importance of the number in the scheme of things is inherent in the human race. What says the Christian? God rested on the *seventh* day from the labors of creation! What says Joshua of the fall of Jericho? 'And *seven* priests shall bear before the ark *seven* trumpets of ram's horns; on the *seventh* day ye shall compass the city *seven* times and the priests shall blow upon the trumpets.' Ah, even in that far time the Mystic Number was felt! Did not Mohammed dream of seven heavens? Was not Rome built on seven hills, and did it not dominate the world? Was it not a cross made by seven nails in the shoe of the cobbler of Jerusalem, that was the mark of the Christian Messiah's curse? It was after pondering these things that I came upon the Secret of the Universe.

"Millions have felt the spell of the Mystic Number. It remained to me—*me*—to be the master of the meaning of the Number!

"Listen! You will say it is all very wonderful. The philosopher tells us that all things have their tunes; that is, they are capable of vibrating to a certain sound and to no other. It is even so with the Universe. Did not David tell of how the morning stars sang together?"

The old man's voice had fallen to a low impressive tone.

"The poets of old dreamed of that which I have proven mathematically. The Universe is sustained by a certain tune—a harmonious vibration, rather. Produce a discord in that tune, and you have *shattered the systems!* And I have discovered the combination of seven notes which alone can produce the cosmic discord! Ah, even now I can feel my fingers trembling at the mystic strings of the smaller harp. The chord is caught up by the next larger harp, hurled on with ever increasing power, until the seventh great harp of the seven strings thunders the terrible sound! I feel the earth totter like a man in his dotage! I see the skies waver like an uncertain image in a disturbed pool! I hear the rending of the planets, the shrieking and hissing of satellites released from their parent spheres! The deeps shiver with the chill of returning Chaos! Light fails! Star ashes shower into the goalless night! Time dies and is swallowed by Eternity! Darkness—silence—insentience!"

The old man had grown momentarily taller in his ecstasy. But immediately he became again an old man, stooped, haggard, weary-eyed. When he spoke again his voice was weak.

"O Waters, I have waited so long for you. I knew you would come. I dreamed it so often. And you have come. You will help me build this engine—won't you? For my body is but flesh and old and worn with too much dreaming. I have not the strength to hew out the frames for the larger harps." The old man's voice lost its confident tone and degenerated into pitiful entreaty.

"Never made a harp, Dad," said Waters, attempting to quiet the old man. "Rather make a steamboat"; and he added mentally, "and get out'n this cussed place." Then softly, soothingly, like a beautiful dream, the memory of the woman of the spring came back.

"Mebbe this old man is just a little bit cracked," he mused to himself. "He's been swallerin' facts so long that he's got indygestion of the information. Guess his girl's a real girl all right. Mebbe I'd better make his cussed machine. I don't know what in thunder it's all about, though. Anyhow, I can get out'n here when I can't stay."

"Yes, Dad," he said aloud; "I can make your moosical instr'ments, and I will make 'em. But let's get out'n here into the sun. I'm catchin' my death of cold." He coughed violently to clench the statement.

The old man snuffed all the candles except one. When the two had reached the outer air, Waters gave a sigh of relief.

"If I work six months or so makin' your moosical instr'ments, what am I gettin' out of it?" he asked, as they strolled out into the afternoon sunlight.

"Getting out of it!" answered the old man; "Poor deluded human being! Why, is it not enough to know that you shall aid in annihilating human suffering—universal pain?"

"If I'd teach you to laugh, wouldn't you like to keep on livin', Dad—and give up the moosical business? Didn't your ma ever tell you about goin' to heaven? Mebbe if I'd teach you to laugh you could remember what she said." The memory of the vision at the spring inclined Waters to optimism.

"Heaven! There is no place in the Universe for heaven!" said the old man. "And if there were, I would not care to dwell there. I would be too restless a spirit. Ah, the poverty of the conception! How faded and cheap it is beside the golden dream of metempsychosis!"

"Me—what?" queried Waters.

"What a precious privilege life would be," continued Ambrosen, "if space were our ancestral residence! How we would enjoy swooping through the mystery of vastness! How we could lave and revel in the paths of day! Space, Eternity, Darkness—to be a soul coëxistent with these! How the thought lures me! Time! It is so pitiful a thing in its incompleteness that I wonder how any can believe that it ever crept into a god's conceptions!"

The two had reached the shore of the island, and they lay down in the warm sand.

"Waters," said Ambrosen, "have you ever dreamed in the sunlight? I have the most terrible dreams at times, even in the glare of the day. At such times I am afraid, and I must hide myself in the dark—out of the glare, where I can see too plainly. But at nights! Waters, at night I dream so quietly. All is pastoral then—green fields with cattle lowing by clear brooks, with the drone of invisible bugs threading the dull music of the noon! But when I open my eyes and feel the day again, I am afraid! The quiet night dreams! Ah, they prove to me that I can not be——" The old man tapped his forehead repeatedly with his fingers, to explain his meaning. Then he threw himself upon his back and sighed. "I should have been the spirit of a rag weed," he went on irrelevantly; "how I would have drooped and sulked in the sun! How I would have loved to feel the drip of the melancholy rain on my face through the sodden days and sullen nights, drinking from the overflowing chalice of the skies!"

"Phew-oo-oo," went Waters; and he followed with his gaze an imaginary cloud of dust issuing with his breath. "I should have been a barrel full of good liquor, a-soakin' for a century or more! I'm dry!" The liquor of the night before had left him very arid.

"Ah," continued Ambrosen in a lugubrious tone; "all the world is thirsty. We are born thirsty. But it isn't water we want; it isn't water."

"Huh uh," agreed Waters affably, thinking of the cargo of good liquor he had left behind.

The old man fell into a silent mood. He was dreaming over again his great dream, and Waters was deep in a soft reverie, through which the glowing woman of the spring flitted like a melody. At length the old man sighed and arose.

"To-morrow we shall begin the great task," he said. "Come."

VI

Concerning Happiness

After the noon meal, which was another feast of wonder for Waters, a vague melancholy seized him. The old man had gone muttering to his books, and the girl had disappeared. Waters wished she had not gone. Now that the bitterness of his debauch on the *Emilie* had passed, he began again to feel the need of human companionship. He went to the mouth of the cave and peered down into it. He saw Ambrosen bent over an old volume. One candle cast a sickly illumination in the dismal place.

"Dad!" cried Waters. The old man heard nothing. "Come out'n your hole, Dad; the sun's shinin'!" Still the old man did not hear.

Waters went out of the house. He remembered the jug of liquor he had left on the shore. Surely he could not have drunk it all. Why hadn't he thought of it before? He hurried along the woodland path, cool in the shade and fringed with flowers. He came to the big spring and approached it cautiously, half expecting to see the luminous body of the girl emerging from it. He knelt down beside it and looked into its clear depths.

"That's you, Waters," he said, intently gazing upon the reflection of his face. "That's the feller the world kicked out. Didn't need him. Took his eye and his leg first, though. Now look at yourself careful, Waters. Hain't you hombly? You're an ornyment to creation—now hain't you? Look at that eye! What're you good for, eh? Oh, you're sort of fillin' space, I guess. There was an ugly hole in the atmosphere, I guess, and so they slung you in to fill it up! There'll be a horrible rip in the unyverst when you die; now won't there?"

He got up from the spring with a sigh and went on down the path, soon reaching the shore. He found the jug of liquor where he left it. He snatched it up, pulled the cork, placed the mouth to his lips. But somehow he felt ashamed and faltered. Something new had crept into him. He put the cork back and beat it in with his fist.

"No, cussed if I will!" he said.

He seized the jug by the handle, swung it above his head and hurled it out into the current. Then with a sudden anger, he gathered a handful of small stones and energetically bombarded it as it sped away southward in the muddy swirl.

"That's right!" he cried to the jug; "go back to the world, you brown devil, and tell 'em Waters sent you!"

He watched the jug bobbing and glinting in the sunlit current until it disappeared. Then he took his pipe and tobacco from his pocket, and hurled both after the jug. When these had also disappeared, he lay down upon his back in the shade of a tree, and gazed into the clear blue of the afternoon sky.

"Well," said he to the universe in general; "me and the World is parted! World kicked Waters out and then Waters kicked the World out. No hard feelin's; suits both of us. Nice place up here! Squirrels and bugs and butterflies and hummin' birds and plenty of blue sky. A feller wasn't made to be such a nice wise animal as he tries to be, I guess. Made to run wild in the woods and sleep in the sun and gnaw roots for a livin'. That's what he was made for! Get big tough muscles on him and growl at t'other animals that tries to steal his grub! Not know no more about dyin' than a tree does! Just growin' and enjoyin' hisself and hollerin' for joy at the sunrise when it's pretty! I guess folks begun havin' trouble when they learnt how to build towns, and got to sayin' 'This land is mine and that's your'n, if you can keep me from gettin' it; and don't you come a-nigh mine!' Now me and the old man and the girl and the squirrels and the bugs and the hummin' birds has got the title to this here end of the unyverst, I guess. God, He made the sky for a tent for the whole tribe, and He fixed it up fine for 'em; but they got selfish and went to buildin' little houses for themselves."

He mused for some time, drawing in great breaths of the Summer air. He heard the dull crooning of the leaves, the rapid beating of a woodpecker, the frisking of squirrels above his head, and the whir of eager wings cleaving the cool shade.

"Old man wants to be God, eh? I guess if he'd crawl out'n his hole and look about careful, things wouldn't seem so bad. He's settin' down there in that hole, a-lookin' at what men done, by the light of a candle that stinks and gets blue in the face a-tryin' to shove the damp dark back; and I'm lollin' out here a-lookin' at what God done, with the yeller day a-lightin' it all up for me, and laughin' all over 'cause it's so easy to shove the night away! Wonder if I hain't nearer right than him."

Waters sighed a deep sigh of contentment, and rolled over on his side, the better to look about him.

"Oh, this is the place for me, I guess," he continued. "I'm too cussed hombly to knock about among folks." As he spoke, his gaze fell upon an ancient oak growing out of the bank and overhanging the river. It was gnarled, and had been disfigured by a stroke of lightning. "But look at that tree, Waters! Now, I reckon that's as hombly for a tree as you are for a man. Been lambasted frightful! But look how it goes on a-reachin' up towards the sun and the blue sky. Don't seem to know or care about bein' hombly. Hain't complainin' none. Just makin' a cool shade for all it's worth. Hain't worryin' about livin' or dyin' or what the other trees is thinkin' about it. Now, if it was cut down, them flowers and ferns and birds and squirrels would miss it, I reckon. When the wind or lightnin' comes along and lops off a limb, it goes right on reachin' up. Guess it ain't so much what a feller looks like."

Waters' flow of optimistic thought made him eminently satisfied. He breathed deep breaths and cast about him for more food for pleasant reflection.

"Oh, there's all kinds of hints for a feller, I guess. They ain't all in the script'res. Now, I reckon that there oak is nigh onto four hundred years old. Say! the way them leaves is clappin' their hands up there in the sunlight, you'd think it was a saplin'! Seen a lot of hard Winters and storms and floods, too. Fergot 'em all, and keeps on lookin' for the sun. So old it's got wens and warts all over its hide; but I'll bet its heart is as full of sweet juice as a saplin'. Oh, I guess there's plenty of hints for a feller!"

He got up, stretched himself with a deep sense of the joy of living, in spite of his late pessimism, and re-entered the woods. He came again to the big spring, and lay down on the ferns, looking into the crystal depths.

"Well, you are hombly, Waters; that's sure. So's that tree. Now look at that spring. Keeps a pictur' of the sky next to its heart. I put my hand into it and rile it up and spoil its pictur', and it goes right on makin' another pictur'. Don't lie to nobody, neither. Shows them just what they look like, and says: 'There's you as hombly as you are—and here's me keepin' the sky next to my heart.' So full of clear pure stuff that it runs over and don't keep none of it. Gives everything it's got to make the world greener. Look at them ferns leanin' over to kiss it!"

He put his lips to the surface and drank a deep draught. As he gazed into the clear water, suddenly a beautiful face grew up from the depths. It was framed in a mass of hanging gold. It seemed the picture of the spirit of the spring, calm and sweet and pure. As he looked, the face seemed slowly rising toward his face, until its cheeks almost touched his cheek. He heard the faint rustle of a garment. He raised his head, looked behind him, and saw the girl.

"W'y—uh—howdy — do — uh — Miss Dinah!" stammered Waters, getting clumsily to his feet. "I've been a-lookin' at your spring. Nice spring. It's yours, ain't it?"

"It's yours, too," answered the girl, smiling. "It belongs to all of us—you and me and everything that gets thirsty. Where did you come from? I wish you would tell me about the place you came from. It must be so strange and wonderful! Come," she said, extending her slender sun-browned hand to Waters with a childish artlessness, as though she had known him always. She seemed so much the child and so little the woman, that Waters felt no more abashed now than if a butterfly had beckoned him to follow. He took the delicate hand, and they were off; she tripping along lightly at a rapid pace, and he following with a hop and a skip as best he could with his wooden leg. At length the girl stopped beneath an overhanging maple where the ground was carpeted with cool mosses and ferns.

"Now let's sit down here and talk," said the girl; and she lay down in front of Waters, resting her chin in her hands and gazing upon him with large blue eyes. "I'm so glad you came. You are never going away, are you?"

"Huh uh," said Waters, leaning his back against the tree and drinking in the fair picture before him —the delicate face, brown-tinted with the sun and wind, and framed in masses of luminous hair; the shapely bronzed arms, slender but strong; the perfect slope of the body downward from the shoulders; the bare feet among the ferns.

"Is the world very big?" asked the girl.

"Tol'able big," answered Waters, still too intent upon the picture before him to talk freely.

"Tell me all about it," said the girl. "It must be very beautiful and happy, too."

"Well," said Waters, sighing, "some of it's b'utiful and some of it ain't; some of it's happy and some of it ain't. But I do think it was made b'utiful and happy clean through, but some folks won't leave it be that way. I spoiled some of it myself. But I didn't go to do it, really. Don't guess the other folks really go to do it. They kind of get onto the wrong tack. Shouldn't wonder if it's because they get too fur away from the woods and the wind and the birds and them kind of things. You take any animal and put him in a cage and he'll get mean. But it'll all come around all right, I guess."

The girl's eyes grew large with wonder, as Waters warmed up to his subject and launched forth into a story of the world as he had seen it; a very little, lopsided world it was—the world of one man, distorted with the little joys and sorrows of one man, but lit with the sunlight of his optimism.

"And haven't you always been happy?" asked the girl, with the light of sympathy in her eyes. "Oh, you will be very happy here, won't you?"

With sudden tenderness, Waters took one of her hands in his, and patted it softly as he would have done with a child.

"Yes, little girl," he said; "yes, yes."

"Because I'll show you all the wonderful things here. I know where there are many nests with birds in them. And I know where the squirrels live, too. Then you'll be very happy, won't you?"

"Yes, yes, little girl," said Waters.

A horizontal beam of light shot through the leaves. The long droning afternoon had passed like a flash of golden light.

"Oh!" cried the girl. "It is almost sunset! Hurry! I will show you the sunset!" Again she reached her hand to Waters, and led him rapidly among the trees to a place where the island rose westward into a bluff. With eager haste she led her hopping, skipping companion up the steep incline among the scrub oaks, until, reaching the summit, all the glorious sun-bathed land, like a revelation, lay beneath them, stretching away in quiet majesty to the rim of sky. The sun, a dull red disc, was sinking in a mass of glowing cloud piled along the horizon. Suddenly it dipped beneath the surface, and many shafts of varicolored light leaped upward half way to the zenith, and faded in the deep quiet blue.

"Oh, sing! sing!" cried the girl in ecstacy; and her clear voice arose in the song of her own making, that had grown up out of her heart as the song of a bird grows. It was the song Waters had heard her singing in the spring. The streamers of light slowly faded; the fired clouds burned into gray ashes, and the dun evening lingered in the West.

"There, it is gone," said the girl. "But aren't you glad it will come back to-morrow?"

"Yes, little girl," said Waters; "I am now."

Hand in hand, like two happy children, they descended the steep hillside.

VII

The Second Notch

That night Waters thought long about the beautiful day that had just passed. A faint night wind came in at the open window with the moonlight, bearing the odor of the woods to his nostrils. It seemed that the spirit of the quiet night was calling him out into the open air. He got up quietly, dressed and went out.

How changed the world was! How strong it was, yet how kind and gentle! The drowsy wind made a lullaby in the leaves, and there was the shrill small chorus of night bugs, glad to be a part of the beautiful plan. How quiet and brilliant the stars were! How magnificently the moon swung westward! The world had become a holy place. Never before had Waters realized so fully the magnificence of the temple of the great outdoors.

He walked on slowly through the woods, until he came to the river, now a stream of living silver. "Oh, it's a great plan you've got for things!" said Waters, as though speaking to some great Ear latent in the beauty about him. "And I'm part of it, too, ain't I? Feller'd ought to be proud of that! I've been a black speck on it all in my time, though. And still it seems I can hear you sayin': 'Fill up your ears and your eyes with it! It's your'n, and I think you'll like it!' "

He lay down and placed his face close to the Earth, and extended his arms as if to pull himself closer to the great warm breast. He did not know that this was prayer; but a great peace came over him.

Suddenly a hoarse shout rang out in the woods. "Waters! Waters!" It was the voice of the old man. Waters ran in the direction of the cry, and soon Ambrosen emerged from the shadows.

"Oh, you have not gone!" gasped the old man. "You have stayed to help me! I dreamed just now —that you went away—and the great scheme failed! I heard the stars laughing—at me! Their laughter was loud as thunder and maddened me! I awoke and you were gone!"

He threw his arms about Waters' neck. "Ah," he whispered; "what if I should be only a man after all—only a man!"

As they returned to the log house, a great kindness grew in Waters. He no longer felt any terror at the memory of his past experiences. He felt the desire to protect this old man who walked beside him, holding his hand like a timid child.

When they had reached the house, Waters carefully arranged the bed for the old man to lie upon.

"Sorry I made you worry, Dad," said Waters; "but don't you be afeerd, Dad. I hain't a-goin' to leave you. And to-morrow I'm goin' to begin to make your moosical instr'ments. You just lay down and sleep. There—that's right."

The old man lay down, looking up appealingly at Waters. "You will stay, Waters?" he said.

"Yes, Dad, you can hold my hand. There, now can you go to sleep?"

The old man closed his eyes like a weary trusting child. His eyelids twitched nervously. Waters stroked the seamed forehead with a hand grown gentle as a woman's. "You hain't goin' to dream bad no more, Dad. 'Cause you know, things'll come out all right; they will."

In a short while the old man was asleep. A cloud-rift sent a ray of light through the window of the room and smote the face of the sleeper. Waters leaned over the illumined face, like a mother watching the sleep of her sick child. The face was a palimpsest—an old dry bit of parchment, upon which some master-hand had left unfinished a brave tale of grace and beauty, to be rendered scarcely legible by the scrawl of a ruthless heavier hand. It was Schopenhauer written over Homer.

As Waters looked upon the face, unquiet even in slumber, a great pity grew in his heart. "Pore old man!" he muttered. "You've got 'em, pore old man! But I'm a-goin' to be good to you. I can't tell just what you want to get about; but you hain't never goin' to get about it, I know. You'll just keep a-wantin' and wantin' and wantin', and havin' them fits 'cause you can't get what you want; and then, some day, you'll kick the bucket; and I reckon then you won't want nothin' no more, and won't have no more fits, pore old man."

He gently loosed his hand from the old man's grasp, and buried his face in his palms. The returning memory of the luminous girl filled his brain with a great soft light. Manlike, he began to plan happiness. Maybe sometime, far off, he would marry her. Then he would build a larger log house for the girl and Dad and himself, and they would be very happy. Why, what else would he need? He would have her and the old man, and he could raise enough to eat. What else would he want? And maybe—afterwhile—well—maybe afterwhile—had not other men been fathers?

"She didn't say nothin' about my leg or my eye," he mused. "She didn't say a word!" And with a sudden inspiration, Waters searched in his pocket for his jack knife. Then, with infinite care, he carved a second notch on his wooden leg.

VIII

The King of the Island

The next morning, Waters was wakened early by the old man shaking him and speaking in his ear. "Come! The great day is beginning to dawn! Let us not waste a minute. Twenty years have passed, and now at last I am beginning to realize my dream. Come! It is dangerous to let the minutes pass; they breed years—and I am getting old!"

Waters rolled out of bed, yawning, still feeling in his drowsy veins the glory of a dream. He dressed hurriedly, and they went out into the kitchen, where breakfast had already been prepared by the old man. Ambrosen ate nervously, and Waters with that good appetite which is at least the companion, if not the parent of optimism. When they had finished eating, the old man brought out an axe from another room where he kept a variety of tools, and they went into the timber, cool in the twilight of the earliest hour of dawn.

As Waters walked along beside the old man, breathing in the odor of the dew-steeped green things, his heart swelled. "Oh, Dad," said he, "can't you see that it ain't all bad? Can't you see somehow, that it's all sweet and pure? Just stop and smell and look around. Hain't it a fine piece of work? W'y, look here at this drop of dew! Cool and pure, and it's got a pictur' of the sky in it!

"Listen! Things is beginnin' to wake up. Hear them birds and them bugs and them frogs! Ain't they glad about the sun a-comin' back? All of 'em a-singin', singin', singin', and us fellers what's a lot smarter, we ain't a-singin'. Oh, Dad, we'd ought to be a-singin'. Look! Listen! Things is beginnin' to happen all over! Sun's wakin' up and rubbin' his eyes and yawnin' and throwin' his big strong pink legs out of bed, and shakin' the kinks out of his long flamin' hair! The whole world is stretchin' its neck to get first sight of his grinnin' face!"

The old man sighed, and his face softened.

"Yes, yes, Waters, I see, I see. I remember, when I was a boy, I could feel all this as you feel it now. But something—came—over me." He stopped and passed his hand across his brow, as though in perplexity. "Something—came—over—me," he repeated falteringly. Then he straightened his body and his face darkened. "Come!" he cried. "The minutes are passing. They breed years—failure!"

They hurried on until they came near the end of the island, where upon their right hand lay the turbulent river dwindling into the South, and before them the green hills with the first light of day upon them. Every moment, as they stood, increased the wonder in the East. A line of dull light lay along the jagged sky rim. Slowly a yellow blur grew up from the horizon, like the glow of a burning straw stack a half day's journey over the hills.

"Dad," said Waters; "if we'd bust it all up, do you reckon we could make somethin' better? I reckon I can't help you none on that end of the job. Let's throw the axe away and go and waller in the sand and laugh and talk about how nice things is!"

The old man stood staring into the growing wonder of the East and did not answer. His face bore the stern expression of a general watching the steady advance of the foe. Suddenly the yellow blur of light brightened and became agitated. Then a dozen flaming rockets shot upward, igniting the clouds of fleece that floated in the pink-shot blue. The East became a riot of colored flame; and then suddenly, like a king heralded by a costly illumination, the sun heaved his glowing head above the hills, and took the steep way to the starless zenith.

Waters, staring in rapture, heard a guttural exclamation from the old man. He turned, and saw a face gloomy and malevolent. Ambrosen shook his clenched fist at the mounting sun. "Boaster!" he muttered. Then, turning to his companion, with all the sinister strength in his face, which had terrified Waters at first, he said, pointing out a tall straight hickory: "There, that is the first. Cut it down. It will do for the largest harp." And Waters fell to work, swinging his axe merrily in the morning sunlight.

"Pore old man," he thought, as he plied the axe and whistled a slow soft air. "He ain't right; but I reckon he won't live long. And I'll humor him. Work don't hurt me none, and he'll feel better when he thinks things is workin' out for him. And then, we can use the trees for wood when the Winter comes. Pore old man."

When the first tree crashed upon the ground, the old man became ecstatic. "Ah!" he cried. "It is the great event of Time; for is it not the first stroke of the death-knell of Time? What were all the puny wars of the Titan brood compared with the subtle attack we have begun to-day? Waters, you have driven that axe through the body of a tree. Only a tree? No!" The old man straightened his body like a bow that has launched its arrow. "You have cut a root of Ygdrasil—the Tree of the Universe!"

Waters worked all day, thinking of the old man and the girl and the island, and of the sweet new influence that had come into his life. The soft low air that he whistled almost continually to the time of his vigorously wielded axe, was the one Specks had heard him whistle that day up the river, when he had carved the first notch in his wooden leg. Toward evening he stopped, and turned to the old man who was sitting near by upon a fallen tree, eagerly watching the progress of the work.

"Phew-oo-oo," he went, mopping his face; "nice

and cool in the shade. Say, Dad, I've been thinkin' some about your big scheme. And I've been thinkin' that we'll have to let these logs lay till Fall before we use 'em. They won't work up good when they're green."

"More wasted time," muttered the old man.

"No, 'tain't wasted, Dad. If I didn't care about your scheme, I'd say, put 'em in green. Then there's another thing. Have you got a block and tackle? You see, these timbers 'll be heavy, and we'll need somethin' to handle 'em with."

The old man's face darkened. "No," he said, "I have none. Oh, the whole scheme will fail."

"No, it won't either," said Waters, " 'cause I've got a plan for gettin' 'em. You know lots of boats passes here goin' to Benton, and I thought mebbe I could sell 'em wood and get what we need for our business."

"Have them stop here!" cried the old man. "No! They will discover my scheme and it will fail!"

"Well, if you'll leave it to me, it'll be all right; and we'll have a block and tackle. If you don't, we can't handle the timbers. Better let me, Dad."

After a long silence, the old man sighed wearily, and said: "I'll leave it to you, Waters."

"That's right, Dad," said Waters; "so I'll finish cuttin' down the timbers and then I'll go at the cord wood."

So it happened that Waters again began listening for the sound of an approaching steamer, and peering up the river for a trail of smoke. But this time it was not with the same longing as in the bitter-sweet Calhoun days.

One day a week later, Waters heard the sound for which he had been listening. He rushed down to the shore, and as the boat came in sight, he began signalling for her to put in. In those days, the sight of a man signalling in the wilderness was so rare that the boat immediately changed her course and swung in to the island. It was the *John H. Lucas.* The captain stood at the bow, smiling broadly.

"Well," said the captain, "we've been looking for this. Met the *Emilie* up stream. So you're Mr. Waters, eh? Been sobering up some? Jump aboard and we'll take you as far as Sioux City anyway."

Waters' face reddened with the memory of the debauch that now seemed ancient history to him. "I don't want to go back, cap'n," he replied. "I'm livin' here now; sort of squatted on the island. I'm king here, and I wasn't nothin' down there; so I'm goin' to stay. You can tell the cap'n of the *Emilie* that I'm glad he kicked me off."

The captain grinned broadly. "Pretty good place to swear off, eh? Well, why did you stop us?"

"Well, you see," said Waters, "I'm settin' up in business. Goin' to run a woodin' station. Woodin' stations is scarce hereabouts, I guess. You can tell some of the others that goes to Benton."

The captain ceased grinning as he gazed upon the earnest face of the castaway. In those days, when the boats of the upper river were obliged to burn wood, much delay was occasioned by "wooding up." It was necessary that the boats tie up and turn out all hands to get fuel for the furnaces. The captain of the *Lucas* became more affable. "We will return to Benton in the Fall," said he. "What can we bring up for you, Mr. Waters?"

Waters began to rack his brain for a list of necessities, that began with a block and tackle, and included not only Winter garments and shoes for two men, but, to the surprise of the captain and all who listened, both Summer and Winter garments for a woman.

"Woman in the case, eh?" queried the captain jovially. "And you're swearing off? Sure sign, Mr. Waters, sure sign! Shall I congratulate you? We'll probably be bringing up an Indian Missionary in the Fall, and we'll have him do the knot tight for you!" And the captain laughed heartily at his own good-humored sally.

" 'Tain't that way," said Waters, grinning pleasantly, "—yet."

"Oh, not yet!" laughed the captain. "Well, you want to have things all ready when the Missionary gets here!"

The captain took a list of the articles desired, and Waters gave the necessary measurements, as best he could, for the garments ordered. When he finished the list, he thought of sending a line to Specks.

He asked the captain for a pencil and paper, and hastily scribbled this note:

"Dear Crony: I'm up here at Old Man's Island. Nice place. Can't you come up? Tell your ma I ain't forgot how kind she was.

"Your Crony,

"WATERS."

"P. S. I'm King of this Island. Don't never drink none."

This he gave to the captain, who promised to deliver it to the post office at Calhoun. The *Lucas* pulled away, and Waters, thinking of the suggestion of the captain, watched the boat growing smaller until it had disappeared down river.

"Wisht it could be that way," he mused.

IX

The Awakening

When Waters had finished cutting the timbers for the harp frames, he launched forth into his own scheme—that of furnishing passing boats with wood. As it would be necessary to let the timbers lie until Winter, he had the Summer before him to be spent in useful toil.

Already he had begun to make vague but pleasant plans for the future. It might be that he would not always live on the island. It might be that he would go back to the world, bearing with him the new light that had come to him in the wilderness. He might not go back alone, and in that case, he would need money with which to begin life again. He often figured how much he could make in a year, and already bore about him that prosperous air of a man who is conscious of filling his niche in the world.

So he went on chopping and splitting and sawing and piling the wood upon the shore, whistling merrily the while. And all the while, the girl hovered about him like a butterfly, talking to him about the wonders of the great world, singing to him in her wild way, and laughing merrily like a playful little girl. And often when Waters would sit down to rest, she would sit beside him and he would repeat to her songs that he had known of old; songs of the sea, rollicking and noisy as the sea; simple songs with old-fashioned melodies. They were the songs that had long been buried under the darkness of his life, and now when the darkness had passed, blossomed forth in the sunlight of his new life. And when she would sing them to him with her full rich voice, in a winsome, artless manner, Waters would stop working, leaning upon his axe, while a new warmth crept into his breast, and a mist passed before him, in which he saw pleasant visions.

Day by day as he watched her playing about him, already a mature physical woman, but as yet only a little girl in soul, Waters' love for her grew. He had never loved in just this way before. She seemed to him rather a young daughter whom he was happy in protecting. It is said that some men are born to be fathers; it was so with Waters.

And yet—why did his heart beat so loudly when she took his big sunburned hand in her thin hands, and said that it was very strong and that he was a very good great man? Often at such times he felt a great desire to seize her and kiss her as he had never yet kissed a woman; but as he looked upon the innocent childhood of her face, he muttered to himself: "Only a little butterfly a-playin' in the sun!" Then he would sigh and go on with his work.

One sunny afternoon she was sitting near him as he worked, weaving ferns and mosses into a crown, and she was singing a song that he had taught her. It was "Afton Water" set to an old-fashioned, crooning air:

"Flow gently, sweet Afton, among thy green braes,
Flow gently, I'll sing thee a song in thy praise;
My Mary's asleep by thy murmuring stream;
Flow gently, sweet Afton, disturb not her dream."

"Yes, yes," muttered Waters, pausing to listen, "the woman in her is sleepin' yet by this old stream, and don't you wake her, Waters. She's only a little girl yet, dreamin' sweet little girl dreams; and don't you wake her."

When she had ceased singing, "Come here, little butterfly," he said. She ran to him and sat down on a log beside him. He gently fondled her long gold hair. "Do you know that I love you, little butterfly?" he said. "Yes," she said, breaking out into a snatch of song; "and I love you," she added, breaking off the song abruptly.

"But do you know, little butterfly, what that means?"

"It means being very glad," she answered; "doesn't it?"

"Yes," answered Waters; "that's what it means, I guess." He gently touched his lips to her forehead. It was the first time he had kissed her. She gave a little cry of surprise.

"Don't you want me to do that any more?" Waters said.

"Oh, yes," she said merrily; "I was asleep one day under a tree; and all at once something touched me on the forehead. It was very kind and warm; and I awoke, and it was a sunray that had stolen down through the leaves. It felt like that."

Waters kissed her gently again, and then returned to his work, muttering to himself, "Only a little butterfly playin' in the sun, that's all."

One evening after they had watched the sun down from the top of the bluff, as was their daily habit, the girl had said, looking across the river to the mainland: "I wonder if the flowers are more beautiful over there than they are here. Can't we go and see?" And Waters had promised that they would go sometime. So he had hewn a rude boat from a cottonwood log, that they might go across together and explore the strange land.

One afternoon, leaving the old man deep in his great scheme, upon which he now spent all his waking hours, Waters and the girl pushed off in the cottonwood canoe and landed on the mysterious shore. The girl was ecstatic over the wonders of the new country. She had never left the island before.

It was late in the afternoon when a deep peal of

thunder aroused them to the fact that the gloom of an approaching storm had fallen, making twilight in the forest.

"Come, little butterfly," said Waters; "it's goin' to rain, I guess." And they hurried to the place where the boat was moored. The air was heavy and a great hush had fallen. Waters looked anxiously up the river to the northwest. Across that quarter of the sky hung a heavy cloud with a regular formation and by fits the blue-black mass was riven with forked lightning. There was not the faintest hint of wind. The river had become a stream of glass. Then the front of the oncoming cloud began to tatter and swing long ragged tentacles of mist before it. A crash of thunder and a sudden puff of wind broke the hush.

"Come, little girl," said Waters, "we'd better be goin'."

He helped her into the boat and pushed off. As the canoe shot through the glassy water, the low rumble of the thunder became an incessant rattle and crash. Then, instantaneously, the wind burst into a gale, driving with it a deluge of rain.

The canoe was now half way across the channel between the mainland and the island. A second and heavier puff of wind caught its prow and hurled it broadside to the blast. Late evening had grown up in the golden afternoon. The river seethed and simmered like heated water under the lash of the wind and rain. With a great effort, Waters again swung the prow of the boat into the wind. The storm now redoubled its fury. The wind burst into a hurricane, lifted the light craft, hurled it upon its side and its occupants went into the river.

When Waters' head emerged above the surface, he saw near him the golden hair of the girl, streaming on the flood like sunlight, as she struggled impotently. The light boat had been whisked out of reach by the wind and current.

Waters was a strong swimmer. With a stroke he reached the girl, and passing his left arm around her body, lifted her head above the surface. In that moment, all the love that had been growing in him since his coming to the island, became a frenzy. The girl shrieked and threw her arms about his neck with her face against his face.

Waters turned himself upon his back, thus throwing the warm beating breast of the girl against his breast, where he supported her. He threw his arms out and turned his head into the current that he might not be swept below the island. With the long back stroke and the backward thrust of the legs, he battled with the flood and wind.

As he swam with the frail arms about his neck, and the warm breast beating against him, he no longer remembered the storm or the dangers of the feat he had undertaken. He felt only the warm frail body close to him; the quick hot breath upon his face; the long wet hair upon his cheeks.

The hot blood pounded at his temples. The dull

hum of the water in his ears became an exquisite melody. It seemed that he had always been swimming; that this same melody had always been in his ears; that this warm body had from the beginning of time clung to him, and would cling endlessly.

But at last, his shoulders struck upon the sand, and exhausted with the strain he had undergone, he dragged the weight at his neck onto the shore and fell beside it.

He did not feel the rain beating in his face; did not hear the trees groaning in the blast. He threw his arms about the panting form beside him, drew it crushingly to him, kissed it with hot lips upon the gasping mouth. She was no longer the little girl to him, the little butterfly playing in the sun. The awakening storm had come.

For a time she lay upon the sand, her wet garments clinging to her body, her eyes closed to the driven rain, wrapped in her wet hair, with her blanched lips—suddenly become the lips of a woman—pressed to the lips of the man.

At length, with a frightened cry, she struggled out of his weakened arms and fled. Then, when his arms were empty, he heard the crash of the thunder, the moaning of the trees, and felt the rain in his face.

X

The Butterfly With the Crushed Wings

The next morning, when Waters sat down to breakfast, his heart sank. She who had only yesterday borne such a frank, childish countenance for him, now avoided his gaze, and something like sorrow had come across her face, where before there had been only joy.

He ate very little, and taking his axe, went out into the timber. His heart was heavy. The storm of the day before had washed the sky a clearer blue; not a cloud marred it. The air was soft; the birds and bees made their music in the sunlight. He alone, it seemed, in all creation had no song at his heart. The work dragged; he had lost interest in it. All the forenoon he forced himself to his task, and when the shadows fell to the north, he hurried to the house with a feverish desire to look into her face again. All forenoon she had no come to him. He entered the house and found the meal waiting, but the girl did not appear. He ate in nervous haste. How terribly still the world had grown! The old man, absorbed in his great scheme, muttered to himself at the opposite side of the table.

Waters left his meal half finished, and hurried out into the woods. He tried to work, but he could not. Repeatedly he would awaken to the fact that she was not there, and that he was leaning upon his axe and gazing at nothing.

At last he dropped his axe and threw himself upon his face in the cool ferns.

"O God!" he moaned. "What have you gone and done, Waters? There ain't no little butterfly a-playin' in the sun any more! You've gone and brushed the gold powder off'n its wings and crushed 'em! You've gone and waked her up when she was dreamin' sweet little girl's dreams, and she'll never laugh and play again like she did! Oh, why didn't you leave the little butterfly a-playin' in the flowers, enjoyin' the sun? Why didn't you let her stay a little girl, and never be no woman at all? What'd you go and show her how to suffer for? She never had no sorrow in her face until to-day. Now it's come there, and you can't never get it clean out again! Pore little sad butterfly without no powder on its spoilt wings! You could've gone on bein' lonesome, Waters, better'n to stop her dreamin'. You've been lonesome so long that it wouldn't 've mattered."

Waters moaned and tossed about upon the ferns. As he lay there, his old dreams of home came back, and he grew calm, as his brain built pictures of happiness. He saw himself returning to a log house in the clearing when the evening was shutting in.

He heard the bass droning of the innumerable little lives about him, threaded with the light arpeggio of children's laughter. He saw in the doorway of his house, a doorway green with vines, the figure of the Girl, with a face grown motherly, like the face of Mrs. Sprangs.

He went on far into the afternoon, fashioning pictures of the future. At last he got up, shook himself as if to throw off a troublesome weight, and smiled at everything in general. The sun of his optimism had again struggled up through the mist.

"I will go and find her," he said. First he traversed the shore, but did not find her. Then he sought in the old nooks which she loved, but still she was not to be seen. At last he climbed the bluff that looked off into the West, and there, sitting in the scant and ragged shade of an isolated scrub oak upon the bleak summit, he saw her.

She was huddled up against the crooked trunk of the tree, with her hands upon her knees and her forehead resting upon her hands. Her long hair fell about her huddled body like a golden mantle.

She had not heard him approaching, and sat motionless. Waters felt a sudden eagerness to clasp her and kiss her. He moved toward her, and with a start, she raised her face, momentarily blank with surprise; then she smiled a vague, sad, timorous smile. Her face was paler than was its wont. Her eyes were dimmed: for she had been crying, and tears still clung to her weary eyelids.

Waters was touched deeply with the change he saw in her face; no more the laughing, sunlit face of the little girl, but ennobled with the first strange pangs of passion, and sublimated with a vague, sweet sadness.

Waters knelt beside her and placed a trembling arm about her shoulders.

"I've been lookin' all over for you, little butterfly, and you never came a-nigh me all day. Don't you like me no more? I didn't mean to hurt you. You've been cryin', too, little butterfly, pore little butterfly."

He brushed the golden hair from her face and kissed her softly upon the eyelids. But she spoke not a word, and trembled like a tired, frightened thing that submits to be caught.

"O little woman!" said Waters, speaking softly, with his lips close to her cheek, and his face bathed in the sun of her hair; "you never knowed before, did you? You never knowed how I've been wantin' you all these days and nights. I've tumbled all over this here world a-lookin' for somethin' I never found, 'cause it was you I was a-lookin' for all the time. And I've been lonesome and mean and bad, 'cause I couldn't never get a sight of you. I knowed allus that if I'd ever see you, it 'd be like the sun a-comin' up out'n a black night—and it was!

"I want you to be my mate. I know I'm hombly and mean lookin', but can't you see under the skin, little woman? When the Winter's over and the

Spring comes, the jays and the bluebirds and the catbirds and the robins and the swallers find 'em mates and go to makin' 'em homes. It's been Winter so long, and now it's Spring, and since I seen you, my heart's been like a robin's, and I want you! You hain't no little girl any more. You're a woman and I'm a man; and, oh, you're so much prettier'n you was; prettier like a warm red rose in the sun is prettier 'n a pink bud sleepin' in the shadders and the dew."

Waters' voice ran on softly like the voice of a spring that overflows and makes low music in the woodland silences.

"And if you'll be my mate, I'll build a nice house for a nest, and we'll live together, not for one Summer, but always. And I'll be good to you and look after you, 'cause I'm stronger'n you, and you're prettier'n me. Won't you?"

He put his hand tenderly under her chin and raised her face that he might look into her eyes. They were filled with tears.

"Hain't you never goin' to be happy no more?" said Waters.

Her lips quivered, and burying her face in his arms, she sobbed:

"I thought I was not happy; but oh, I am! I never knew before that it hurts to be happy!"

XI

Fuel for the Winter

That night was one of enchantment for Waters. He lay awake far into the small hours, listening to the beautiful words spoken by the girl on the bleak summit, that sang themselves through his brain in endless repetition. When he closed his eyes, it seemed to him that the universe was only a great endless darkness and a great holy stillness, but with the woman's face and the thrill of her voice potential in the night and hush.

His dreams toiled powerfully in the dark beneath his eyelids. Like young gods they shouldered away all that was dark in his mind and cleared a space for day. And through the new day, like singing winds, ran the words sobbed in his ear beneath the isolated oak.

In the morning he arose early and called Ambrosen.

"Dad," said Waters, "I want to talk to you. I've listened to you and now I want you to listen to me." Waters waited while the old man dressed. "Let's go out into the cool sweet morning before I tell you what I got to say," said he.

They went out into the open air, twilit with the early dawn.

"Dad," said Waters at last, "me and your girl loves each other."

The old man stopped and stared upon the face of Waters with lowering brows.

"Yes, we do," continued Waters. "Oh, won't you git young again jest for a minute, Dad, so's you'll understand? You mind what you told me about her mother? It's jest like that."

A soft momentary light came upon the face of Ambrosen.

"Oh, I see you hain't quite fergot!" continued Waters with trembling voice. "You hain't fergot how the gold of her hair and the light of her face got into your blood; and how thinkin' of her was like hearin' a song! You know, I've allus been alone, Dad, and I've lived rough because it didn't seem no use to be good. I've been hombly allus, 'cause I got a bad eye and a wooden leg, and folks can't all see under the hide what a feller'd like to be. And I allus felt ugly and acted ugly. I've drunk a river of liquor tryin' to drown sorrow, but sorrow's a good swimmer, and it don't drown that way. Yesterday I kissed her and it was like drinkin' a big mug of warm light. That's the only thing sorrow can't swim in—light.

"Look at me, Dad! Am I as hombly as I was?"

Could it have been the dawn that made the disfigured face of the man suffused with light?

"I can't be," continued Waters; "I don't feel hombly no more. I feel b'utiful! Hain't a feller pretty much like he feels?"

Ambrosen stared long into the brilliant eye of Waters with a penetrating glance, as though he looked deeper than the retina can register.

"You *are* beautiful!" said the old man slowly. He placed his bony hands over his eyes and bowed his head. "Even as I was once," he added.

For many minutes the two stood silent, while the morning grew.

"Let me marry her then!" said Waters at length.

The old man removed his hands from his face, and saw Waters leaning toward him, his body and face tense, his lips quivering. At length he said wearily:

"With all my philosophies, Waters, I can not banish this thing called Love. Ah, if the world could know its meaning better, there would be no need to wait for the heavens; there would be no need to dream of grotesque gods; there would be no need of maddening philosophies; and I would not have been here with a great dream eating my brain like a cancer. When I allow this thing to creep into my great plan, it fails as a bitter dream fails before the memory of better things; and I am only a man lost in wonder—lost in wonder!"

Both were silent for some time, while the dawn slowly expanded.

"Ah!" exclaimed Ambrosen, breaking the silence

with a start; "it is not love I seek to annihilate; it is hate. Perhaps if I succeed in shattering the systems into dust, this thing shall live and sing new worlds out of chaos!"

"Yes," said the old man at length, "take her, Waters. I would not wish to take one beautiful chord from among the cosmic jangles. Take her; and if my plan should fail, be happy as a man can be. And if I do not fail, who knows? Perhaps this thing shall sing—sing like the memory of an old song in the silence. I had thought to see her grow and bud and blossom like a flower, without the flower's hot, shrivelling, fatal desire for the seed. Ah, even perfume and color exist but for that one end. But maybe I am wrong! These dreams! these dreams!"

"Thanks, Dad! thanks!" cried Waters, when the old man had ceased speaking. But a change came over the face of Ambrosen. He scowled and his eyes took on a steely glitter.

"Oh, don't thank me, Waters!" he said, in a voice that was almost a snarl. "Thank the poor weak wretch that I once was! Thank the poor fool that I was when I believed in all the painted lies of life! You have fallen into the old trap, and you kiss that which has ensnared you. The ever-successful trick of Nature! Faugh!"

And he turned and strode away, clenching his fists and muttering: "Fool! Fool! I almost became a man again! Fool! Fool!"

"Pore Dad," muttered Waters; "pore ol' man!

His old heart is like a fireplace when the logs has burned into ashes. The yeller blaze spurts up now and then, but gits blue and falls back, 'cause they hain't nothin' left to burn. And by and by a cold wind'll come a-whinin' down the chimley, and then they won't be nothin' left but ashes. Pore ol' man!

"Oh, a feller's got to keep his fire goin'! When he's happy he'd ought to be layin' away fuel to warm his hands by when the cold wind comes down the chimley!"

From that morning a quiet and continuous joy dwelt in Waters. Another branch was added to his industry. He began building a larger log house on a grassy knoll of the bluff that overlooked the sunset. Here he had resolved to make his happiness, and lay away that fuel of the heart that its fire might not fail when the cold winds should come.

Two steamboats had already put in at Old Man's Island for wood, and Waters had begun laying away the basis of a modest little fortune which he meant to have some day. For had not other men been fathers?

So the dream went on, and the work progressed until in the latter part of August the new house was ready for occupancy, and Waters began looking for the returning *Lucas*. The joking words of the captain had grown into a meaning. Waters had decided that he would need the Missionary.

XII

The Wedding in the Wilderness

Near the close of a day in early September, the *John H. Lucas,* bound for Fort Benton, pulled up to the Island and made fast. Waters, who for several weeks had been listening and looking with supersensitive ear and eye for the boat, was at the shore when she pulled in. The haloed smile, beloved of Specks, made his face a picture of joy.

"Hello, Mr. Waters!" said the captain, coming down the gang-plank with hand extended; "how's the wood business?"

"Plenty of it," replied Waters laconically, for he was thinking of something else.

"Well, we brought your stuff along. We'll lay up here for the night and wood up, if the King doesn't object," said the captain, laughing pleasantly.

"Didn't fergit the Missionary?" queried Waters.

The captain's face was momentarily clouded with perplexity; then a light broke upon it and he laughed aloud.

"Is it time for congratulations?" he said, extending his hand to Waters, who nodded affirmatively.

"Well, shake on it! You're certainly prospering up here. So there's going to be a Queen, eh? Yes, the Missionary's aboard. Shall I arrange for it to take place to-morrow morning at sunrise?"

"Wisht you would," said Waters.

"Well, you're prospering! Shake again! Won't come and have a drink on that, will you?"

Waters shook his head negatively.

"That's right; stick to it. You leave the arrangements to me and there'll be a wedding. Where do you want it to take place? On the boat? Or has the King a palace?"

"I'd rather have it up on the bluff on the west side of the Island," said Waters; "clean up on the peak where the scrub oak is."

"It shall be as the King wishes," replied the captain. "And the guests? Shall it be private or public?"

"Bring the whole crew!" said Waters.

"All right," replied the captain. "If the King will appear with the Queen at this place a half hour before sun-up, we will be ready. Now you'd better come on board and take a shave and clean up. I'll have the men carry your goods ashore this evening. We'll wood up to-night and be ready to start north as soon as the ceremony is over."

The next morning at the peep of day, the shore of the Island near the moored boat presented a most unusual spectacle. The boat's entire crew of twenty men sat about among the ferns, chatting pleasantly and awaiting the coming of the bridal couple. The captain, mate, pilots and engineers were dressed elegantly for the occasion, while the deckhands wore their working clothes and a general air of having been thoroughly shaved and combed.

A pilot, removed a short distance from the rest, sat cross-legged with a fiddle placed to his chin, meditatively drawing the bow across the strings. The Missionary, a priest of the Catholic Church, clad in the robes of his office, with a book in hand, sat among the awaiting guests.

It was a clear, quiet morning. The hush of the dying night was broken only by the happy call and answer of the awakening birds. Suddenly out of the gloom of the forest, Waters and the girl emerged into the twilight. He was dressed in the new suit just received from the *Lucas,* and his freshly shaved face glowed. She wore a simple garment of the kind worn when Waters first saw her. Her delicate face bore a look of anxiety as she clung timorously to Waters' arm. Her hair hung loosely about her shoulders.

As the couple appeared, a murmur of surprise ran among the awaiting guests, who stared with wonder upon the unexpected beauty of the "Queen."

Simultaneously they all arose. The captain bearing a fern wreath in his hand, approached the couple and, bowing, said: "Mr. Waters, I think I have not yet had the pleasure of meeting the Queen."

"Cap'n," replied Waters simply, "this is her—

Miss—uh—Ambrosen." The captain bowed low with his hand at his heart. Half in fun, but genuinely captivated by the peculiar wild beauty of the young woman, he surpassed himself in politeness: "I am delighted to meet you, Miss Ambrosen. Allow me to place this wreath upon a head where it can scarcely regret the absence of the sun!"

He crowned her with the wreath, then turning to those who still stared with admiration upon the woman, he announced:

"Gentlemen, the Queen!"

The men bowed low and the Island Girl, bewildered by these strange ceremonies, clung closely to Waters. The captain again turned to the bride and groom.

"You will now please take your places behind the reverend Father," he said, "whom I have instructed as to the place of ceremonies." Then turning to his crew: "Gentlemen, fall in!"

And the bridal procession began.

At the head, with a slow, majestic pace, went the priest, followed by the bride and groom, then the captain and mate, then the two pilots, the two engineers and the deckhands, walking two and two.

As the procession started, the pilot, with the violin, began to play a slow, majestic march upon his instrument.

Never before in the wilderness had such a spectacle presented itself. Crowned with flowers, with a solemn, measured tread, they passed on through the ferns and flowers, in and out among the trees, with the ever-increasing light of the coming day upon their animated faces.

Suddenly, as the procession proceeded, the majestic march tune was broken off and the sweet strains of an old familiar air came from the violin. It was "Annie Laurie."

The pilot who played, began singing the familiar words in a rich baritone voice. At once the whole procession caught up the song and made the forest echo.

"Maxwelton's braes are bonny
Where early fa's the dew;
And 'twas there that Annie Laurie
Ga'e me her promise true.
Ga'e me her promise true,
That ne'er forgot shall be;
And for bonnie Annie Laurie
I'd lay me down and dee.

"Her brow was like the snaw drift,
Her neck was like the swan;
And her face it was the fairest
That e'er the sun shone on."

As the singers proceeded, rapt in the ecstasy of the song, an old man, unseen by the bridal company, watched their approach from the cover of a thicket. He held a rifle in his trembling hands. Closer and closer to where he lay concealed came the singers. He cocked the rifle and held a nervous finger on the trigger, and his face became dark.

> "And for bonnie Annie Laurie
> I'd lay me down and dee."

As the singers passed where he lay, the refrain, sung by twenty deep voices, arose in ecstasy. The old man's face changed. He carefully let down the hammer of his rifle. His lips quivered, his eyes softened. He buried his face in his hands and sobbed.

> "That e'er the sun shone on,
> And a dark blue was her ee;
> And for bonnie Annie Laurie,
> I'd lay me down and dee."

The singers passed on and the song became muffled in the depths of the forest. The procession reached the bluff, and mounted its steep incline with a measured tread. They reached the summit and halted beneath the isolated oak, with the broad landscape, lit by the slowly growing dawn, spread out before them.

According to a plan pre-arranged by the captain, the crew of the *Lucas* formed in a semicircle about the priest, who stood facing the bridal couple; and the ceremony began.

Far over the green hills to the East the miracle

of dawn was in progress. As the priest's voice arose sonorously in the hush, the yellow blur at the horizon flashed into crimson and gold. The morning mists arose from the river, and grew scintillant in the glow of dawn. The scent of the dew-steeped green things filled the air like the perfume of some unseen censer.

"Kneel, my children!" said the priest, extending his arms above the two before him and raising his face to the sky.

A great hush like that which follows the dying notes of an organ closed about the summit.

Then the sun peered above the hills, throwing out horizontal paths of gold through the river mists and wrapping the bleak bluff in a glow of light.

The voice of the priest continued amid the glory and the hush.

"And now, in this vast, green sanctuary of God, with the sunlight of his love about you and the clear blue of his heaven above you, I pronounce you man and wife. May the beauty of this hour dwell in you hereafter. May your hearts remain pure and fresh as the dew about you. In the name of Him whose spirit is the goodness and beauty of this vast wilderness, I bless you!"

After the crew had filed past the couple, offering their congratulations to Mr. and Mrs. Waters, which the Island Girl received with shyness, the procession began the descent of the bluff and proceeded to the boat.

At the moment of his going aboard, the captain produced a small bundle from his pocket and gave it to Waters. Then the cables were taken in, the gang plank was raised, and the *John Lucas* with grunting and snoring pulled out into the stream.

The man and woman stood upon the shore with clasped hands, watching the boat. The crew stood bunched at the stern, waving farewell; and as the steamer gained speed, they began singing "Annie Laurie." Fainter and fainter grew the snoring of the steamer and the song.

"And her face it was the fairest
That e'er the sun shone on;
That e'er the sun shone on,
And a dark blue was her ee—"

The words of the song became unintelligible in the distance. Only the air, sung with strong lungs, came to the ears of Waters and his heart supplied the words:

"And for bonnie Annie Laurie
I'd lay me down and dee."

XIII

The Autumn

The package which Waters had received from the captain at the last moment contained a letter from Specks and a copy of the Fort Calhoun *Trumpet.* The letter ran as follows:

"Dear Crony—Pa died; he was sick when he come home and never lived long. I feel bad, but he was gone so long that he didn't seem like my pa. I wisht you was my pa. Don't you suppose you could come down and be? Or can't you leave being King of the island? Sometimes ma looks out of the window a long time and then she talks about you. I am setting type for Mr. Simpson again. He don't like you, but I do. Ma says tell you she ain't forgot how good you was neither. You better quit being King and come down. If you don't, I'm coming up there next summer. I have got your money hid and I keep the buffit locked. For a while ma cried lots, but now she don't. Don't you think you could come back?

"Your crony,

"Henry Sprangs.

"P.S.—Could I be King part of the time if I'd come up?"

The *Trumpet* contained a notice of the death of the returned adventurer, Mr. Sprangs, with the usual extravagant encomium which is the portion of the recently deceased, who become for the moment immensely important in the public eye, just as they have passed out of it.

In his great happiness, Waters had forgotten the package for several days, and had taken it from his pocket one afternoon while at work with the axe. When he had finished reading these messages from the world which he had cast away, he sat long upon a log with his face in his hands, thinking it over.

How strange it all seemed! A short time ago he had wanted something with all his soul, and it had slipped out of his grasp just when he was about to touch it. Now he no longer needed it, and it suddenly became possible to gain; as though Happiness fled from him who pursued and pursued him who fled!

All the old Calhoun days came back in a bitter-sweet flood. He remembered the days and nights of feverish longing. All the words he had spoken to Mrs. Sprangs and all she had spoken to him ran mockingly in his head now. He remembered the herculean struggles he had waged with the demon of his past; all the effort he had spent in piling back the dark, and building a sunrise in the rift of night

—a vain Sisyphean toil! He remembered all the beautiful dreams he had dreamed, and how they were tossed with his cork leg into the swirl of the river at midnight, when he skulked away like a wild beast, out into the starlit night to the south.

Suddenly, as all these old memories (they seemed very ancient now) ran in his head, like cloud piling upon cloud in an angry night sky, the vision of the sun-bathed girl, standing waist-deep in a cool spring, shot through his troubled brain like a flash of sunlight.

Waters raised his head and saw how the good, quiet afternoon made gold about him.

"Oh, I guess God knows what He's doin'!" he said aloud. "I guess He knows. Feller fergits that he ain't runnin' this unyverst. A feller like me thinks that if he had the runnin' of the whole business, he'd put a big stationary moon in the sky, and have the whole world a-walkin' paired off in the moonlight, with a fiddle a-squeakin' in every bunch of brush! But it takes black clouds and thunder and lightnin' to bring rain and make things grow, I guess.

"A feller's allus tryin' to have his flowers without clouds and rain. And then he whines at the thunder and dodges the lightnin' and frets 'cause it's dark! You had your clouds, Waters, and now the flowers is growin'. That's the way of it. You jest pick your flowers and fergit the clouds!"

Having restored his optimism completely, he began plying his axe merrily and whistling the while.

The Summer passed; the quiet, golden days of Autumn came with the first frosts, and the forest became a riot of garish color. The forest, unlike man, imbued so deeply with the optimism of the sun, dresses itself more brilliantly at the death of the season than at its birth. So strong and sure seems the hope of its magnificent spirit, that it makes a gala day for its dying, and expires in royal robes.

Since his coming to the island, Waters had unconsciously absorbed something of the spirit of the wilderness. He looked forward to the Winter with joy, thinking of the snug comforts of the fireplace. He had gathered the small crop of corn and potatoes which had been planted in the Spring by the old man. Also, he had laid in a good supply of other necessities for the Winter, purchased with wood from northbound steamers.

In late October, he began working upon Ambrosen's great scheme. And when Winter closed in, the three inhabitants of the little island kingdom were very happy.

XIV

The Cutting of the Third Notch

Spring had come to the island. The ice had broken up in the river, and the flood leaped Summerward with a giant's shout. The first Spring rain had fallen. What song is sweeter than the music of the first Spring rain? It is the answer to the first bee; the sky's cry of kinship to the first audacious robin. It is the most exquisite music in the orchestration of the seasons. Its song is the song of relentance, and its touch is the caress of pity. It is as though the great Mother-Soul, long estranged, had grown tender again, and wept.

The first rain is more than a condensation of vapors. Should you ask a scientist to explain the matter to you, he would weary you with discussions concerning the thermometer and barometer. He would be correct, no doubt. But giving you the facts without the truth, he would make the mistake of leaving the heart out of the thing.

The first bee was abroad seeking the first flower, and the silent spaces were filled with its exquisite droning melody, like a small prelude to the mightier song of the thunder storm. Light was abroad—the warm, friendly, yellow light of Spring. The scientist says that light and sound are merely different modes of molecular motion; then may not light and sound bear the same meaning to different senses?

And now between the fitful thunder showers, the Spring sunlight filled the silent places of the wilderness, as in an overture the low, woman-singing of the violins succeeds a storm of horns and cymbals.

Amid the audible and visible melody of the Spring, the Girl dreamed an ancient dream. The mystery of motherhood was upon her. Day by day the mystery deepened. She sought the lonesome places where the sunlight filtered through the young leaves, and brooded in wonderment. At times she was seized with a great soul-deep ecstasy as instinct whispered to her how the sweet load she carried would soon lie huddled at her breast. She felt that it would be something dearer than sunlight and bird-song, more marvellous and fairer than the dawn. And often she was terrified with strange but sweet pangs, when she would throw herself upon the ground beneath the kindly shade of a tree, as though she sought protection upon the warm breast of Earth, the great, kind, pregnant mother, wise with the memory of much love and many children.

As the Spring developed into Summer, the girl lost something of the diaphanous beauty of her Springtime. As the prairies grow sallow under the midsummer sun, her face grew sallow. Her eyes lost some of their lustre and her limbs their fleetness. When she sang at evening, it was no longer the wild pæan to the setting sun, but a low, caressing croon. She sang as if to that which soon should hear.

One June night Waters sat by her bed in the house which he had built for them the preceding Fall. She slept uneasily and muttered in her sleep. Waters gazed upon her face, already marked with the patient suffering of the mother. In all his half-starved life, this was the supreme hour. He had become a King in this wilderness, and his kingdom lay before him; a creator, and the sunlight of his love lay upon his cosmos.

With a great rapture he gazed upon her. He scanned the haggard eyes, the cheeks that had lost some of their bloom, the slight fullness of the throat, the bosom becoming full and soft to be the pillow of a sensitive little head; and it was like scanning the irregular lines of some beautiful poem.

When her breathing had become more regular with a deeper sleep, he leaned over the bed and placed his lips tenderly to her forehead. Then, whistling a low soft air under his breath, he took out his knife, opened it, and with almost religious care he carved a third notch upon his wooden leg.

XV

The Seventh Day of the Seventh Month

Late in the month of June an heiress had been born to the little island kingdom. Waters named her June, perhaps so more because of the month of her birth than that her advent had brought the season of roses to his heart. It was now with a great effort that he continued a show of interest in the accomplishment of Ambrosen's great dream.

The supreme event of Waters' life barely served to gain a passing notice from Ambrosen, who toiled daily with nervous energy, placing the strings upon the series of harp structures. He went about silently and with an air of abstraction that was incomprehensible to Waters. Often he toiled far into the night in the dismal cave, setting and tuning the strings, and would not leave his task until Waters forced him away to bed. His sleep was restless and broken with mutterings, as he still endeavored in his dreams to tune the giant strings.

At last the seventh day of the seventh month came. Ambrosen arose early and awakened Waters.

"Come," he said in a strange whisper; "it is the dawn of the last day."

Waters dressed himself while the old man paced nervously up and down the room, muttering: "Hurry, hurry, what if I should die—and it should fail!"

Waters placed his hand upon the shoulder of the old man. "Look," he said, pointing to the child still asleep beside its mother.

Ambrosen laughed a low, dry, nervous laugh. "Hurry," he muttered; "I feel strange. I may die before it is accomplished."

They went out into the early morning together. A heavy mist lay upon the river, and the east was blood-red. Ambrosen led, walking rapidly. He stopped suddenly near an old oak tree shattered at the top by lightning.

"Behold me!" he said wearily, pointing to the top riven by the mysterious fire. "If I should fail," he said slowly, "dig here at the base. It will arm you against the world. But I will not fail!" he continued, speaking rapidly. "Come, let us hurry!"

Ambrosen and Waters together entered the subterranean library that led to the great cavern. Both were silent as they walked. Waters thought to himself: "What'll Dad do when he hits the strings and nothin' happens? What in thunder will he do? Pore ol' man!" When they had reached the mouth of the cavern, the old man stopped and nervously grasped the arm of his companion. Waters noted that Ambrosen's teeth were chattering.

"Cold, Dad?" he said, almost affectionately.

The old man straightened himself and said: "I am feeling ill this morning, Waters; feeling ill. Caught some cold perhaps."

Ambrosen lit a candle. "Come," he said, his voice trembling strangely. "Come! The last bitter cup of darkness and silence awaits us yonder in the shadows! Give me the cup!" he cried, a wild light coming into his eye. He ended with a low, inhuman cackle far down in his throat.

As they proceeded, there was the weird sound as of a light wind blowing through the strings of a mighty harp. The light of day came faintly through an opening in the roof at the far end of the cavern.

The old man passed his flickering candle along the walls as he went, and lit other candles placed in the crevices. The place became illuminated with an eerie twilight, discovering a series of seven harp-like structures, increasing in size from that of an ordinary harp to one of colossal proportions far down the cavern.

"See!" cried the old man. "My Dream! It has materialized! It is the lever of Archimedes! I control the universe with the weight of my little finger! Ah, listen! Is it not a very wonderful engine?"

He touched a string of the smallest harp. The metallic snarl filled the place with echoes.

As the sound died away, Waters looked upon the face of Ambrosen. He thought it had turned paler. The eyes were luminous with excitement.

"Did you hear it?" said the old man, in a voice of awe. "And it was only one string smitten lightly. Ah, if it had been the Master Chord of seven!"

He dropped his head upon his breast and mused awhile. When at length he spoke, it was as one in a dream, softly, in a low, strange, monotonous tone.

"And there shall be no more singing of birds at dawn; no more droning of bees in the sullen noon; no more trilling of crickets in the lonesome night. And there shall be no more sunlight! Ah, it is very beautiful upon the crest of an evening cloud. No more rainfall droning dully through the melancholy hours of the night. No more scent of green things, sweetening the lazy winds of afternoon. No more dreams—no more dreams!"

His voice had become slower and softer.

"No—more dreams."

He remained some minutes silent and motionless.

"Let us go out into the sunlight once again, Waters," he said quietly. And they went out together.

They reached the sandy shore, and saw the good sunlight sweep the glittering waters. In their mental state, the two men drank in the generous light as though it had but lately leapt out of ancient darkness.

Waters felt that the time had come to fight against

the inevitable maddening failure of the old man's dream.

"Goin' to spoil all that, Dad?" he said.

The old man sighed, and was silent for some moments.

"It used to shine like that," he said at length, with a melancholy weariness in his voice. "It used to glitter that way on her hair, Waters! See! where the water ripples about the bar!"

Then he continued ramblingly in a monotonous undertone. "Will it be all dark? Will there be innumerable centres of bodiless intelligence floating in the black spaces, yearning for light, longing for material manifestation? Or only blackness, stillness, blackness, stillness? Shall the ego be destroyed utterly, or live and remember? Ah, remember light and sound, and yearn for them; sicken with an eternal home-ache! What if there should be Something dreadful *moving in the darkness? Oh!"*

The exclamation was uttered sharply like the cry of one awakening from a nightmare! Ambrosen grasped the arm of Waters convulsively.

"Did you see anything? Hear anything? What was it?" he whispered, his whole body shaking violently. "Hold my hand, Waters. I'm afraid! Afraid—of—nothing!"

"You're feelin' wrong, Dad," said Waters soothingly. "Caught cold, you know."

"Yes, that's it, Waters; because nothing really happened, did it, Waters?"

Waters felt a chill at his marrow. He tenderly stroked the forehead of the old man, who seemed to waken with a start.

"Let's walk on down the sand," said Ambrosen, his voice growing steady again. "Ah," he soliloquized, "I am striving to be God! Egotism? Of course. That is the secret of power. It is the vital principle of Nature. Did you ever see a rag-weed ashamed to grow beside a rose? The shabbiest blossom believes the sun exists to warm its petals. It struggles upward among the oaks, and the oaks—they reach for the stars! If there should exist a God, and you should say to Him, 'Who are you?' God would answer, 'I am!' It is the vital principle."

Twice the two approached the entrance of the cavern. Twice they turned back into the sunlight. The third time they reached the entrance, Ambrosen faltered.

"Let us wait until the west darkens for the last time," he said. And they waited, silently walking on the sunlit sand.

When the sun had slipped beneath the western hills and the darkness had crept quietly out of the East, the two entered the cavern. The candles in the crevices had burned to their sockets, and their odor lingered in the dark like the bitter memory of a dead joy. Both were silent, and Ambrosen leading with the candle above his head, trembled violently as he went.

When they had reached the smallest harp of the series, the old man handed the candle to Waters.

"Look upon light for the—last—time!" he said. Feeling amid the maze of strings, Ambrosen placed his fingers upon seven of them.

"Are you ready?" he said to Waters. Waters did not answer.

"Then——"

The withered fingers trembled impotently upon the unstricken strings. The emaciated body of the old man shook as with an ague. He staggered and leaned against Waters. His voice came gaspingly.

"*I—am—a—fraid!*"

Waters felt a strange chill. He endeavored to speak calmly.

"Le's leave these here moosical instr'ments and be jest men, Dad; come on, le's."

"Fail now!" cried the old man, something of the god welling up in his shrunken form. "Look at me! I have toiled upon this dream until a faint wind shakes me like a leaf! No! You shall strike the chord! *You,* I say!"

Ambrosen's eyes blazed into the eye of Waters, who felt a strangeness under the wild gaze.

"Yes, Dad," he said.

"Here," said the old man excitedly. "These are the strings! Place your fingers upon the strings—so. There!"

Waters did as he was commanded. Ambrosen buried his face in his arms.

"*Strike!*" he cried.

A strange wild combination of notes leaped from the strings; a weird chord with the snarl of anger, the cry of pain, dominated by a yearning note of a world-old grief. It was the voice of the old man's soul.

The supreme hour had come.

For a moment, Ambrosen stood transfixed. His eyes glared in the twilight of the taper. His body was straightened. His hands were clenched, his jaws set.

Then amid the reverberations of the terrible chord, the old man's voice was raised in a hoarse, choking cry.

"*Listen! It is done! The sun is shattering into dust! Can't you hear the crackling, rending sound? It is the breaking up of the systems! It works! The chord!*"

Suddenly the light died in the old man's eyes. His arms relaxed and hung limply. His head drooped. He staggered, reeled, and sank languidly to the floor of the cavern.

"It works!" he muttered. "The chord! I have——"

The voice sank into a rattle. The face twitched slightly. Waters stooped and held the candle near the old man's face.

There was now not the slightest twitching of the eyelids. The face was bloodless and haggard.

"Dad! Dad!" cried Waters pleadingly. "Wake up, Dad, and we'll clean out'n here and be jest men! Come on, Dad."

Ambrosen did not move.

Waters placed his hand upon the old man's breast. The heart was still. He grasped the languid hands; they were rapidly growing cold.

"Pore ol' man—pore ol' man."

XVI

The Face of Death

Waters stooped beside the languid form and tenderly grasping the emaciated hands, drew the arms across his shoulders. He staggered to his feet, and leaving the taper where it sputtered blue upon the damp floor, he stumped into the darkness that crushed heavily about the candle.

He shivered nervously as he walked, his shadow preceding him, huge, vague, dancing hideously as he swayed with the melancholy weight at his back. Having reached the low entrance to the cavern, he stooped, dragged the body through the aperture, and clambered with his burden up into the log hut. He lit a candle, and laid the old man upon the couch. Then he sat down beside the quiet form and waited for the day.

"Pore ol' man," he muttered. "You hain't never goin' to want nothin' no more, nor have no more fits 'cause you can't get what you want. You wanted and wanted to do somethin' or other for over twenty years, but nothin' much happened 'ceptin' you give out. I reckon the sun'll come up all right in the mornin'. Crickets are all singin' yet. Wind's blowin'. Stars're shinin'. Nothin' don't seem to know you're dead but me. Pore ol' man!"

He stroked the straggling gray hairs from the cold forehead, and gazed with dim eye into the horribly haggard face.

"Wonder how you do feel, pore ol' man. Don't ache no more, do you? Hain't thirsty nor hungry nor lonesome nor skeered, nor nothin'. Jest quiet and done fer; hain't you that away, dad?"

Waters half expected to see the lips open for answer. The night wind awakened and moaned outside, like the sigh of a sleeper who has bad dreams.

"Wonder if the wind's sorry. Oh, I don't reckon it minds much," muttered Waters. Then he sat quietly for an hour gazing at the thing before him.

Suddenly in his lonesome vigil, he was aware of a soft footstep at the open door of the hut. He looked up and saw his wife standing in the doorway. The night wind tossed her glorious hair about her face. Breathlessly the woman gazed with her eyes riveted upon the silent form of her father. With a spasmodic catching of the breath, she cautiously approached the couch. She leaned over and gazed. A deep line gathered on her brow. Her eyes contracted as with fear. Her arms were raised and her hands clenched.

"What is it?" she whispered hoarsely.

"Dead," said Waters quietly.

"How dead?" she queried plaintively; "as a flower dies to come back again in the Spring? Then, when will it be Spring?"

"Dunno," answered Waters, hiding his face in his big hands to conceal tears.

"No," said the woman, "it does not seem that way."

With a strange mixed expression of curiosity and tenderness, she touched the forehead of Ambrosen, but withdrew her hand with a startled cry.

"Ah, why have you not covered him? *He is cold!*"

"Set down," said Waters; "set down till mornin' —mebbe——"

Then again he buried his face in his hands. When he uncovered his face, he saw by the faint day coming in at the door, the woman standing over the corpse, gazing curiously upon the face of death. Her face during the night had grown white and haggard. There was a strange light in her eyes.

"Stay here till I come back," said Waters, getting up from his chair. But the woman gazed steadily upon the mysterious face and did not hear.

Waters went out into the early dawn, breathed in deep draughts of the scented air, and bathed his face in the dew of the grass. The vast kindness in the world about him stimulated his shaken nerves. He went back into the hut. The woman still gazed upon the haggard, discolored face.

As Waters entered with a quiet smile, she turned and said in a voice that was a ghost of her full rich voice: "He has not wakened yet!"

"No," said Waters, "he's done for. Look at that." He pointed to a candle upon the table that had burned to the socket during the long night watch. "That's the way he is; burnt clean down to the end of the wick! But the fire hain't dead; it's only left 'cause the wick burnt down. That's all."

"Ah," she said in a weak voice, gazing again upon the quiet body; "he will never see the sun again? Never feel the wind when it blows sweet from the south? Never smell the perfume of flowers again? Never speak? Never hear? It seems strange! But, maybe, in some mysterious way he will be in the wind when it blows from the south; in the light of the morning; in the scent of the flowers; in the silence of the night. And maybe I shall hear him talking in the crooning of the leaves or in the singing of birds. Will it be that way, do you think?"

"Yes, little woman," said Waters tenderly, "somethin' like that, I dunno. You better go back to your baby, and I'll look after dad. There, don't cry. See how quiet his face is! Quiet and white as the prairie is in Winter. Don't cry, 'cause I guess he's found the way to Spring after all. Go to your baby and take her out and let her laugh in the sun. When I'm ready, I'll call you."

She went out, and Waters began to prepare the

body for its long sleep. He undressed it and washed it with the tenderness of a woman caring for a sick child.

"Pore ol' man," he mused half aloud, as he worked over the body. "I'm a-goin' to put you down there with your books and your harps, 'cause you loved 'em so much. Goin' to put you right near your playthings, with your big dream. 'Twasn't the best in you that dreamed that dream and loved them playthings. It was only your pore ol' body that loved 'em, and I 'm goin' to put 'em where they can be together. Pore ol' wrinkled child that wanted too much! Pore ol' man! I guess there's all kinds of hints for a feller. He'd ought to be glad for what he can git, and not want too much. Pore ol' man, if you'd put half your strength on makin' things that is, better, there'd been a big track of sunlight and flowers a-follerin' you through the world. But I don't blame you, pore ol' man; and it'll be all right with you, I guess. God's so big!"

He tenderly stroked the hair back from the cold brow. "There, now, sleep, pore ol' man."

Waters went out, closing the door behind him, and hurried to his home. He found his wife sitting on the doorstep, holding her child in her arms, and staring with unseeing eyes ahead of her into the sunlight.

"Come," he said, "and see him again."

She arose and followed mechanically. As they entered the quiet room where the old man lay, she shuddered and would not look upon his face. Waters tenderly lifted the emaciated body in his arms and descended with it into the cavern through the opening in the floor of the room.

When he had reached the subterranean library, he shuddered at the sound of the cave-draught sighing through the strings of the giant harps in the damp and dark. It was like the wail of the great dream that had died.

He laid the old man upon the rocky floor and placed a large volume under his head; an ancient folio over which the dreamer had so often pored.

"Good-bye, dad," whispered Waters; "good-bye."

As he hurried out of the place, the forlorn wail of the many strings fled after him out of the darkness where the dead lay. When he had reached the room again, he hurriedly rolled a broad flat stone, which the old man had shaped for a covering, across the mouth of the cave. Then he turned to the woman and child. She lay huddled against the wall.

XVII

THE THUNDER'S VOICE

That night Waters sat beside the bed where his young wife lay, tossing and muttering in delirium. A fitful night wind arose and moaned about the hut. It blew in through an open window, and made the lamp flame smoke and sputter, casting dismal moving shadows through the room.

A nameless fear had seized Waters. Would she die, too? Where would he go then? His thoughts wandered back to the old man, and he shivered with a strange cold.

"Pore ol' man," he mused; "he wanted so much, that he didn't git nothin'. Wanted to bust up the whole business, and wipe it out like a boy wipes figgers off'n a slate. Well, mebbe he did; mebbe everybody does when they quit livin'. I don't know. Wisht I did—wisht I did."

Waters leaned over the bed and listened intently for the breathing of the sick woman. She had fallen into a deep sleep.

"Mebbe she'll sleep it off," he muttered. He got up and went to the door. The sky was covered with clouds, moving ponderously northward, driven by a damp wind. Somewhere deep in the dark south the thunder rumbled, and the forked lightning followed like whips after the flying clouds. The smell of the coming storm oppressed him, and gave him a dim sense of impending calamity.

"God! It's lonesome!" he said aloud. He thought again of the old man lying alone among his books, with the wail of the great futile dream about him.

A heavy hush succeeded a long roll of thunder. The ominous silence was torture to Waters' tense nerves. He closed the door with a strange fear of the hush out in the shadows. He walked lightly back to the bed. She still slept. Her face was paler than it should have been, and there was a haggard look about her eyes.

Was this strange calm in the elements and about the woman he loved, but a forerunner of death? He heard his heart beating strainedly in the silence. He had an appalling sense of the terrible emptiness of the world. He felt that the last beautiful thing was slipping out of his weakened grasp.

Where was God? Surely if there was a God, He could 'iear the beating of a heart in this awful hush.

Suddenly the hush and the dark were shattered. A wild light flashed simultaneous with a sharp crash of thunder. It seemed like an answer to the silent question of Waters. Had God heard the strained beating of the heart?

Perhaps it was the effect of the sudden shock; but Waters felt a sense of security rushing through his veins, steadying him as many a drink of liquor had done in the old bitter days. A great kindness toward Something big and powerful dominated him. He took the child in his arms and fell upon his knees beside the sleeping woman.

"O God, did you say somethin' then? Seems like you said somethin', only I don't seem to understand. What'd you say? Did you say I've been ornery and deserved somethin' bad? But you know I don't allus go to be ornery, don't you? I hain't goin' to ask you to keep her for me, less 'n you're a mind to. But I'm goin' to be different with you from now on. I don't want to try to make a trade with you; but let me keep her, if you can, 'thout hurtin' your business much. Can't you?"

The rush of the wind, the driving of the rain and the continuous rumble of the thunder swallowed up his words as they dropped warmly from his quivering lips, as though to bear them somewhere far off where they would reach a great kind Ear in the sunlight and the calm.

It was far after midnight when the storm died. During its fury Waters had knelt by the bed. A lightness of heart that he could not understand had come to him.

He felt a stir beside him. He raised his head and saw his wife leaning upon her arm and gazing with calm tired eyes upon him.

"I dreamed about sunlight," she said wearily. "It seemed as though there was only a little speck of darkness, and it was swimming in a great warm sea of light. And then after awhile the speck of darkness faded away, and there was only sunlight. I wonder if it isn't that way."

Waters' ears drank in the sound as a thirsty mouth drinks water. It was as though music had grown up out of the night.

"The day dies," she continued wearily, "and it comes back again brighter and fresher. Flowers die, and they bloom again. But while I was asleep, it seemed I learned that dying is only another kind of Autumn or evening. Does your wonderful world know this?"

Waters stroked her tangled hair, and laid her head upon the pillow.

"Some knows it," he said with a soft voice; "the others suffers. Can't you sleep some more?" He stroked her head gently until she slept again like a tired child.

He got up and opened the door. The first touch of the warm, fresh air after the storm was like a caress to him. The half light of morning was abroad. In the East the dawn heaved a flaming head out of the night and mist, like the soul of a strong man struggling dayward out of the dark.

Waters drew a deep breath that thrilled him like an elixir. Was it because the morning air had changed, that he felt joy in the very act of breathing?

He looked again upon the sleeping woman. Her face was calm, and something of the glow of health had returned. He went softly out into the new day.

XVIII

The Call of the World

Waters strolled on through the soothing air, with a great peace at his heart. The whole world had a new significance for him. It was no longer a place fit only for wolves, from which the wolves had been driven. It was to him the abode of erring beings, pitiable for their failings.

He thought of the old time wonderingly. How blind he had been! A new beauty was in the morning. Song birds sang louder and sweeter. He no longer felt a dread of remembering the tragic passing of the old man. It seemed right somehow.

Was it right that he should remain hidden in the wilderness? Should he conceal this new light from the world? For it seemed so new to Waters that he had a sense of absolute ownership by right of discovery. After these many feverish years of bad, might he not do something good? Would it not be better to go back to Calhoun and live down his old life there? And then, there was the girl, June. Should she not be taught how to live among men and be pure?

Yes, he thought he should go back to Calhoun. He could surely get some sort of employment. He was a good carpenter, and Omaha City was growing rapidly; he could get work there. He thought of his "bad" eye and his wooden leg, but not with bitterness. He felt a strange pride in them now, because he would have the opportunity to show how good a man could be with such a handicap. In the old days Waters had always allowed his disfigurement to justify his debauchery.

As he walked and thought, he looked up and found himself at the foot of the old lightning-riven oak which Ambrosen had pointed out to him two days before; or was it a year—five years? It seemed longer than two days.

"Dig here, it will arm you against the world!" What had the old man meant? He would see. He went to the deserted hut to get a spade. How strange it seemed that bitterness had left the place. Now he felt only a great pity for the old man whose dream had failed. He went back to the tree and began to dig, thinking all the while of his new life that was just beginning.

The striking of his spade against something, broke his train of thought. He began to dig with renewed energy. In a few moments he had uncovered a strong box. Then he remembered that Ambrosen had spoken of having had great wealth before coming to the island. Could it be——?

With great effort he lifted the box from the hole.

It was very heavy. With several strokes of the spade he shattered the worm-eaten top.

The box was filled with coins!

He grasped a handful and stared at it giddily. It was gold!

He lifted the box to his shoulder, and staggering with the weight, he hurried to the house. His wife had dressed and was sitting upon the edge of the bed holding the child.

Waters dropped the box upon the floor.

"See!" he cried. "Look! It's money! Thousands of dollars. We're rich—rich! We'll go back into the world and live! Don't you see? Look!"

She sat unmoved and stared at the box of coins.

"What is it?" she said languidly.

"It's money!" cried Waters.

"Money?" she said softly and without the least agitation; "what is money, dear?"

"*Money?*" Waters fairly shrieked the magic name. "Money? W'y money's everything in the world jammed into a little bunch so's you kin carry it in your pocket! It kin do anything good and anything bad. If you're hungry, it'll feed you; if you're sick, it'll take care of you! If you've got it, men'll woller in the dust for you; and if you hain't got it, you'll woller in the dust for them! It's everything!"

"Everything?" she queried wonderingly. "It must be very wonderful!"

She laid the child upon the bed, and cautiously

approached the magic heap. She stooped and grasped a handful of it. With knit brows she examined it carefully.

"It *is* pretty," she said naïvely. "It has a great bird upon one side and the bird is singing, I think."

"No," said Waters, smiling at the woman's curiosity; " 'tain't singin'; jest clawin'."

"Ah, and it has a woman's picture on the other side," she continued, half in glee; "a great, kind, strong woman; I think she would be very beautiful walking in the sunlight."

"That's Mrs. Liberty," mused Waters half aloud; "but she don't walk about much; stays pretty clost to her money most always."

"Ah, see! It says *In God We Trust* at the top! Then the great world trusts in the God of sunlight and bird-song and wind just the same as I do here?"

"Some of 'em does," sighed Waters; "most of 'em trusts in the money."

"Ah, then it must be *very* wonderful. Make it do something, dear. Let me see it do something, won't you? Why did you not get it before and have it keep *him* with us?"

"W'y, you don't get what I mean," said Waters excitedly; "it can't dance a jig, but it can make folks dance 'em. It can't walk and it can't swim and it can't talk nor nothin', but it can make folks do 'em all to onct if that'll make 'em own it. Men fights for it and folks dies for it when they can't get none of it."

"It *is* wonderful," she said with the marvel of a child. "Where did you get it?"

"I dug it up," said Waters, hopeless of explaining.

"Why doesn't the big world dig it up?" she queried, gazing at Waters with wide questioning eyes.

"That's all they're tryin' to do all the time," said Waters. "They're borned diggin', and they die diggin'."

"Tell me everything about this great wonderful world that lives for these magic things, dear."

"I can't," said Waters. "It's too big. We'll go and live there and then you'll know. But we won't make folks woller in the dust with our money. We'll help 'em git off'n their bellies, and stand up and be good."

"Oh, I do want to see this big world! It must be very good and beautiful," said the woman.

"God, He made it that a-way, but there's some folks as didn't want to leave it that a-way," said Waters.

PART THREE

THE BIG WORLD

I

The Grocery Store

Sylvanus Coppers was the proprietor of the Green Tree Grocery Store of Fort Calhoun. He was a little wiry man, whose fifty-odd years had slipped harmlessly off his body to leave their record wholly upon his face. His features, which had always been small, had shrunken to a leathery minimum. This, however, applied only to the *breadth* of his nose, which managed to creep out from the narrow space between his small gray eyes, and extended bravely for a considerable distance into the world, but ended in a melancholy droop at the end. This conspicuous but faint-hearted feature had a timid air of alertness about it, as though it were always nervously expectant of some ominous smell; and one observing it for the first time, half expected at any moment to see it turn like a scared thing, and run in a panic back into the head with some horrible scent in close pursuit. Mr. Coppers wore side-burns, worthy of their name, for they burned a dull red flame upon the sides of his face, and added much to the alert atmosphere that the nose contributed to the facial ensemble. His ears stood out from his head rather conspicuously. They also added to the whole expression of alertness; for they seemed waiting with a mixture of boldness and timidity for some sudden sound.

It was the habit of Coppers when he was thinking (a process for which he felt himself admirably fit) to stroke his nose with a forefinger and thumb, and comb his side-burns with his bony fingers. This morning in August he paced up and down his dingy store, stroking his nose with his left hand, and a side-burn with his right, which double sign indicated that Mr. Coppers' brain was doing an unusual amount of work.

The Green Tree Grocery Store had a significance deeper than canned goods, and more expansive than prunes. It was not simply a place for sordid bargains; it was an emporium of ideas. The unemployed intellectuality of Calhoun was wont to gather there, and exchange items of vital news and opinions of grave moment. The *Trumpet,* blowing only at intervals of a week, always found itself miserably "scooped." Before it came out, the most recent sensation had been relegated to ancient history by the convention at the grocery store. This institution had long since established its position as the ablest exponent of current opinion, and Mr. Sylvanus Coppers, with his nose ever ready to smell, his ears ever extended to hear, and his lips ever quivering to speak, might have been aptly called the Editor-in-Chief. This sultry morning in August he felt a sense of depression, for the cause of which the heat was wholly inadequate.

Something startling had happened—and the convention had failed to assemble! He was seriously considering the advisability of locking his store, and going in search of the assembly, when matters brightened up a bit. Mohammed was relieved of going to the mountain; the mountain came to Mohammed.

In through the front door, puffing and perspiring, waddled Mrs. Griggs with her two hundred comfortable pounds and her round, anxious face.

"Well, well, good morning, Mrs. Griggs!" said Coppers, rubbing his hands together, an act of preliminary conciliation that always foreran a sale of goods. "How are you this hot morning? Children well, I presume?"

Mrs. Griggs beamed pleasantly and answered puffingly.

"Well, folks shouldn't complain, I always say, Mr. Coppers, even if it *is* work, work, work. I declare I've been on the trot shameful for the last week, and now comes that quiltin' bee for Hank and Sary. But I'm not complainin' about that, *although*

Hank ain't hardly worth us a-slavin' our lives away makin' kivers for the likes of him! But Sary's a good, hard-workin' girl, and we felt as if we'd ought to do somethin' for 'em, she bein' in the church and singin' so sweet in the choir. It's really the Lord's work after all, Mr. Coppers," said Mrs. Griggs with a sudden acquisition of facial devoutness. "And a body owes so much to Him, you know. I wanted to get some yarn for tyin' the comforters. I *de*clare it's money, money, money all the time!"

Mr. Coppers produced several skeins of yarn, but, strangely enough, forgot to sing his usual song of praise over the article, which always began: "Very cheap at the price; direct from the factory; no middle-man profit."

"*Haven't* you heard about Waters comin' back?" he said, oblivious of the imminent sale.

"Waters!" Mrs. Griggs gasped in horror. "*He* come back. That miserable, one-eyed, wooden-legged sot? Well, do tell! What'll happen next? Thought the town had got shut of *him!* I suppose Mrs. Sprangs 'll be oglin' round him like she did before he left, now since Sprangs died last year of slavin' his life away for her out in the gold mines!"

"He's brought a wife back with him!" Mr. Coppers dropped this sentence like a bomb. Mrs. Griggs gasped again.

"A *wife?* What sort of a woman *could* she be to go marryin' the likes of him? Poor thing! Maybe she didn't know." Mrs. Griggs' face became the picture of commiseration.

"They're stayin' at Sprangses. Come last night on the *Lucy*. They say Waters is worth all *sorts* of money! Captain of the boat said Waters discovered *immense* wealth in an island up the river!"

Mrs. Griggs' face softened.

"Well, well, I reckon it's us women-folks' duty to go and see Mrs. Waters. Wrap up that skein—the yeller one—Mr. Coppers. Ten cents, you say? Well, Mr. Griggs'll settle when his boat gets back from the trip."

Mrs. Griggs took her parcel from the hands of Mr. Coppers and hurried out into the August glare. Coppers' spirits fell from their temporary elevation, as his little gray eyes followed the waddling figure up the street. It was positively torturing to him—this terrible quiet at a time when so much might be said. As he was again about to lock his door and go in pursuit of the sensation, a bunch of men came hurriedly up the street from the direction of the river, and entered the store.

"Good morning, gentlemen; good morning, sirs!" Coppers cried excitedly. "What's the news?"

"Waters is back!" ejaculated the foremost, as he threw himself puffing into a chair.

"I knowed it!" Coppers felt the least resentment when anyone presumed to tell *him* news. His question was always given in the nature of a plummet to sound the depths and shallows of the public's information. It was meant to be simply a small prelude to his own song.

"He brought a wife with him—and a baby!" added one.

"Hm! I knowed it!"

"And he's rollin' *rich!*" exclaimed the most reticent of them all, in a tone that accompanies a clinching statement.

"I knowed that, *too!*" Coppers' little gray eyes twinkled with self-congratulation.

"We just come back from the buffet that he used to run and we seen him——"

"You did?" Coppers' self-congratulation was swallowed up in curiosity.

"Seen him go into the buffet——"

"And drink a gallon of liquor!" added Coppers, again resuming his self-congratulatory air.

"No, sir! Seen him roll the kegs out one to a time and bust 'em with a axe, and pour it out onto the sand!"

Coppers gasped and wilted into a chair. "The deuce he did!"

"That's what he done!"

"Well, I do say! 'Tain't like him! Seen his wife?" Coppers leaned forward, braced against the probable worst. "I didn't get down to the boat till they was gone," he added, by way of explaining his woeful lack of intelligence in the matter. "They wasn't nobody to stay at the store, you know."

"Seen her? Yes, sir! But you can't be sure you've seen her when you have. She ain't like common women folks. She's more like a picture of somethin' you've dreamp about. Long kind of yeller, kind of red hair. Looked like fire in the boat's light; but when she got into the moonlight, looked like water runnin' in a starry night." The speaker hesitated as he brought back to himself the vivid picture. The eager assembly breathed hard. "But the funniest actin' thing you ever see," continued the speaker; "snivelled and hung on to Waters like a young'n—'cause we was a-follerin' her, I guess."

"Where'd he get her?" asked Coppers, now casting off his entire burden of self-congratulation, the better to pursue the flying sensation.

"Nobody don't seem to be able to gather," replied the spokesman.

II

Mrs. Griggs' Call

When Mrs. Griggs left the Green Tree Grocery Store, she felt a sense of exhilaration in spite of the hot day. If there was one thing in the world Mrs. Griggs needed, it was sensation. Perhaps this was due to her undeniable habit of being busy. She prided herself upon her industry throughout the devious ways of domesticity, from baking superior bread to weaning precocious babies. She had a continual longing to see things go, that amounted to mania; and when the course of events dwindled into a listless singsong, Mrs. Griggs temporarily lost her grip on life.

The recrudescence of Waters made Mrs. Griggs' long-weary spirit prick up its figurative ears, as must have done the scriptural horse that sniffed the battle from afar and "cried ha-ha to the trumpets."

Yes, indeed, she assured herself as she waddled and puffed through the scorching dust toward her home, it was clearly the duty of the women-folks to go and see Mrs. Waters. Folks shouldn't condemn the wife for the failings of the husband. Folks should have charity. Goodness knew! Most women would be mighty lonesome if folks visited them because they had good husbands! She would go that afternoon. And into the idea of neighborly duty crept the least shade of premeditated glory, as she thought of what she could tell the folks that night at Sary's quilting bee.

At half past two, clad in her best calico and a distinguished air, radiant in a carefully ironed pink sunbonnet and a spotless apron, she knocked at Mrs. Sprangs' front door. Mrs. Sprangs greeted her neighbor cordially. The lines of her face, always motherly and sympathetic, were deepened with care.

Anything not totally imperceptible was perceptible to Mrs. Griggs.

"Well, well, Mrs. Sprangs, you're lookin' like you was more'n half sick! Seein' as how I got my bakin' and scrubbin' and ironin' did up, and the children's clothes mended, not to mention the runnin' about I done to get things for the quiltin' bee, I thought I'd drop in on you awhile. You've had a heap enough of trouble, goodness knows, with Sprangs goin' before, and that boy of your'n, with*out* bein' called on to take in strangers. And it's tellin' on you, Mrs. Sprangs! You mark my word, you'll be follerin' your man before long, if you don't get shut of your worries somehow. Us women folks has a mighty hard time of it. Work, work, work! And meechin' little we ever get for it! I declare, I get so throughother thinkin' about it sometimes!"

Mrs. Griggs often found it necessary to go more or less extensively into word coinage to express the woes of life.

Mrs. Sprangs allowed the silence to settle before remarking that the weather was very hot, and she did hope it would rain.

"Oh, goodness gracious, *no!* Don't have it rain, for pity's sake!" cried the silently suffering Mrs. Griggs, with horror in her fat-obstructed eyes. "Think of the mud the children 'd bring in onto my nice clean floor I just scrubbed and nearly broke my back a-scrubbin' it! A body *can* sweep dust, gracious knows; but *mud!*"

Mud was sudden death. Mrs. Griggs' expression proved it.

"Are *they* here now?" asked Mrs. Griggs in a subdued voice, switching the conversation to things vital.

"You mean Mr. and Mrs. Waters?" said Mrs. Sprangs. "Mr. Waters and Henry went to the printing office together. The boy thinks so much of Mr. Waters. I declare all the time Mr. Waters was gone, the boy hardly whistled once."

"I'd be careful about a boy of mine and his comp'ny, Mrs. Sprangs," reproved Mrs. Griggs. "I always wondered at you a-lettin' him run with that—well, with a immoral man."

"I did worry about that before, but Mr. Waters is so different now. He doesn't drink any more, and he was always so kind to the boy," said Mrs. Sprangs, and Mrs. Griggs sighed as one who knew and could speak if she would.

"But *Mrs.!*" urged Mrs. Griggs; "I come part to get acquainted with her."

"She's in the bedroom putting her baby to sleep."

"Do have her come out, Mrs. Sprangs, *and* bring the baby. If there's anything I do like, it's babies."

"Well, I'll call her."

Mrs. Griggs' two hundred pounds quivered with anticipation as she waited for the sensation to develop. Presently Mrs. Sprangs returned from the bedroom leading by the hand a woman who clung timorously to her. Mrs. Waters was of middle height and slender. Her dress of calico, unable entirely to conceal her symmetry of form, would have been unnoticed upon many a figure, but was grotesque upon hers. It was as if some prude had dared to clothe a sculptured Diana.

As the sensation reached its climax, Mrs. Griggs gasped wide-mouthed and wide-eyed.

"This is Mrs. Griggs, Mrs. Waters," said Mrs. Sprangs in her gentle way.

"Very happy to meet you," gasped Mrs. Griggs, arising stiffly, surrounded by her "company" atmosphere.

Mrs. Waters smiled a sweet, trusting smile, and approaching Mrs. Griggs, she placed her arms about the woman's neck and kissed the ample perspiring cheek. Mrs. Griggs was a woman of dignity. She recoiled as though she had been bitten by a snake, and stared coldly at this most startling acquaintance.

Mrs. Waters shrank back to Mrs. Sprangs, clinging to her as a protector. After a breathless moment of horror, Mrs. Griggs managed to hang a faded rag of a smile upon her perspiring countenance, which was answered by a returning smile from the momentarily startled Mrs. Waters.

"Well, Mrs. Waters, how are you beginning to like the town?" began Mrs. Griggs, endeavoring to drag the conversation into a comfortable channel. Mrs. Waters gazed questioningly into the little fat eyes.

"I say, how do you like livin' here by this time, though you hain't only just come?" persisted Mrs. Griggs.

"I wonder why they cut all the trees down and drove the birds away," answered Mrs. Waters, with the light of home-longing in her eyes, and a slight nervous tremor in her musical voice. Mrs. Griggs stared aghast.

"Mrs. Waters has always lived in an island in the upper Missouri," explained Mrs. Sprangs; "it's hard for her to get used to the prairie, I think."

"Well, well, I declare! In an island? It must have been terrible lonesome. What on earth *did* you do when you wanted to talk to somebody? I always think I'd just bust sometimes if I didn't unburden my soul to somebody," said Mrs. Griggs;

and the expression of her face bore witness that she was fully aware of how horrible such a catastrophe would be. "What on earth *did* you do?"

"I talked to the birds, and listened to the wind and the river singing. And I sang to Apollo in the morning and the evening; I was so happy then."

"Oh!" ejaculated Mrs. Griggs triumphantly. "Then there *was* a young man there all the time!"

"My father was there—and God," answered Mrs. Waters with a troubled, questioning face. "Is God here? I have not felt him."

Mrs. Griggs gasped and pushed her chair back from an imaginary zone of contamination.

"W'y, Mrs. Waters! You sur-*prise* me! God is *every*-where! He lives in *our* breasts!" And Mrs. Griggs placed her hand upon that ample abode of deity.

"What church do you worship in, if any, Mrs. Waters?" Mrs. Griggs was hot upon the scent of the new sensation.

"Church?"

"Where did you go to talk to God?" explained Mrs. Griggs condescendingly.

"Anywhere," answered the beautiful heathen, with the troubled expression increased. "In the still night out under the stars; at the burning of the dawn; in the quiet evening; in the thunder-storms and when the snow wailed through the bare branches. Does not everyone do so?"

Mrs. Griggs suddenly felt that the zone of contamination had widened, and she hurriedly slid her chair backward.

"W'y, goodness me! How you do talk!" she exclaimed. "All decent folks worships their God and Savior of a Sunday. They go to the House of the Lord and beg forgiveness for their mis'rable sins!"

Mrs. Waters passed a hand across her brow, as if endeavoring to brush something away. Her eyes became large with wonder, and a troubled light went across her face.

"Do they keep God in a house?" she said simply.

"I must be a-goin', Mrs. Sprangs," said Mrs. Griggs, rising hurriedly. "It's no tellin' what them children 'll be trackin' in on my nice clean floor before I get back."

And she waddled precipitately to the door.

III

The Old Time Clings

When Mrs. Griggs had gone, Mrs. Waters, haunted with a new fear, went into her room and, lying down, buried her face in the pillows. It was the instinct of the wild animal that hides in its den when it is frightened. She thought longingly of her old haunts; of the peaceful starlit nights; of the long, quiet, droning days of Summer; of the song of bird and wind and river. She tried to imagine herself untroubled as of old, dreaming golden dreams in some shady nook or bathing in the great spring. But ever through the dreams, she saw the face of Mrs. Griggs like the face of a nightmare, blotting out the scenes of peace. To her, Mrs. Griggs was the embodied spirit of the great new world which she had thought would be as kind and beautiful as it was great; and she wept softly as a child who wakes from a bad dream when all the house is hopelessly dark and still.

The foundations of her life had fallen away. Everything seemed out of proportion; grotesque as the world of delirium. It was as though she had gone to gaze in the great spring, formerly so clear and quiet, and had found its surface troubled, distorting her own image hideously. Her child lay asleep beside her. She took it into her arms and held it very close to her face. In all the unreality of things, this one seemed real. It was like touching an incarnate memory of the old quiet life that was dead.

Her thoughts wandered longingly back to him who lay in the wilderness. How lonesome it must be there, she thought, waiting for the coming of that mystic Springtime, infinitely further away than April and not to be understood. And yet for the first time in her life she longed for such a sleep. Even the gentle words of Mrs. Sprangs were unavailing. When Waters returned, he found her crying softly.

"I thought the great world would be so kind and beautiful," she said to him. "Oh, it is so ugly and so sad."

"Don't cry," he said, stroking her forehead gently. "It 'll get beautifuller afterwhile, when you git used to it. It means to be beautiful, I guess; but it fergits how sometimes."

"Why do they keep God in a house?" she asked wonderingly. "He lived everywhere in the old days. I think that was why the world was so beautiful there."

"Don't worry, dear," he said, "I guess they don't keep much of Him in a house." Under the gentle touch of Waters' hand she fell asleep. He arranged her hair about her head, and tenderly gazed upon her face, now smiling faintly with some pleasant dream.

"She's up in the Island, I guess," he said to Mrs. Sprangs; "wonder if I'd ought to took her away?"

When they had reached the sitting room, Waters sat down and buried his face in his hands. Had he done wrong in bringing her into a world that she could never understand? She would have been happy there. Was he not selfish in bringing her? Was it only a desire to flaunt his new wealth before the world that had made him do it? No, it really was not that. He thought of the thunder-storm in the night after the old man died. Was it not then that he had heard the Voice that changed him?

Had he not come back to the world he had left so shamefully, that he might do good where before he had done only evil? How could he do good if he made her suffer? Well, he would do all the good he could, and then if she did not learn the strange new life, he would take her back.

All day he had been planning ways of doing good. He had thought of beginning by sending Specks to school; that would be a start.

"Mrs. Sprangs," he said at length. "I've been thinkin' all day about the boy. He was my first crony, and he didn't hate me 'cause I was ugly and mean. Don't you think he'd ought to go to school?"

"I've been wanting to send him this long time,"

said Mrs. Sprangs, "but I couldn't see how it was to be done. What Sprangs left us is barely enough to keep things up."

"Well, you see," began Waters, and ended in embarrassment. Instinctively he felt in his pocket for his pipe, although he did not smoke now; for it seemed that this moment was simply a continuation of that other time when he had driven himself to ask to help Mrs. Sprangs, and had been able to come to the point only when his face was hidden in a cloud of smoke. Finding no pipe, he turned his face to the window, and looked out into the dusk of evening closing slowly in about a patch of amber sky. Why did he feel this strange embarrassment in her presence? Was not the old time dead, with all its midnight dreams of sunrise? Had not day come? Or was it because a man, once having experienced love for a good woman, finds evolved within him an impersonal love for the idea in universal womanhood, deeper than the heat of blood and purer than any desire?

It was with a new tenderness upon his face and a new softness in his voice, that he turned to Mrs. Sprangs.

"Well, you see, I've got more money than I deserve to have; it ain't mine, 'cause I didn't give nothin' for it. If I spent it all on myself I'd feel like a thief. Some of it 's Specks's."

"Why, Mr. Waters, you don't owe the boy anything!"

Waters turned again to the window, and gazed thoughtfully into the quiet dusk. Did she mean to ignore his kindness? It did not seem like Mrs. Sprangs. He turned to her again, and spoke rapidly and with a harsher tone.

"He'd ought to go to school. He can't 'thout money. I've got money. 'Tain't mine. He needs it. I don't. It's his'n!"

"Oh, if the whole world were like you!" said Mrs. Sprangs.

Waters felt the blood rush to his face; he could hear it singing in his ears. He turned his face again to the window, and studiously noted the change in the sky. It had been amber before; now it was dun. It would be a dull blue in half an hour. All the while he was thinking how such words would have changed him in the old dark time. How they would have shattered the night with riotous dawn! And yet, as he thought thus, he was ashamed of his own thoughts. The memory of the glowing woman of the spring flashed through his brain, and threw a searching light upon his guilty thoughts. Why did the old time cling? He did not want it back.

"I ain't good!" he said defiantly. "You don't have to be good to give away what ain't your'n. I want to send Specks to school, and you'd ought to let me. I'd let him pay it back to me or somebody else that needed it."

"If you really want to, Mr. Waters," said Mrs.

Sprangs, "and if you'll let him pay it back, I'd be so glad."

"And you see, Mrs. Sprangs," said Waters musingly; "mebbe if he knowed more, he wouldn't think the world was queer. I never knowed much, and I thought it was queer; and it was me, jest me. Did you ever strike a match in a dark night, and see how much darker that made things? That's the way it is. Takes a bonfire or nothin'!"

"And then," said Waters at length, speaking very low and slowly, "the boy kind of seems like he's part my boy now, since his pa died. Wisht I was good enough and smart enough to be everybody's pa."

IV

The Needle Club

Owing to her mania for seeing things go, Mrs. Griggs had long since been elevated to the presidency of the Needle Society of Fort Calhoun. This organization was only secondarily a needle club. Its basic reason for being (though never openly acknowledged) was broader than a quilt, and more intricate than fancy work. So it happened that the needle had lost its material meaning, and had become merely symbolical of sharper things.

The Needle Society of Fort Calhoun met regularly on Tuesday evenings. This regularity, however commendable as a principle, was bad as a policy, in that it precluded the immediate discussion of current topics, thus placing the organization as a news exchange upon the vulgar level of the *Trumpet* that was able to blow only weekly echoes, owing to the daily convention at the grocery store.

And yet, to do the Needle Club justice, it must be said that while the policy of the Grocery Store was rather a destructive one, and the blasts of the *Trumpet* merely echoes, the Needle Club was not only a combination of the two, but a great deal more. Though it rarely had the opportunity of working upon the raw material in a destructive manner, it always builded anew upon the wreck of the old. It ripped open threadbare reputations, and applied deft patches where they were most needed. It did not merely stand aghast at horrible rents, as the Grocery Store did; but it went at them with a vim, and stitched them stoutly.

When the needle workers arrived at the house of Mrs. Griggs, they found their president with a face of care. She greeted them with a business-like brevity that said plainly: "No frivolities; there is work to be done!"

When the quilting frame had been placed in the kitchen (for Mrs. Griggs just could not stand a litter on the carpet of her best room) the murmur of talk increased to a merry babble, through which the usual prenuptial jokes were bandied back and forth like shuttles weaving a gaudy cloth.

"I *suppose* Sary's heart is jest thumpin' with joy, poor thing!" said a slim, angular woman with matrimonial failure written upon a face of sunken eyes, protruding cheek bones, long slender nose and thin, nervous lips; "but she'll sing a different tune by and by, if I don't miss *my* guess!"

"Lawsy me, yes!" sighed a little self-effaced woman slavishly plying her needle.

"Well, if she's got the right sort of spunk she'll pull through in one piece, I reckon," waspishly added a heavy muscular woman whose every movement suggested belligerency.

Mrs. Griggs smiled with the superiority of latent knowledge.

"*Leastwise,*" she observed with deliberation, "Hank hain't no ugly sot and Sary hain't a *heathen!*" At the last word her voice sharpened into vocal italics. Then she closed her lips tightly, with an air that said plainly: "I could say more if you'd dig it out of me."

"Gracious, no!" said the belligerent woman. "What can you mean, Mrs. Griggs?"

"Well," answered the president, "mebbe I'd oughtn't to've brought Sary and Hank into it, them jest a startin' out fresh and joyous on life's stony highway."

It? Bring Sary and Hank into *what?* The Needle Society of Fort Calhoun wanted to know!

"We've got *heathen* in our very midst!" Mrs. Griggs delivered herself of this in a voice of awe. Her round face was a travesty of sublimity.

"Heathen?"

"Heathen!"

"*Heathen!!*"

"Hea-*then!!!*"

These four exclamations ran the gamut of vocal emphasis.

"I was up to Sprangses this afternoon and called on Mrs. Waters."

The society forgot its quilt and waited breathlessly for the president to display the shameless rent.

"I seen her."

Mrs. Griggs' marvellous taciturnity suggested the restraint of the master.

"You did?" (The self-effaced woman.)

"Come, Mrs. Griggs, don't be so tantalizin'!" (The woman with the face of matrimonial failure.)

"If we've got heathen amongst us, we've got a right to know, I guess!" (The belligerent woman.)

"Well," sighed Mrs. Griggs, "we've got that very thing amongst us, and may the Lord deliver us! Mrs. Waters is a heathen!"

Every hearer gasped in horror.

"It's no more'n a body could look for, goodness knows! Who but a heathen would've married that ugly drunken monster, I'd like to know?" said the woman upon whose face the tale of connubial infelicity was written. She had never been known to miss a chance for dealing a blow at her natural enemy, the male.

"Well, to begin with," said Mrs. Griggs, "I must say for her that she's a curiosity. She don't look nothin' like me nor you, and still she hain't what you'd call hombly. She's got eyes and nose and mouth and ears, but she don't look like nobody but herself, and that ain't flatterin' her, goodness knows! Lets her hair hang down her back—the longest, greasiest, yallerish, reddish hair! When I first see her I said to myself: 'Gracious me, I'd make you do that up or cut it off if you was at *my* house'. 'Cause I always say there's nothin' works agin the peace of a family like hair in the victuals!"

"Hm!" sniffed the woman with the face of marital woe. By which she interposed that *she* could say a thing or two on the subject of domestic peace, if she were not so long suffering and patient.

"But that hain't really the worst," continued Mrs. Griggs. "She's never been into a church in her life! Jest as good as *said* so! I daresay she don't know she's got a Saviour as died on the cross for the likes of her!"

The little self-effaced woman opened her mouth, raised her hands in awe, gasped, closed her mouth hopelessly, and dropped her hands limply in her lap.

"And she said what did we shut God up in a house for, think of that! Like as if He was a jack-in-the-box a-bobbin' up of a Sabbath with a spring! W'y I trembled for fear she'd be struck down with lightnin' on the spot! I did that. And Mrs. Sprangs jest sided right in with her. She said Mrs. Waters had always lived wild like a red Injun in an island up the river somewheres!"

"And to *think!*" ejaculated the belligerent woman, with her large fists set firmly on her protruding hips, "that this enlightened community has got to have heathen in its midst!"

"Well, for my part," ventured the little self-effaced woman, "I think we'd ought to pray for her soul. It's a body's Christian duty."

This opinion entered into the spirit of the Needle Society and chastened it.

"I suppose we'd all ought to pray for her," sighed Mrs. Griggs; "and what's more, I think we'd ought to appoint a committee to go to her and *yank* her soul out'n the slough of sin!"

Everyone thought this was a good idea. It was certainly the duty of the women folks to battle for the high moral standard of the community. Goodness knew! It could go to smash for all the men cared!

Thus it happened that the Needle Society of Fort Calhoun appointed a committee to look after the spiritual welfare of Mrs. Waters. It consisted of the belligerent woman, the matrimonial failure and Mrs. Griggs. It requires strong natures to fight Sin.

V

The Committee On Salvation

It was Sunday afternoon. Mrs. Sprangs and Mrs. Waters sat in the front room. During the week, Waters and Specks had taken a southbound packet for St. Louis, where Specks was to go to school; and there was an air of lonesomeness about the place.

Since her coming to Calhoun, the Island Girl had grown paler. She rarely spoke, and her voice had become fainter. Her experiences of the past month had developed symptoms of that nervous malady which had destroyed her father. She walked with a quick spasmodic motion, and the slightest sound made her start. The sense of the dropping away of the foundations of her life had been intensified since the visit of Mrs. Griggs. Her delicate face bore a tense expression as of a vague fear.

"You say he can not be back by sunset?" she said wearily to her companion.

"No, dear, it will be a month before he can be back. You must not worry about him. Just think, my boy will be gone all Winter."

"A month? There are many sunsets in a month. I wish it were only one sunset, and then a long, long night. Then he would come back in the morning."

Mrs. Waters abruptly ceased speaking and clutched her companion's arm. Three women were approaching the house, and the foremost was Mrs. Griggs.

Mrs. Waters sat rigidly in her chair, like a bird charmed by a snake, as Mrs. Sprangs ushered in the three visitors and seated them.

"It's a very hot afternoon," remarked Mrs. Sprangs, by way of breaking the awkward silence.

"Yes, indeed," puffed Mrs. Griggs, and the silence closed in again.

The belligerent woman with tense brows and a sharp nod of her head, commanded the president of the Needle Club to begin. Mrs. Griggs, with the same signs, endeavored to push the responsibility upon the woman with the face of marital woe, who shook her head sidewise and bit her thin colorless lips. Then Mrs. Griggs sighed, coughed, mopped her drenched brows, and began.

"Mrs. Sprangs," she said with a martyred air, "we've come to do the work of the Lord in your own house, and mebbe we'd ought to beg your pardon, for not askin' you if we could. But we thought you'd be glad to have the work of salvation did under your own roof. You know that our sister here, Mrs. Waters, hain't had the benefits of a early Christian trainin' as we've had, and us three proposes to open the door of mercy, and let the sunlight in onto her. We will begin with a hymn or two, and after dispensin' with a few truths from the Script'res, we will close with prayer."

With her choicest expression of facial devoutness, Mrs. Griggs arose to her feet and producing a hymnal, opened it to a page marked with a turned-down corner. The attack upon Satan had been carefully planned.

The belligerent sister and the sister of marital discontent simultaneously arose and leaned, from either side of Mrs. Griggs, over the hymnal. Mrs. Griggs, as leader, gave the pitch.

"Tra-a (very high and strained). No! Tra-tra-tra (rather lofty still, but seemingly satisfactory) tra-tra-a-a. Now!"

"Comethou foun tof fev ry bles-sing,
Tunemy har to sing-thy-gra-ce."

A burst of strident voices filled the little room and rushed out at the doors and windows into the dull unoffending August afternoon. The belligerent woman stood with her calloused hands upon her hips, and defiantly jerked her heavy under-jaw up and down as she bit off the joy of praise in great chunks. The woman with the face of woe leaned forward, squinting with eyes that much weeping had made dim, and seemed to be picking the words of glory off the printed page with the point of her attenuated nose. Mrs. Griggs leaned backward with all her perspiring stoutness, her little eyes hidden under their fat lids and her diminutive stub nose plainly pointing the way to the skies. She made it very plain that *she* did not need the book at all. *She* knew the hymn verbatim and sang it from her heart!

"Te chme some——"

At this point in the hymn, where the very notes (exalted in the start) insisted stubbornly upon climbing forthwith into the empyrean, dragging "some melodious sonnet" with them, the faces of the singers grew purple with the strain of endeavoring to follow the aspiring air. It was a flat failure; they couldn't possibly soar so high. The voices faltered, floundered—and died in a squawk.

Mrs. Griggs let her head drop upon her agitated breast. The nose of the woman of woe withdrew from its vain toil, and the belligerent sister let her heavy under-jaw drop, as though she had been hanging to the soaring tune with her teeth, and desisted from sheer fatigue. The two looked at Mrs. Griggs and scowled. They suspected from the first she had set the pitch too high.

"Tra tra tra-a-a," hummed Mrs. Griggs, puffingly, in a lower key. "Second verse," she added.

The possible altitude of the new pitch encouraged her sisters in song. The woman of woe again inserted her nose among the notes, and the belligerent woman, refreshed by the breathing spell, grasped the hymn firmly between her teeth with a light in her eye that said plainly how she meant to shake it to death this time.

"Here rile ra-smine Neb-en-ne-zer.
Hi-ther by thy hel pI'm co-me;
And dI ho pby thy good plea-sure,
Safely to ar-rive vat ho-me."

When they had reached the end of the hymn, Mrs. Griggs with an air of devout resignation, closed the book leisurely, and sought the face of the heathen for the possible effect of her first glimpse into glory. The woman of woe dropped her hands languidly by her sides, and the tense expression vanished into the look of chronic weariness. She looked as though her Ebenezer had been very difficult to raise indeed. The belligerent woman showed no signs of weariness. Her under-jaw was yet very firm. She looked as though she meant to say: "I could do it all over again, and don't know but I shall."

During the hymn, the Island Girl had stared aghast. She had never heard anything in all the music of the wilderness like this. As she listened and gazed at the singers, the sense of her own identity became dim. It was like a nightmare, so utterly impossible to her; and yet it seemed to be happening. When the song ceased, she still stared blankly at the three women. Mrs. Sprangs smiled kindly and waited nervously for the next.

It was not long in coming. The attack upon the devil was to be rapid and decisive. It was not to be a siege—the devil isn't taken that way. It was to be a storming—sudden and violent and pitiless. Mrs. Griggs remained standing, and the two sisters seated themselves.

"I will read," announced Mrs. Griggs, fitting her spectacles to her eyes, and opening a Bible at a marked passage, "from the Holy Script-res; the prophet Malachi, chapter four.

"For, behold, the day cometh that shall burn as an oven; and all the proud, yea, and all that do wickedly shall be as stubble, and the day that cometh shall burn them up, saith the Lord of Hosts, that it shall leave them neither root nor branch."

Mrs. Griggs read in a nasal singsong, dwelling with terrible emphasis upon the allusions to fire. She closed the book with a sigh, removed her spectacles, and fixed her little gray eyes, now as stern as possible, upon the white face of Mrs. Waters.

"My dear sister," she began ominously, "you have sinned against the Most High, because you have never praised Him. Nay, you have said hard words of your Lord. Repent, or you shall be damned! Ah, think of what that means, my sister! It means that God has prepared a place of torture for them as doesn't serve Him; and that place is Hell! Repent or He will cast you into the fire that never goes out and burn you for all eternity! O my sister, my sister!"

Tears of utter love stole sneakingly out of the eyes of Mrs. Griggs and, lodging in the wrinkles of fat in her cheeks, made little lakes of sorrow.

"You must change your ways or you will die. And if that only meant dyin' and havin' yourself put into the cold, cold grave, w'y then it wouldn't be so bad." Mrs. Griggs was weeping softly. "But it don't!" Mrs. Griggs sobbed aloud, and the woman of woes hid her eyes in her handkerchief and snivelled. "It don't! It don't!" sobbed Mrs. Griggs, the overpowering sense of the eternal truth harrowing up her soul. "It means a-burnin' and fryin' and sizzlin' always! And them as loves you mebbe'll be up in heaven a-watchin' you! O my sister!"

Mrs. Griggs' grief became uncontrollable, and she sobbed in a manner worthy of a hysterical funeral. The Island Woman, unskilled to look beneath appearances, and moved by the great incomprehensible grief before her, wept, hiding her face on Mrs. Sprangs' shoulder and clinging to her desperately.

"She's gettin' the spirit," whispered Mrs. Griggs to the belligerent sister. "Let us pray while the spirit is onto her." And the three knelt.

"O Lord," snivelled Mrs. Griggs, "send Thy spirit down onto us and bless us a-workin' for Thee! Thou saidest inasmuch as we did it unto one of the least of these, we was a-doin' it to Thee; and we want to do it to Thee, O Lord. If we seem to be a-workin' hard for Thee, don't pity us, Lord; we'd give our lives for Thee who gave Thine for us. Bless us and help us to drive the heathen out'n the land."

With one eye, Mrs. Griggs had been covertly watching the effect of her attack upon the devil. Therefore, when she saw Mrs. Sprangs get up from her chair and lead the broken heathen away, she closed her prayer abruptly.

"Amen!"

The Needle Society's committee on salvation was alone in the room.

"There it is!" said the belligerent woman in disgust; "Mrs. Sprangs is just a-doin' all she can for the heathen!"

And the committee obstreperously left the house of the devil.

VI

The Judgment

"Well, things has come to the worst," announced Mrs. Griggs to the Needle Society, assembled for its weekly task; "and it ain't any more than I expected, although the judgments of the Lord hain't often so sudden as I'd make 'em if I was Him, which I hain't. But He knows best, and goodness knows, this judgment was suddent enough!"

"Why, what's happened?" asked the little self-effaced woman. Her domestic duties so engrossed her that she was often known to display alarming ignorance of current events.

"You don't say that you haven't heard? Why, it's all over town long ago!" Mrs. Griggs' face was superior and contemptuous. "We went over to Sprangses last Sunday to bring Mrs. Waters to the true light; and didn't Mrs. Sprangs take her heathen and get out of the room while we was on our *knees* a-beggin' for her at the Throne of Mercy? And so I say, it's happened!"

"What?" persisted the self-effaced woman.

"W'y, the judgment as was to be expected has

come down onto the head of the heathen, though it hain't touched Mrs. Sprangs yet. When I heard a-Monday that Mrs. Waters was sick abed and delirious, it come to me like a flash—It's the judgment! And then when Sary run over and said that it was bein' told that Mrs. Waters wasn't just delirious but plum crazy, I knowed I was right. You know God always makes them crazy that he wishes to destroy. Well," sighed conscientious Mrs. Griggs, "we done all we could for her, and we can rest easy and let the Lord take His course.

"We hain't hid our light under a bushel," she continued. "We took it to her and she wouldn't have none of it." She remained silent for a moment by way of deepening the impression of a peaceful conscience. "Well, this morning I thought to myself I'd go over to Sprangses and see if I couldn't be of some help with the sick, because I always think when folks is sick they'd ought to be took care of, whether they'd ought to get well or not. 'Tain't more'n a body's Christian duty. So I put on my sunbonnet and run over; and do you think Mrs. Sprangs would let me in? Not her! She met me at the door and says in them simperin' tones of her'n she's got since she don't wash for a livin'; 'Mrs. Waters is quite sick, Mrs. Griggs,' she says, just that way; 'it was very kind of you to enquire. I've sent for the doctor; he'll be up on to-morrow's stage. I think in her state no one should see her.' Just that way she said it, and me a-leavin' my work and puttin' myself out! I could've spit in her face, I was that *throughother!* But I didn't; I just turned around without sayin' a word, I was that beat, and walked away. Well," sighed Mrs. Griggs, "things can go as they will for all me!" The needle of the president worked spitefully for several minutes.

"Well," snapped the belligerent woman, "if Mrs. Waters dies, which she most likely will, I guess Mrs. Sprangs won't bawl her eyes out! Goodness knows she tried hard enough to get that Waters to propose before he had money. And what wouldn't she do now? It beats me what she ever see in him! I always think it's hard enough to put up with a *whole* man, let alone a man that hain't got all his eyes and legs and things!"

"Gracious me, yes!" sighed the woman of marital woe.

"I daresay," pursued the belligerent woman, "if you see a funeral, you'll see a weddin' before snow flies! It's sickenin' the way them two goes on. Her a coddlin' his baby like it was her'n; and him a-hangin' around that freckled boy of her'n like it was his'n! I think Mrs. Waters 'd do well to get out of their road and let them put their families together; poor thing!"

This placing of Mrs. Waters in the light of an abused wife, infused a new spirit into the conversation.

"Yes, I say poor thing!" said the woman of matrimonial infelicity. "I say poor thing! She looks so innocent and trusting. I daresay she leads a hard life with him. There's no doubting it'd be a blessing to her to get shut of him by dying."

"Yes, indeed," sighed Mrs. Griggs; "for though the young thing *is* a heathen, her early trainin' prob'bly wasn't of the best; and folks should have charity. I declare I don't know which is the worst, Mrs. Sprangs or Mrs. Waters. Mrs. Sprangs has lived in a enlightened community, leastways. I really guess she's the worst. But she'll get her judgment later, I reckon. 'Specially if she gets Waters. That'd be judgment enough for a most anybody!"

VII

A Cloud Across the Sunrise

It was in the evening of a mid-September day that Waters alighted from the Omaha City stage that stopped in front of the Green Tree Grocery.

The arrival of a stage at Calhoun was one of the events of the week which (with the occasional steamboat) vied with the sunrise and the sunset in giving life that variety which is alleged to be its spice. Consequently a mixed crowd of men and boys had congregated at the store.

When Waters, the odd, the rich, the mysterious, the food for gossip, stepped from the coach, a murmur of surprise and wonder went through the crowd. For Mr. Waters was no longer Mr. Waters. To be sure, the alighting passenger had the curling hair of Mr. Waters, although it had evidently undergone some refining process. Also, he had the face of Waters, all but the eyeless socket; the socket was no longer eyeless. It contained an eye of an unusually bold and penetrating stare, and a sort of frank defiance of physiological laws. An independent eye it was, placidly refusing to follow the roving gaze of its more versatile companion.

Also the body of the man, although neatly clothed, was the body of Waters; but the left leg was no longer wooden. It was a leg with a foot at its extremity, and it was decently clothed in trousers. But as it moved, it demonstrated an independent if not rebellious nature like the eye.

Therefore the little crowd simply gazed in wonder at this seeming hallucination, as the man passed, smiling kindly and with a glow on his face that was not cast from the brilliant west where the day was passing.

"Is *that* him?" said one.

"It's him all right; but him with another cork leg and a glass eye!"

"I'll be danged!" exclaimed another. "Waters is made over!"

And so he was. In the joy of his new life, Waters had rediscovered his self-respect. During his stay in St. Louis he had not been idle. He had placed Specks in a boarding school. He had deposited his considerable wealth in a bank. He had bought a steamboat, and ordered it to be refitted; for he had decided to go into business for himself. And finally he had "made himself over" with a glass eye and a cork leg.

And so it was not without a certain innocent pride that he hurried toward the house of Mrs. Sprangs, with his wooden leg,—the tangible past, too dear to be discarded utterly—in a bundle under one arm;

and under the other arm a bundle (tangibly representative of the future) containing material for new garments for Mrs. Waters. As he neared the Sprangs home, his heart was very light within him. The last glorious flood of light from the passing day seemed to him to emanate from his own soul. Now at last his sunrise had begun. He had gained the respect of men, and he was in a fair way to do much good, and consequently be very happy.

Many brave, beautiful plans ran in his head like music. He would build a house yet that Fall. His young wife would become accustomed to the strange new life, and people would love her and honor her. Then in the Spring he would make his first trip as owner and captain of a steamboat. He knew how large the profits from such an enterprise could be, and he would make much money, and thus gain greater power for helping those who suffered as he had done.

He arrived at the door, and was met by Mrs. Sprangs. Although her face was gentle as ever, he noted a new weariness and anxiety upon it. Also, he noted with pleasure the look of surprise as she saw the changes he had made in his personal appearance.

"Well, I've gone and made myself over, Mrs. Sprangs," he said, smiling pleasantly and glad as a boy. "But you'll be wantin' to know about the boy first, I reckon. Well, he's in a nice place, and he'll learn a lot, too. Said for me to tell you not to worry more'n you could help. Good boy that, Mrs. Sprangs."

Mrs. Sprangs put her finger to her lips and said quietly: "Tell me about him afterwhile; Mrs. Waters is quite sick."

A little cloud went over Waters' sunrise. Nervously he followed Mrs. Sprangs to the little bedroom. There lay the Island Girl, white and languid, her delicate face, now grown pale, framed in her sunny hair. She was staring blankly at the wall. Waters went quietly to the side of the bed and spoke to her.

"You been sick, dear?" he said tenderly.

At the sound of the familiar voice that she had always been hearing in her delirium, she turned her strangely staring eyes upon Waters and gazed at him, at first with a faint light of recognition that changed gradually into questioning, then into terror.

"Oh, go away!" she said gaspingly. "You are not—you are—oh, go away."

With the strength of terror she lifted herself in her bed and crouched against the wall.

"Don't you know me, dear?" said Waters caressingly. "Don't you remember when we was up in the island? It's me; can't you see? Of course you do!"

He leaned across the bed, and reached trembling arms out for her. She shrank back closer against the wall, and stared with eyes glazed with terror.

"No" she gasped, "you are not the one!" She placed her thin hands over her eyes and shook with fear.

"She don't know me this way," muttered Waters, and he went out of the room.

"What was it?" gasped the sick woman to Mrs. Sprangs. "Was it only another terrible dream come to torture me? When will he come back?"

"Soon," said Mrs. Sprangs, stroking the luminous hair.

In a few minutes Waters returned. He had removed his artificial eye and replaced his wooden leg. When he entered the room, the sick woman gave a feeble cry of joy, and tried to arise from the bed to meet him, but fell back exhausted upon her pillow.

"You know me now, don't you, little woman?"

"Yes," she said, feeling his face with her weak hands and speaking brokenly; "It—is—you. There was another—another here just now. It tried to look like you. But—it was not—so beautiful."

In her days of longing, the very disfigurement of Waters had become a fetich to her.

"I can hear the wind singing in the trees back in the old place," she said languidly. "I can hear the river washing on the sand. It left with you, but I can hear it now. And I am not sick any more, am I? Why do I hear it, so sweet and low and soothing, when I touch you?"

"You must get well right away," said Waters

caressingly, "and mebbe we'll go back there afterwhile."

"Yes," she said wearily, "I will sleep now and get well, then we will go back. I am not afraid to sleep now; I will not see ugly things now. I will hear the wind and the river back there."

Waters laid her head gently on the pillow, and stroked her forehead. Like a tired child, she closed her eyes and sank into a sleep. Waters sat beside the bed, holding one of the thin, blue-veined hands. He heard nothing but her light, spasmodic breathing; saw nothing but the thin pale face, grown frail and delicate as a Spring flower growing in a deep shade. Her slender nose was pinched with suffering; her eyes were sunken and the lids were traced with thin threads of blue.

As Waters sat and watched he lived over the island life again, from the bitterness of his waking there to the joyous hope of his leaving. His conscience accused him bitterly. He should never have brought her away. What if she should die? The awful thought aroused him. He turned to Mrs. Sprangs, sitting near the bed holding his sleeping child.

"We'd ought to have a doctor," he said in a hoarse whisper.

"I had a doctor a week ago," said Mrs. Sprangs; "he said the only thing to do was to keep her quiet. He said the sudden change in her life had shaken her nerves."

"Is he coming back again?"

"He said there was no use in his coming back."

"No use, no use;" the words ran monotonously in Water's head. He gazed at the woman holding his child, with an eye that seemed searching something at a great distance. Once he had dreamed of this woman holding his child, and it was denied him. Now that the old desire had passed, and he had a child, it was sleeping in her arms. How strange it all seemed! What he did not want, he had; and what he wanted was slowly, slowly slipping from him.

With a sudden movement, he turned to the bed again, and placing one arm under the frail head, he clung to the sick woman as though with the strength of desperation, to hold her back from the dreadful silence into which she seemed slowly slipping from him. Never before had time seemed so terrible to him; not even in the old days of long, weary watching for the northbound steamer that should bring him his happiness.

All night Waters and Mrs. Sprangs sat together beside the bed of the woman sick with the home-ache. He held the frail, languid hand, counting the slow throbbing of the pulse. She, with her calm, sleepless mother-eyes, hovered about, busying herself with the application of homely remedies; speaking soft words of cheer to the man who watched.

"Mrs. Sprangs," said Waters; "I guess I'll take her back. She's jest a little delicate flower, and she can't live here. Don't you think I'd better take her back?"

Mrs. Sprang placed her strong, capable mother's hand upon the golden locks of the man.

"Yes," she said, "and you must let me go back, too. She needs a woman to wait upon her, and I will be her baby's mother until she gets well. Won't you let me go?"

Waters raised his face to the quiet, careworn face of Mrs. Sprangs and smiled.

"O Mrs. Sprangs, you're an angel!"

"No," she said quietly; "I'm just a woman."

He took her hand in his, and placed the tips of her fingers to his lips.

"It's all the same," he said.

VIII

As They Saw It

"Gracious me!" said Mrs. Griggs, closing her fat eyelids with a sigh of benevolence. "There you have it! I'd never have thought it of Mrs. Sprangs, though I always did think there was something sly about her. You never could get her to talk free about things. Think of her a-going up there into a savage island with Waters and his half dead heathen wife! The way she does foller that yeller-headed, one-eyed, wooden-legged—well, folks should be careful of what they say! Little she thinks that Mrs. Waters 'll ever get well. Not her! She's got it all planned out, the sly, designin' creature! I daresay they're both a-holdin their breaths till the poor little innocent thing dies!"

The Needle Society had not even touched a needle as yet; for a boat bound for the north had that day taken with it the three burning topics of conversation, and everything else was forgotten.

The little self-effaced woman sighed a wretched sigh, and wilted into a non-combatant heap, at the thought of the overpowering badness of the world. The woman of marital woe wrapped her face in a frozen grin, and remained locked in a Winter silence.

"Well!" snapped the belligerent woman, biting her words off with powerful jaws; "I'd like to see him get *me!*" And she straightened herself, placed her strong hands firmly upon her hips, and with a face of battle, stared down an imaginary host of Messrs. Waters advancing to the siege.

At the Grocery Store the convention was at work.

"It does beat a certain hot inland settlement," said Mr. Coppers, "how that there Waters has played the devil with the heart of the widder and orphan! I'll bet poor old Sprangs is turnin' over in his grave something furious about now! You see, this here's the way of it. Waters comes up here to work for Simpson. The widder's boy works for Simpson, too. Widder's boy likes Waters. Waters goes home with widder's boy. Widder gets sweet onto Waters, and 'tother way just as bad. Sprangs comes back, and Waters leaves. Waters comes back with a woman, and Sprangs is dead! Nothin' in the road but the other woman! Other woman gets sick—can't get well, folks has it. Mrs. Sprangs says: 'Mr. Waters, she's dyin' of homesickness; let's take her back to the island.' Then Waters and Mrs. Sprangs trades winks, and says: 'Yes, we'll take her back.'

"Draw your own conclusions, gentlemen. It ain't Coppers that would say a word against any woman on earth!"

And the convention became one knowing grin.

IX

The Growing Mystery

On a quiet evening in early October, a steamboat pulled in at Old Man's Island, and made fast. Immediately after, a gang of deck hands began unloading a considerable quantity of household goods, various articles of furniture and food; for the wilderness that had for a few months been left uninhabited, was again to be occupied.

After the unloading of the goods, four deck hands appeared from the cabin, bearing a cot upon which lay the sick Queen now returning to her kingdom after exile. Beside the cot walked Waters and Mrs. Sprangs, carrying the child in her arms.

As they left the gang plank and entered the timber, a great joy lit up the frail face of the Island Girl. With a great effort, she lifted herself from the cot and sat up, leaning upon a trembling arm, and drinking in the scene about her.

"Oh!" she cried, "how kind and beautiful it all is! See my old trees clapping their hands and shaking with laughter because I have come back! Oh, the odor of the flowers growing in the shade! How they send their fragrant souls out to welcome me! I wonder if they were fragrant while I was gone!

"Lower the cot," she said, "and let me touch them again. There! Ah, they bend their little heads and kiss my hand. I am so happy!"

She fell back exhausted upon her pillow, panting with the effort.

"I can feel God again," she said. "Dearest," turning to Waters her languid eyes, wet with tears of joy; "give me your hand to touch. There! It has all come back to me—all the beautiful, quiet dreams that I had lost. I shall get well now; I am so happy."

"Yes, yes, little girl," said Waters, "you will get well right away, and play again, you pretty golden-headed little butterfly!"

They had reached the log house that Waters had built as a palace for their happiness. The girl made an effort to raise herself again, but fell back with a little cry of joy.

The Autumn grew old apace. The leaves turned crimson and gold, and the silence of the golden end of the year dwelt everywhere. The Island Girl lay all day on her cot, too weak to be out with the play-mates of her childhood. Everyday she grew frailer, more like a tender little flower that pales in a shadow.

Mrs. Sprangs and Waters were unwearying in their attentions to her, and she thanked them with her deep, quiet eyes; for she seldom spoke now.

She seemed brooding over some great mystery that deepened about her.

One morning she awoke early and called Waters.

"Won't you take me out and let me see the sun come up," she said, "brave and glad and good as it used to be? I think I shall be stronger then. You can carry me, can't you? You are so strong and good, and golden-headed like the sun."

Waters wrapped her carefully, and took her in his arms. She had become very light,—more spirit than flesh. He carried her out into the crisp Autumn morning, with her thin arms about his neck.

"Do you remember," she whispered at his ear, "how you swam with my arms about your neck like this, dear? You were so strong and brave! That was when I learned that happiness hurts."

"Yes, yes, little woman," he said. "I can't fergit that. I'll always feel your arms a-clingin' there; always feel you breathin' on my face! That was when my little butterfly changed into a woman, my little golden butterfly!"

"Always, dear?" she whispered; "you will always remember? For I feel as though I am going a long way off soon—so far away!—where he is. Remember it always, and I will be so happy there, even though it is all Winter and the Spring never comes."

Waters sobbed, and kissed the weak clinging arms.

They had reached the summit of the bluff, sanctified with memories.

"Now we'll set down here under this lonesome old scrub oak and wait for the sun," Waters said; and he sat down, holding her to his breast like a little child.

"Do you remember how you came to me under this tree, dear?" she said. "It seems so long ago, so long ago; although it was not long, was it?"

They talked together like old people who had played together in youth, going over all the little things that they had done together. And Waters' heart ached; for he felt the deepening of the mystery.

As they talked, the dawn slipped up out of the clear, autumnal sky and bathed them in light. The girl gave a little cry of joy and endeavored to stand up, but could not.

"Oh, the good old Sun!" she cried, with a voice grown thin; "how kind and warm and strong he is!"

And she began to sing in a plaintive, quavering voice the pæan to the sun which Waters had heard her singing at sunset in the Spring. Her voice broke as it arose to an ecstatic note.

"I can not sing any more," she gasped, as if in fright. "I feel so old—so old that I can not sing. Take me back and let me lie down. I am so old, so tired." And Waters bore her back to the house.

X

The Sunset

The Fall passed and the cold winds came, wrapping the great valley in fog. The sick girl did not leave the house now. She lay all day exhausted upon her couch; and Waters watched over her continually, trying to be sunny, for a dull light, as of a fog, was slowly settling over her face.

The Winter came, and the great river was locked with ice. The cold fingers of the snow hushed the wilderness, and Waters kept the fireplace roaring merrily; but he could not drive away the subtler Winter of the heart that grew apace even in the heat of the dancing flames.

Christmas passed, and January came with storms that howled and moaned down the valley. Day by day the sick girl had grown weaker, until at last she lay for hours in a lethargy, staring with unmeaning eyes at the ceiling. Mrs. Sprangs ever moved about in her patient, quiet way, looking after Mrs. Waters and the child, cooking, cleaning, always kind and capable.

The child, June, had grown to look upon her as

its mother. She alone could quiet it; and Waters often sat in the awful quiet that clung about the place, watching with wistful eyes the kind, careworn, motherly face bent above the baby nestled at her breast.

Late one night in February, as Waters and Mrs. Sprangs sat beside the bed, the girl opened her eyes wearily, and reached out a hand to Waters. "I think," she said slowly and faintly, "I am going far off to-night. I feel so quiet and tired and old. Hold my hand till I go."

She closed her eyes, and a strange light went across her face. She fell into a nervous sleep. Waters sat holding her hand until midnight. The strange light still dwelt upon her face. A thought that she would never waken came to Waters. He kissed her and a teardrop fell upon her face. The sick girl wearily opened her eyes, and smiled. She began speaking slowly, and her voice seemed to come from some great distance, weirdly musical as the faint wailing of the violins in an orchestra when the last act passes on the dimly lighted stage.

"I dreamed the sweetest dream just now. I was a windflower growing by the great spring; and I was the only one in all the world, and it was Spring-time. There was a soft southwind blowing, and it blew for me alone; for I was the only flower in all the world. I heard it singing far above me in the trees; and I saw it stoop and kiss the pool beside me, until the water rippled and smiled. The sun looked in through a rift in the leaves and kissed me, for I was the only flower there was left. It was all my sun. But I was only a little windflower and the sun's kisses were so hot. I felt my petals wilt; but the pain was so sweet, because the sun did not mean to hurt me. And then, when it seemed I was about to die, a raindrop fell upon my face, and I was so happy that I awoke—and I am not sick any more—am I?"

Waters wiped his eye with his big rough hand, and struggled with a sob far down in his throat. With a great effort he smiled upon her, but did not answer.

"Ah," she said, her face lighting up, "that is the way the sun smiled when I was a little flower by the great spring, the only little flower in all the world."

"You are the only little flower of all the world," said Waters, kissing her. "And I went and pulled you up where you was a-growin' happy," he said to himself.

"Listen!" whispered the sick girl, endeavoring vainly to raise herself upon her elbows; "don't you hear it?"

"What, little woman?" said Waters.

"The river lapping on the sand. Why, you must hear it; it is so plain." She listened intently for some time, with a soft light in her eyes. "And the wind is singing in the trees. It must be evening, because the birds are chirping low as they do in the evening. Why, of course it is evening. *See!*"

With a great effort she raised herself upon her elbows, and gazed at the wall with wide, glaring eyes as if a great light had dazzled her.

"It's the sun setting!" she cried. "See! It burns the hills and sets the river aflame. There! It slips under the hills! Look where the cloud catches fire! Ah—it has—died—the fire. The river—is growing—black. When the dull red dies it will soon be night. Look! The sky has faded, it is growing pale. It—is—gone."

Exhausted, she fell back upon her pillow, with short, rapid breaths that momentarily grew feebler. She closed her eyes and drew a deep sigh. Her eyelids and lips twitched feebly, and then were still.

Waters placed his lips to the white lips of the girl, but felt no breath. He dropped his head upon the quiet breast of the girl and sobbed.

It might have been ten minutes; it might have been ten years; for Waters had lost the sense of time, when he was aroused from his dumb grief by a hand laid gently upon his shoulder, and a soft voice behind him.

"Mr. Waters, you must go away awhile; I will look after her. Please go away."

Waters heard the words as in a dream. Dazedly he arose and stared at Mrs. Sprangs. Slowly the meaning of the words crept into his brain like a command to be obeyed. Staring straight ahead of him, he walked out of the room and out of the house. He was conscious only of a command; the gentle words pushed him as from behind. Like a somnambulist, he took the path leading out to the frozen river and the night. He felt nothing but a terrible vague sense of uneasiness, like that the heavy silence produces in one lying half awake at midnight. Only this and some strong but gentle words commanding him to go.

Wearily his brain seemed endeavoring to arouse some latent memory. What was he trying to think of? He stopped and rubbed his brow in bewilderment. Ah yes; go away; that was it. He began walking rapidly, then broke into a trot, his wooden stump thumping weirdly in the crisp, starlit night. Soon his hop and skip increased to a breathless run. He ran out onto the snow-clad, frozen river. There was something behind him that he was fleeing from. He could not think what it was; but it was terrible. He had a strong desire to turn his head and look behind, but the thought sent cold chills up his spine.

As he ran, the exertion sent the blood to his brain, and slowly his normal consciousness returned. He slackened his pace to a slow walk, feeling as a man who has been stunned by a blow on the head. He stopped and looked about him. Where was he? A white waste and the night were about him. Why had he wandered out here? Someone had told him to come. Why? He passed his hand across his brow; it was cold and damp. Something had happened; what was it? Then slowly like the memory of an old bitterness, the whole thing came back. He sobbed, and feeling a sudden weakness, sat down in the frozen snow.

How different the world had been a few months before. Then it was swathed in the flame of sunrise; now it was wrapped in still, pale night, awful as death. In the painful hush, the complaining cries of coyotes arose like the voices of his own soul. How still and empty the night was—and the world!

Suddenly the face of the dead girl grew up before him. He got up totteringly. The face moved away from him down the river. He followed, walking rapidly. Still the face went ahead, faster than he could follow. He ran, and it fled dizzily ahead of him into the night, eluding his nervous hands extended to touch it. His speed became a panic flight. Once he stumbled and fell; he got to his feet with the strange terror increased. Breathing heavily, he proceeded in his vain pursuit. The pain of labored breathing aroused him. The face vanished, and there was only the star-lit, empty night, the silent, white spaces, ironically calm.

Where had he been going, that he should go so fast? Who could run fast enough to overtake a soul released? He stopped and stared into the sky. There was no change in the heavens. Orion, in the breathless pause of midnight, gazed complacently toward dawn. A big star in the south looked upon him like a quiet eye. With luminous gasconade, a sudden meteor flaunted its tawdry flame before a myriad stars—and disappeared. Clothed in the awful sublimity of isolation, each far sun conjured its own light in the universe of darkness. Austere and alone, they cast about them each its own sufficient day. Calmly they looked down upon him, as if to say: "Trouble exists at the centres of horizons: we see so far that we are calm!"

And Waters wondered at their quietness. Could they not see her lying there, pale and still? He sat down again to gather his wits. He drew his watch from his pocket, but could not see the time, so he lit a match and held it within the housing of his hands until it burned big. It was one o'clock. The match went out.

How dark it had made the night—the little match flame! It blotted out the stars. Ah, the darkness of a little light!

Again he looked upward. The darkening effect of the brief flame passed slowly, but one tear choked the heavens with mist. As he sat and gazed, the tear slipped from his eyelids, and lo! the heavens were vast and clear and kind!

A great peace descended upon him. It was the same peace that had come to him out of the thunderstorm. Something great and warm wrapped him about. He got to his feet and walked back to the island.

When he entered the room of death, he found Mrs. Sprangs sitting beside the bed, holding his sleeping child. Upon the bed lay the one little flower of all the world, cold and colorless as a lily. During his absence, Mrs. Sprangs, ever practical and capable, had washed and dressed the frail form. The thin hands were crossed upon the quiet breast, and the glorious hair was arranged carefully about her face, that seemed a wedge of carved ivory in a mass of gold.

Without a word, Waters sat down beside the bed, and looked upon the beautiful dead. He rested his face in his hands, and became lost in reverie. Some time after, he felt a soft hand laid upon his hair. He lifted his head and looked into the patient, sympathetic face of Mrs. Sprangs. In her left arm she held his child, and her right hand still rested on his head.

In that moment a something, like and unlike love, went out from his soul to the woman before him. It was not the burning love that he had felt for the girl now quiet before him. It was more the child's yearning toward the mother, such as he had felt when he first met her.

And as Waters sat between the living and the dead, with his soul yearning toward both, he felt no shame. For he knew that she, who lay so still and white beside him, could not be jealous if she knew.

XI

The Resurrection

Waters made a grave on the summit of the bluff, where the frail flower, that had left the mysterious Winter of the world to seek the Spring further away than April, might feel the sunrise and the sunset that she loved. The isolated scrub oak, bent and gnarled with the stress of many storms, stood a patient guard above her resting-place.

The lonesome latter days of the Winter moved slowly, and the great optimistic Heart of the World beat bravely toward the Spring. Waters wandered about, lost in reverie; exhausting his strength in long aimless rambles up and down the frozen river and in the snow-hushed timber. He seemed seeking something hidden in the haze of distance—something pure and sweet that ever eluded him. But when he returned from his long rambles to gaze upon the face of Mrs. Sprangs bent above his child, his heart softened, and he felt toward her as a child that cries for its mother in the night.

"Come and play with June," she would say in her low, softly modulated voice. "See, she has the great blue innocent eyes of her mother, and she will have the hair, too. You will be allowed to live it all over again."

And Waters would smile, gazing with dimmed eyes upon the kind face. Day by day it seemed to him that he discovered something new and beautiful in the face of Mrs. Sprangs—the something sweet and pure that eluded him in his long rambles. Could it be that the spirit of the dead mother had re-arisen in the face of the older woman who had become as the mother of his child?

The feeling grew upon Waters until it became so strong that he was afraid of it. Could it be possible that he had so soon forgotten the little flower that he had laid away? Ah, no; it seemed rather that the faded flower re-blossomed in the face of the good woman, and he loved it. "Not Mrs. Sprangs," he would mutter to himself; "no, not her; it's jest because I can half see the little dead woman a-lookin' out of her eyes; that's all."

And yet he felt a thrill of warmth, and found peace only when he was near her. He spent many hours out of doors examining his own thoughts. He would pace for hours up and down on the bleak, cold summit of the bluff, talking in a low voice, as if to her who could no longer hear. Or did she hear? It almost seemed that she could.

"Do you blame me, little butterfly?" he would say. "You know I hain't fergot you. You know I can't never ferget you. She seems jest like you was in her a-callin' to me, little woman, and I can't help hearin! Shall I tell her sometime? Would it make you sad where you are? Can't you let me know some way?

"No, no," he would mutter, "I must run away; I must finish up livin' alone, like I begun. Oh, I wisht the ice'd break up and the Spring'd come! Then I'd run away from myself, 'cause I don't want to do what ain't right."

Many long hours, when the warm days came, he watched the river for the first signs of breaking up, the rending of the chains, the liberation of the sleeping giant. It would not be long after the ice cleared, until some boat that wintered in the north would pass; and then he would take Mrs. Sprangs back to Calhoun. He would pay her well to take care of his child. She would not need to work. Then he would go on to St. Louis, and take charge of his own boat. He would hide himself far away from his temptation.

March came, and the northward moving sun made the days soft and warm. The popping and groaning and whining of the ice-bound river heralded the Spring like trumpets. The great stream struggled prodigiously, hurling its clanking chains aside, fighting with all of its gigantic optimism toward the Summer; roaring and growling with the good lust of strength, as it rode down all obstacles, and ran to meet the coming sun with boisterous laughter.

"That's right!" Waters would cry; "kick it out'n

the way, you good old shaggy feller! Smash it up and shake yourself, you old Sleepy Head! It's been holdin' you down too long! You're too big and strong and brave to lay tied onto your back! Bully for you! Toss it up, and show it how strong you are, you big, good-natured old giant!

"Bully! Bully! Bully! Oh, you got a strong heart, and you're a good fighter. You won't never give up till you get to the Summer. Bully for you! Bully! Bully!"

The colossal struggle went on for days, until at last the cause of Summer won, and the great giant purred in the contentment that follows a worthy victory. And Waters began straining ear and eye for a south-bound steamer. All had been prepared for leaving the island, and Waters spent many hours upon the summit, saying farewell to her who slept under the thin shade of the gnarled old sentinel.

One afternoon, when the leaves were beginning to burst from the bud, and the faint fragrance of early blossoms grew up out of the woodland depths, the steamboat came. Waters hailed it, and the three went aboard.

As it pulled away into the current, with the engine groaning and moaning, he stood at the stern, and watched the island dwindle into a strip of green. Then at last it became but a blur, above which the bald bluff reared its head, glinting in the afternoon sun that dwelt upon its summit like a golden memory. Then this passed, and there were only the monotonous bluffs on either side, and stretches of lonesome prairie; the heavy sigh of the waters rushing from the wheels, and the sobbing of the engine.

For a long time Waters stood leaning on the stern-railing, gazing into the boiling, yellow wake. His reverie was broken by his own sobbing. He straightened himself, shook his shoulders, as if tossing off some heavy weight.

"Come, Waters," he said, half aloud, "you got to shake it off like the river did. You've got to keep on livin' and doin' the best you can, and go on huntin' for the Summer. You wouldn't be good enough to remember her, if you went on settin' up there on that bluff, and cryin' bitter into the lonesome sky."

And he turned and walked with a firm tread forward to where Mrs. Sprangs sat on the forward deck, holding his child, and gazing down the yellow expanse of the river.

"Mrs. Sprangs," he said, sitting down beside her; "I'm goin' on to St. Louis, and get my boat and make the trip north this Summer. If you'll take care of the little girl, I'll pay you good for it, and then I'll make some way for takin' her off your hands."

Mrs. Sprangs turned to him with eyes suddenly grown dim.

"Will you take her away from me, Mr. Waters? You said you felt like a father to the boy; let me be a mother to the girl, won't you?"

Waters looked upon the winsome, motherly face, and a great wild desire to take her in his arms shook him like a strong wind.

"Yes, yes," he said. "God made such women as you for mothers." And he got up and hurried away to the stern again.

"I seen her then!" he said aloud to the yellow, boiling wake, "I seen her in Mrs. Sprangs' face!"

PART FOUR

TOWARD THE SUMMER

I

The Race With Dread

Waters' freight steamboat, *Island Girl,* had made a prosperous trip. Starting from St. Louis late in the Spring, she had delivered her cargo of freight at various points along the river, and arrived at Fort Benton in the early part of July. Waters had spent the remainder of the Summer trading his stock of merchandise for furs.

As the Fall was now far advanced, and the *Island Girl,* a slow boat, heavily laden with a valuable cargo, Waters hesitated to begin the trip south, as there was always the possibility of delays, and the prairie Winter might come down sooner than expected, blocking the river with ice.

A great lonesomeness had come upon Waters. Now that his Summer's task was finished, he longed to be back at Calhoun. One picture was continually before him—the picture of Mrs. Sprangs holding his child. He gazed often upon the first notch in his wooden leg, and dreamed vague, golden dreams. What could she have meant that Spring afternoon, when she spoke so tenderly of his child?

Did it mean that the same sun, which had set when the mother of his child died, had risen in the eyes of the mother who lived? In the isolation of his thoughts, the idea grew stronger and more beautiful. It became dominant; it was with him all through the day, and at night it did not sleep.

The thought of the lonesome Winter of waiting was terrible. At times he felt a foolish desire to leave the boat and cargo at Benton, and fly across the prairies afoot. At times he felt a strange anger at the sixteen hundred sordid miles that lay between him and her who had become as an incarnation of the dead woman of the island.

But was it not wrong for him to think so? Had he not fled from his temptation, and should he be conquered now?

Waters strolled about, day after day, and still the longing for the south and what it held for him grew stronger. Among the boats that lay in the river, was the *John H. Lucas.* Waters renewed his acquaintance with the captain, a jovial companion, and they were much together. In his lonesomeness and longing, he made a confidant of the captain, telling him, in long rambles together, the story of his life.

"Do you think I'd ought to go back, cap'n?" asked Waters.

The captain slapped Waters upon the back and laughed merrily.

"Go back?" said he; "why, yes, man! Should a man run from happiness? If the *Lucas* was going south this Fall, I'd have you gagged and chained and brought aboard; and I'd deliver you with care to the enchanting widow of Calhoun! Go back? Do you think *she* wants you to stay away?" And he laughed pleasantly.

So, as the golden days of October ran slowly toward the Winter, Waters became more and more impatient. One morning when he approached the *Lucas,* lying at the bank, to take his habitual stroll with the captain, he saw that the boat had steam up, and that she gave signs of life after her long nap.

The captain met him at the gang-plank.

"Going to force me to bind and gag you, Mr. Waters?" he said. "We're starting south on unexpected business for the Fort. We'll cast off at noon, and I'm determined to deliver you up at Calhoun!"

Waters hesitated for a moment.

"I'll go," he said at length. "The mate can bring the *Island Girl* down in the Spring."

As the *Lucas* pulled out into the stream at noon, Waters felt the lightness of heart that a carrier pigeon must feel when it is released in a strange land. The home-sense seemed compelling him southward. The *Lucas* being a small boat with no cargo to handle on the trip, carried but ten men;

the captain, two pilots, two engineers, three deck hands, a cook, and Waters, the only passenger. During the first few days the boat made good time, running far into the night by moonlight. But one night a submerged snag struck a paddle-wheel, shattering it and carrying away the wheel-house. During the five days the *Lucas* was laying up at the bank for repairs, Waters contributed his skill as ship carpenter toward building a new wheel and replacing the house. Thus he became acquainted with the head engineer, James Hanway.

Hanway was a man of about forty years; flat-chested, short in stature and slenderly built. He walked and talked nervously. His face was one of almost feminine delicacy, strangely out of harmony with the element about him. From the broad, high, prominent forehead, that overhung deep-set sad eyes, it narrowed regularly to the chin, the weakness of which contrasted strongly with the upper part of the face. His nose was long and delicately formed, with a slight fullness at the nostrils. And over all the face lingered an expression of nervous expectancy, that seemed like a veil ever about to be lifted, displaying some terrible latent passion. Something in the man's face won Waters' heart. Perhaps this was because his own life of soul-hunger seemed mirrored in the wan face and sad eyes of Hanway.

After the repairing of the shattered wheel-house, the two were much together, Waters spending many hours in the engine room. With their growing friendship, Hanway, ordinarily taciturn, talked much. He betrayed a breadth of culture rarely found in a river engineer. Yet he seemed to be swayed by one thought. His conversation turned inevitably to his son, Lucien, whom he had left in St. Louis.

"An unusual boy, Mr. Waters," said Hanway one day; "an unusual boy, I think. He is only eight years old, and yet he has displayed rare gifts. You are near the gauge, Mr. Waters. How much steam are we carrying?

"He will be a great man some day," continued Hanway; "and then all I have hoped for myself, and failed, will not matter. How much did you say?"

"One hundred sixty-five pounds!" said Waters, who had been studying the steam-gauge with a troubled face. "How much do you gener'ly carry?"

"One hundred fifty," muttered Hanway dreamily, as though his thoughts were far away.

"My God, man! Who tied the valve down? She'll blow up!" cried Waters.

"I did," Hanway answered quietly. "And still it was not Hanway the engineer; Hanway the father, I guess; Hanway the mother, too, for his mother is dead. You may release the valve. You see," he continued in the same nervous weary voice, "a strange premonition tortures me at times. It seems I will never get back to St. Louis again; never see the boy again. At those times I want to give wings to the old *Lucas*. God! how she creeps! If the ice should catch us, I know I should never——" The rushing of steam from the released valve drowned the words. "How she creeps!" muttered Hanway, pacing up and down the engine room.

The next day another delay occurred. A defective boiler made it necessary for the *Lucas* to lay up for repairs again. Hanway worked at the boilers nervously. When anyone spoke to him, he answered peevishly like a child, or stared blankly.

During the second delay, a damp cold wind blew up from the northeast, and by evening a heavy snow storm had set in. All night the two engineers and Waters worked at the boilers. Hanway grew more nervous and abstracted. "Hurry, hurry!" he would mutter to himself; "the ice is coming."

The next morning the *Lucas* again started south, now obliged to feel her way on account of the heavy snow. She had already left Benton 400 miles behind. The sudden cold wave might not last long, as it was only the middle of November. Two days passed; the cold increased and the snow stopped. The nights were cloudy, and the *Lucas* was obliged to run only by day. Hanway grew more excited, though he said nothing. He did not leave his engine, but continually inspected every part of the strained machinery, carrying every pound of steam she would hold. He was racing with Dread. The boat flying down stream like a chip in a flood, trembled with the throb of the plethoric chests. Once the captain, startled by the quivering of the boat, went down into the engine room. Hanway, his face flushed with the heat of the boiler, stood before the steam-gauge with his eyes riveted upon the rising indicator.

"How much are you carrying, Mr. Hanway?" asked the captain. Hanway threw his hat over the gauge, picked up a shovel, and his face was demoniacal as he turned menacingly toward the captain. His voice was low and vibrant.

"*Go to hell!*" he said, his upper lip raised, exposing his teeth like a wolf at bay.

The captain withdrew, walking backward.

"Something's gone wrong with Hanway," said the captain to a group on deck. "He's going to blow her up. Mr. Waters, won't you go down and see if you can do something with him? Maybe he'll listen to you. If he don't, something must be done."

In the old river days a licensed engineer was an autocrat in the engine room, and frequently took matters in his own hands.

When Waters entered the engine room, he saw that the valve had been tied down again. Hanway stood staring at the gauge with a strange smile on his face. He was talking to the engine: "Don't give up again! I know it's a lot to stand," he was saying appealingly; "but don't give up again! You know what it means!" And he laid his hand upon the engine that panted with its mighty effort, patting it caressingly as a kind rider might pat the neck of a thoroughbred in a long hard race.

Waters went quietly to the man, and laid a hand upon his shoulder. Hanway turned with a start, and looked haggardly at Waters.

"It's too much, Jim," he said quietly. He released the valve, and the steam escaped like the sigh of a weary monster. Hanway sat down limply, and buried his face in his hands. "She creeps!" he muttered.

Since the snow had stopped, the temperature had been falling rapidly before a keen wind driving from the north. Hanway's uneasiness increased with the falling of the mercury. He vibrated like a pendulum between the steam-gauge and the thermometer on deck. Hour by hour he noted the ominous dwindling of the degrees toward zero, that seemed like doom to him. 36 degrees—34 degrees—32 degrees! It was freezing now. Hanway returned to his engine and threw quantities of lubricating oil into the fire. Then he stood before the gauge, watching the pulse of the engine rise to a dangerous fever heat.

The captain haunted the engine room. "Hold her up, Mr. Hanway; but for God's sake, be careful!" he would say.

"Captain," Hanway would answer quietly, "I am a licensed engineer."

31 degrees—30 degrees—28 degrees! The mer-

cury fell steadily. On the morning of the 21st of November, it had reached two degrees, and the bitter wind still blew from the north. Zero seemed like death to Hanway. Two degrees left for life! Hanway was racing with Winter and Death—swift and pitiless competitors.

Now in what seemed the supreme hour to Hanway, his nervousness apparently left him. He spoke to no one. Even when Waters entered the engine room, he seemed to have no knowledge of his friend's presence. He stared at the gauge, with his gloved hand upon the lever of the safety valve. When the indicator rose to 166, he released steam until it had fallen back to 165—no lower. His face had taken on something that was almost sublimity. It was no common fight—this struggle of Hanway's. He fought huge foes; subtle insidious Titans! The frail, neurotic pigmy struggled with the ancient giant-foe of his race, the Spirit of the North; and there could be no truce.

Waters stood by, watching the bitter struggle, yet he could give no aid. He, too, wanted to get back south, and could understand the intense anxiety of his friend. As he studied the face of the dread-ridden engineer, he felt a great pity; because he read there a something that he had found in the face of Ambrosen—the longing of the magnificent fool.

As Waters stood studying the face of the man, Hanway suddenly turned and said:

"Do you believe in God?"

"W'y, yes," said Waters wonderingly.

"I don't. There's too much bitterness," said Hanway.

Waters made no answer. For several minutes the sounds of the furiously chugging paddle-wheels and the sobbing and groaning of the engine seemed terribly loud. They were like the tumult of the battle that was being fought—great blows dealt, and groans and sobs of giant pain!

"Then if you do," said Hanway, turning again to Waters with an intense white face; "swear this before your God to me. Swear that if I die and you live, you will look after my boy; for he has no mother."

"W'y, Jim, you hain't goin' to die! Brace up!" Waters tried to laugh but failed dismally.

"Swear that!" cried Hanway.

Waters reached for the hand of the engineer, his eye soft and dimmed.

"Of course I'll swear that, Jim; I do before God!"

Hanway took a piece of notepaper from his pocket, and wrote an address upon it. This he gave to Waters, who put it in his pocket carelessly.

"If I should never get through this, I have given you everything," he said; then quietly turned toward his engine, and the pitiless fight went on.

During the night of the 23rd of November, the *Lucas,* flying down stream under heavy pressure, suddenly stopped. She had run onto a bar, and her great speed had driven her bows far upon the sand. Hanway, standing before his engine, was thrown down. He got up feeling a strange dizziness, and mechanically shut down the engine. The meaning of the sudden stop came to him as a heavy blow on the head. His pitiless foes were upon him. He was conquered—in the dust! He felt a strange weakness, now that the intense strain of the long struggle was past. The engine room swam before him. He sank to the floor in a heap, and, in the utter night that engulfed him, even despair passed.

After a time he awoke dizzily. Everything seemed changed; even he himself. The stillness was like death. He lay still for some time, wondering. He could hear voices above; they came faintly to him. He was seized with a sick fancy. It seemed that he was already dead, and heard, in some unaccountable way, someone talking over his grave. Then he heard the creak of spars, and the groaning of windlasses. The crew was making ready to spar her off.

A faint light came to him. They would need steam, he thought—steam for the capstan. *They* would need it. He had forgotten about the struggle he had lost. All hands were on deck, so he got up, staggered to the engine and fired up. Then he set the pumps to working, and filled the boilers. All this he did as one in his sleep. Nothing really mattered now; only *they* would need steam. When the boilers were filled, he stopped the pumps, and sat down with his head in his hands. He heard dimly the shouting of the crew, the creaking of the windlasses, the groaning of the spars. It was all like the sound from another world. His fight was done.

He slept feverishly and awoke with a start. A pale light shone through the room, and the lamps burned sickly in the disconsolate morning. He got up and went on deck. His face was pale, and there were blue circles under his haggard eyes.

The *Lucas* was in a hopeless plight. During the night, the sand had collected about the boat, and she now lay on a broad, dry bar. It was useless to try to spar her off.

Hanway went listlessly to where the thermometer was hung. *Five below zero!* With a ghastly humor, he smiled as he thought that he had now been dead five degrees!

Out of the haggard east the sick sun rose. Hanway stared into the sunrise as though it were an unheard of phenomenon. He had become the ghost of the man who fought with Titans.

On the 26th of November the ice began running, making useless any further attempts at releasing the boat. All the night the crew heard the crunching and grinding of the ice about the bar, like the sounds of the forging of a mighty chain. The Winter had won, and was placing manacles upon the conquered!

On the morning of the 27th, the great stream was choked with ice from bank to bank, except in the narrow channel where the current was swiftest. By the next morning this had closed in, and the whole was frozen into a solid mass. The point at which the *Lucas* was grounded was nine hundred miles from Fort Benton and nine hundred from Sioux City. For hundreds of miles to the east and the west lay the desolate prairie.

II

The New Captain

During the first week of December, the temperature rose, and it began to snow again. The mighty river, a few weeks before masterful and brooking no restraint, now lay quiet in its chains. There was no longer a river; there was only a broad flat valley; upon one side the white bleak bluffs, made more lonesome and desolate with their straggling growth of scrub oaks; and upon the other side a long gentle slope of white, ending at the indistinct rim of clouded Winter skies.

Quietly, steadily the snow fell. It was as the insistent taunting of the Conqueror Winter, speaking with ironical kindness to the vanquished in their chains. The crew of the *Lucas,* crushed by the sudden descent of the Winter, succumbed to apathy. The northern trip was tedious and lonesome, and their hearts had been glad with the thought of reaching St. Louis before the Winter set in, some longing to be with their families, and others thinking of the Winter's round of pleasures in the western metropolis.

There was no little doubt as to the boat's provisions lasting until Spring, unless game could be found, and the heavy fall of snow made this dubious. For a week none stirred outside the boat which had suddenly been transformed from a refuge to a prison. The prisoners did not wish to see the completeness of their bondage.

The quiet snow fell two feet deep upon the decks, and lay undisturbed. Only the smoke from the fires, blending with the snow maze, gave signs of life in all that silent, white immensity.

During this time Waters fought bravely against the gloom that pressed about him. He was constantly with Hanway, who lay always in his bunk, eating little, speaking to none. His face was expressionless, and his eyes stared nervelessly at the wall. All Waters' attempts to be jovial were met with a gaze that meant nothing. It was only when Waters spoke of Lucien, that the engineer, who had fought and lost, gave signs of intelligence.

"Now don't be worryin' yourself sick, Jim," Waters would say kindly. "W'y, you hain't in a bad way. You've jest got a confounded notion, that's all. We'll get through this all right, Jim; and then you'll see him in the Spring. I've got a little girl I want to see pretty bad myself, and I hain't gettin' sick over it, am I?"

Hanway merely stared and shook his head.

But in the long nights when he was lying alone, the dreadful hush of the snowbound world terrified

Waters. Four months and a thousand miles between him and Calhoun; between him and his little girl; between him and—— Then a something sweet and caressing went into his blood, and he became strong; and in the awful hush he heard a kind voice, and in the darkness his brain conjured radiance. At such times the haunting fears that were bred of the Silence and the Dark, ceased to torture him. He believed no more in the possible dangers of the Winter—famine, disease, and with these, death.

But again when he awoke to feel the faded, disconsolate dawn creeping in through the white silence, the radiance of his dreams died. Then nothing but duty moved him. He had become for the third time a father—the father of a child he had never seen; the father of a name, Lucien Hanway. He must not give up; he must live if all the others died, to fulfil his vows made to Hanway; for he felt that the engineer would not get through the Winter.

But why did the whole world remain so silent? Why did not the wind blow and howl about the *Lucas?* Not even a coyote called over the snowbound prairie. Why did not someone shout or sing or swear aloud? Even he could not drive himself to shout or sing, so awful was the seemingly ancient hush.

But one afternoon someone did break the silence. The crew, huddled indoors, talking over the situation in low voices, was suddenly aroused by the sound of shouting and singing. It seemed to come from above. The dreadful spell was broken. The crew rushed out onto the deck and looked about. Who had dared to shout or sing in the stillness? It seemed like crying defiance to some monstrous sleeping foe!

They looked up and beheld the captain of the *Lucas*. He had climbed to the top of the pilot house. His hatless, coatless figure loomed big against the illimitable white spaces. His face was red and bloated; his eyes wild. Dangerously near the edge of the snow-covered roof, he was executing a grotesque dance, the while he accompanied himself with a maudlin song.

As the captain beheld the suddenly appearing audience, he ceased singing and dancing. Approaching the edge of the roof and grinning, he poised himself on his toes after the manner of a dancer at the footlights.

"Kind of entertainin' the coyotes! (hic)," he explained grandiloquently. "Good of me, dontcha think? Preshative aujence! None of 'em's showed up yet. (hic) Goin' to encore myself; goin' to do it all over! Say, why don't you fellers get some of it—song and dance water? A-hic?"

At the end of his speech, the drunken captain bowed very low, kicked away the snow about him, again poised himself upon his toes and grinned pleasantly. Then he extended his arms like a ballet dancer, and whirled off in a maze of maudlin ecstasy, the snow caught up in his rapid evolutions flying about him like filmy skirts.

He pirouetted, he *chasséd.* He balanced dizzily upon one foot, and with the other kicked extravagantly at the imaginary bald-heads in the front row. His wild song, varying from the catchy strains of a ballet to the measured moaning of an Indian chant, outraged the silence.

The crew, so long under the spell of the hush, went wild with sudden joy.

"Go it, cap! Go it!" they yelled as the captain's dancing degenerated into a clog to the tune of "Old Aunt Kate she's good enough for anybody." The audience joined in with the entertainer, whistling and singing the rousing air, and keeping time by clapping their hands and stamping their feet.

"Go it, cap! You're good enough for a most anybody! Go it!"

Encouraged by the liberal appreciation of the audience, the captain, growing rapidly drunker with his liquor and his whirling combined, indulged in more extravagant motions.

"Bravo! Bravo!" shouted a pilot, as though he were watching from the gallery of a St. Louis vaudeville. "Bravo!"

Nearer and nearer the edge of the roof the captain danced. Then in a maze of flying snow, he went over the side, struck far out on the hurricane deck, and bounded off at the feet of the hushed spectators.

He lay quiet. A thin stream of blood from his head reddened the snow. The dreadful hush came back. When he was lifted to his feet, he sighed, opened his eyes for a moment, and hung limply in the arms of Waters. His skull was crushed, and he was dead.

No one spoke. All seemed to fear to break the spell of the silence again. In the great stillness sound seemed to bear with it a curse.

As Waters stood and gazed upon the limp body of the captain, he thought of that happier hour when the silent form before him had taken charge of his island wedding. The memory made his heart beat warmly for this man who had died in folly. He looked about him at the semicircle of blanched faces, and read terror there; for, to the heart-sick crew, the white face lying in the reddened snow seemed the visible form of the awful hush that had so long oppressed them.

The night was coming on, and the white waste had already begun to grow eerie with the death of day. Waters' own voice sounded strangely to him as he broke the silence.

"Someone take hold of his feet, and I'll take his head, and we'll take him in and let him rest till to-morrow."

One of the pilots obeyed. and they laid him on a couch in the cabin. The long night closed in with the hush. Waters and the pilot sat watching beside the dead by the light of a dim lamp. As

Waters sat again in the presence of death, thinking over all the sadness and gladness of his past, life seemed to him a sweet frail blossom to be guarded jealously from the ever-lurking frost. How glad one should be that he could feel the sun and the wind and the warm blood in his breast! What a priceless thing it was to breathe, and be conscious of the illimitable mystery of skies and stars and fields and flowers and seas and streams! How kind one should be in thankfulness for all this! What a duty one should feel it to be happy!

The long night dragged its black shadow slowly through the silence. At intervals a careful step, muffled in the deep snow, would approach the door of the cabin, and the blanched face of one of the crew would peer silently in at the door where lay the thing that seemed the generative centre of the quiet.

Midnight passed and there was no sound; not even a coyote mourned with the Winter and hunger pinching its vitals.

In the tenseness of his nerves, the figure of Mrs. Sprangs holding his child grew up vividly before Waters. How far away it seemed, yet how much to be desired, grasped and clung to! How desperately one should cling to happiness! How obstinately one should remain in the sun! For after all, this awful stillness comes. He resolved in his heart that he would live through the Winter and seek her in the Spring. How foolish it seemed to him that he had tried to run away from himself, to flee from the sun, to seek shadow, to commit wilfully the sin of unhappiness! He saw it all now in the presence of this thing that was so quiet and cold.

And the weak white dawn coming in at the cabin window, found him stronger with his resolve.

When the day had come, Waters got up from his long watch and taking a pick and a shovel, went some distance from the boat and clearing the snow away, cut a hole in the ice. It was the grave of the captain. Then he went back and resumed his watch until afternoon, when he rang the boat's bell calling all hands. At the melancholy sound, the crew turned out and assembled in the cabin about the body of the captain. Waters stood beside the couch and lifted the covering from the white face.

"Look," he said in a low voice. The sound of the heavy breathing of the crew filled the place, as they stared upon him who had passed so suddenly from loud drunken mirth into this stillness. "Yesterday he was singin' and laughin'. Does it pay to do like him? Let's be good and really happy today; to-morrow we might be like him. That's all. Now let's put him in the river."

Four men lifted the body and bore it out of the cabin into the rapidly falling afternoon.

It was a dismal procession that followed Waters, with faces looking to the snow. When he had reached the grave of ice, Waters knelt beside the body and muttered a prayer. There was no other sound but his muttering and the heavy breathing of the men clustered about the hole. Then the body was lowered into the river, and it was lost in the current.

Waters at once hurried from the place; but the others stood as if fixed to the spot, staring into the black current beneath.

As Waters stepped upon the deck, the sound of his own footsteps frightened him. He started and looked behind him nervously. The seven men still stood transfixed, by the hole in the ice. Waters shuddered at the sight.

"Come away!" he cried.

The shout seemed prodigiously loud. He saw the group of men start, and turn their blank faces toward the boat.

"Got to shake this off!" muttered Waters. "Got to shake it off!"

He closed his eye involuntarily as he passed the red stain in the snow where the head of the captain had lain.

"Got to shake this off, I say!" he said aloud as he hurried into his room and locked the door.

The dusk was deepening in the silence. Waters lit a lamp, and tried to pull himself together. He forced himself to think of his little girl, of Specks, of Mrs. Sprangs, of Lucien Hanway. He said their names aloud, endeavoring to clear away the horror of the silence.

"Mrs. Sprangs, June, Specks," he said aloud.

"Little butterfly—little butterfly." He dwelt upon the latter, and saw again the diaphanous girl of the island standing waist-deep in the glowing spring. Then he thought of the night when something strong and kind had come to him out of the thunderstorm.

Was it not also in the silence?

The thought dispelled his dread. Then he began calmly thinking over the situation, and continued far into the night, when he was aroused from his thoughts by the sounds of muffled voices.

He got up, dressed and went out on deck. The voices came from the engine room. He went back to the cabin and lit a lantern; then he descended the aft stairs, up which the voices came in intermittent snatches of discordant song.

He reached the door and carefully opening it, looked in. There he beheld the seven men huddled about a keg of liquor. Hanway alone was absent. Their faces were wild, and they were making a pitiful effort to sing. As the door creaked, they leaped to their feet and gasped.

"God, Waters!" mumbled one, "thought you was the cap'n!"

Waters closed the door and went back to the cabin. What he did then was the result of his hours of thinking, and this recent discovery. He saw the need of law in the *Lucas,* and he had formed a bold plan. He entered every room and ransacked them for fireams, finding a number of revolvers, rifles, and a shotgun. He took them to his room, and concealed under his bunk, all but two revolvers. Then he went out, locking the door behind him.

He went into the hold where the liquor was stored, and found five kegs. With a half hour's work, he carried these also into his room. Then again locking the door, he slung the lantern over his arm, and returned to the engine room. He threw open the door and went in. The seven still sat huddled about the keg, their faces haggard with drunkenness.

"I want you to go to bed," said Waters quietly.

"Who go tha bed?" mumbled one, deep in liquor. "You go tha bed, Wooden Leg! Don' have tha go. Cap'n's dead."

"Cap'n's dead," muttered the others like a chorus.

A burly deck hand, his brutal features bloated and inflamed with drink, got staggeringly to his feet and seized a shovel.

"You go," he mumbled with thick lips; "no—go to hell! Cap'n's dead. *Lucas* goin' to be a pir't'. Who made you cap'n?"

The man staggered toward Waters, with the shovel upraised. The others stared witlessly.

"I was 'lected unanimous by my friends," said Waters quietly. "Here's one of 'em," he said, pulling a six-shooter from its holster; "and here's another one of 'em," producing the other. "I want you to go to bed."

The man dropped his shovel. One by one the drunken seven got up muttering, and staggered out of the room. When they had gone, Waters took a hammer and shattered the head of the keg of liquor, and poured the contents out. Then he went on deck, and after satisfying himself that all had gone to bed, and that Hanway was sleeping, he went into his room and locked the door.

III

The Return of Gloom

The next morning Waters got up early, and rang the boat's bell to call all hands on deck. Through habit, the men obeyed the familiar call, and turned out, still drowsy with their night's debauch. Waters with his two "friends" in plain sight at his belt, talked to the men:

"Gen'lemen," he said, "I told you last night that I was cap'n of this boat, 'cause none of you looked like you'd make good cap'ns. Now did you?" Some grinned and others scowled. "Now I was doin' this for the good of us all. You fellers all want to get back to St. Louis; so do I. But we'll never get there bein' hogs. We've got some tough times ahead of us, and we've got to run under low pressure, and feel our way with the lead or we'll run aground worse'n we have. Now, whenever you fellers act like you'd make better cap'ns than I am, then you can be cap'n. Bill," he said, addressing the cook, "I want you to keep on doin' the cookin'. I'll pay you what you've been gettin', and settle every week. Now there's got to be wood chopped, and timbers put around the *Lucas* to save her from the ice in the Spring. I'll pay two dollars a day for doin' this, and pay it every week. I've got the money, and a bankful more of it at St. Louis, not mentionin' a cargo of furs at Benton. Flecto and Cabney," he continued, addressing the pilots, who were the most intelligent of the seven, "I want you to oversee this work of gettin' timbers for the boat, and cuttin' wood to burn. You can meet me in the cap'n's room in ten minutes, and we'll talk it over."

The new captain's proposition to pay for all work done infused spirit into the formerly dejected crew.

"Hooray for Cap'n Waters!" cried the deck hand with the brutal face, who had looked down the mouths of Waters' friends the night before, and consequently felt the new authority.

When Waters met the two pilots in the cabin, he took them into his confidence, and readily won them over. They agreed to serve as overseers of the men, without pay.

"Now which one of you fellers has been on the river longest?" asked Waters.

"Flecto has," said Cabney.

"Then I want Mr. Flecto to be my first mate, and Mr. Cabney second mate," said Waters.

By noon the new organization was complete and in working order. The men lost their dread as they worked, and when they returned from the bluffs in the evening, their appetites had returned with their good spirits. For several weeks the work went on merrily. The snow had stopped, and the sun came out, bleared and pale; for the temperature had fallen after the ceasing of the snow. It was hard but wholesome work, cutting timber at the edge of the bluffs, and dragging it to the boat. But the dreadful hush had been broken with the sound of axe and saw; and the men sang and laughed in the exhilarating frosty air.

Waters' *coup* had succeeded perfectly. Even Hanway seemed to shake off some of the lethargy that had hung upon him so long. A slight fever that had seemed to be slowly wasting him away, disappeared, and he ate with better appetite. Still he talked much of Lucien, laughing at his childish pranks as he remembered them, and growing enthusiastic over the possible future of the boy. Waters managed to take him for walks over the timber trail to the bluffs, and noted with joy how the haggard face had gained color and a more peaceful expression.

But one day in the early part of January, Waters foresaw a coming danger. The stock of potatoes and flour was exhausted, and there was nothing left for food but cured meats. Even this supply would scarcely be adequate for the balance of the Winter, and it became necessary that fresh meat should be supplied.

Waters called the men together and explained the situation. Flecto and Cabney at once volunteered to go on a hunt. So on the morning following, the two pilots, armed with a shotgun and a rifle, which Waters produced from their hiding place, set out in search of jack-rabbits and antelope.

They took the timber trail for the bluffs, and disappeared over the indistinct sky line. It was a cold still morning, the temperature below zero. The many days of continuous cold had made the heavy fall of snow like dry powder. By noon the sky clouded, and the far sky line disappeared in a gray haze. A light wind came up from the north, scurrying the feathery snow like dust across the drear expanse.

Anxiously the men in the *Lucas* gazed at the hazy summits of the bluffs, straining their eyes to see the returning hunters suddenly loom out of the sky. All afternoon they gazed; still nothing moved upon the summits but the snow writhing under the lash of the wind. By evening the wind had increased. Slowly the great expanses had grown smaller and smaller with the rising of the wind, until there was but a small circle of day left about the *Lucas*, and beyond that the dizzy twilight of the storm.

The night came almost unnoticed; and with it the wind rose higher, and the lessening circle of vision closed in, leaving the *Lucas* in impenetrable night.

All through the night the men on the boat sat huddled about the furnace in the engine room. The burning logs popped, the wind howled, and the watchers sat silent, listening, listening. When a sudden puff of wind shook the smokestacks outside, the watchers by the fire invariably started, thinking they had heard the footsteps of the returning hunters. The dread of noise became even more terrible than the former dread of the hush.

Once the howl of the wind in the stacks sounded like the hoarse shout of a desperate man. Hanway leaped to his feet.

"There!" he cried. "*Flecto!*"

The watchers stared into each other's faces, and did not move. After years of waiting, as it seemed, morning came; but it was not day; only the seething gray twilight of the blizzard, a travesty of dawn.

The gloom that had been dispelled by the efforts of the new captain now descended again upon the *Lucas*. Waters fought with the incubus of dread. He tried to appear cheerful; he joked, but no one laughed. It seemed that some stern fatality followed the *Lucas*.

Failing in his jokes, Waters began talking about the wedding in the wilderness, in which the crew had taken part.

"You fellers remember my weddin', don't you?" he said, attempting to speak affably. "Never was a weddin' like it before, was there? Say, let's sing 'Annie Laurie' again, jest like we sung it then." And he began:

"Maxwelton's braes are bonny
Where early fa's the dew,

And 'twas there that Annie Laurie
G'ae me her promise true."

The men caught up the song, and sang falteringly until they reached the refrain:

"And for bonnie Annie Laurie
I'd lay me down and dee."

At the words, tears came into the eye of Waters, in spite of his efforts. The song died.

"What became of the beautiful girl?" whispered one of the men.

Waters hesitated long, and then said quietly: "Died."

"Ah," said one, "it all comes to that!" And a quiet fell upon the assembled crew.

Still Waters made a final effort to dispel the gloom. He announced that he would open a poker game in the engine room, and that he was going to be the "house." Although he had long since put away his old rough life, he feigned a deep interest in the game. All the players had the greater part of their Summer's wages with them. They drew cards and hazarded their money with listless unconcern, always listening, listening for the sound of footsteps that never came.

Waters almost wished that someone would be caught with an ace up his sleeve; but there was no desire to win. Once when a considerable jackpot had just been opened with everybody staying, an unusually heavy gust of wind made something clatter on deck. The players dropped their cards face upward upon the table, and leaped from their chairs.

But when at last the second engineer called a large bet with a pair of deuces, Waters closed the game.

And the gloom deepened.

At the end of the third day the storm died, and the white waste emerged from the shadow, glittering in the sickly sun that went down smiling like a cynic.

IV

The Coyote

With the dying of the storm, the hush returned with increased intensity. The men huddled about the furnace in the engine room, and spoke little. Hanway had again taken to his bunk. The general depression had made him irritable. He refused to eat regularly, and with petulant outcries resented all attempts at persuasion, often cursing even Waters.

One evening Waters went out on deck for a breath of fresh air, walking rapidly around the cabin. Suddenly he came upon the brutal faced deck-hand, who was leaning over the stern railing, his hard face savage with hate, as he stared into the white emptiness. His arms were raised menacingly, and his fists were clenched.

"Damn you, damn you, damn you!" he was muttering fiercely, as if challenging some invisible enemy.

"They'll all get luny," said Waters that night as he lay thinking over the matter. So the next morning he gave orders for the chopping of more wood, although a large supply still remained.

"We don't want to chop wood," growled the second engineer.

"Plenty wood," muttered the others.

"But I'll pay for it," urged Waters.

"Pay be damned!" said they.

Waters' nerves, tense with the strain they had long borne in patience, gave way. His face became devilish. His cheeks blanched and his lips whitened. His one eye glared. He pulled his guns and made the hammers quiver beneath his nervous thumbs.

"Chop wood!" he cried. "Will you chop?"

The men obeyed doggedly. But when they returned in the evening, their spirits were no better. They went about muttering, with their heads hung.

During the scanty supper of fried bacon, the second engineer spoke for the men.

"Cap," he said, "we want liquor; you've got it hid, and we want it."

The others all shook their heads in assent. Waters made no answer for some time. He foresaw the danger that lay in drunkenness. He wished he had shattered all the kegs the night he concealed them in his room.

"Well," said he at length, "of course you can have liquor." He felt that the time had come when his authority could be sustained only by lenience. After supper he brought to the engine room, where the men had congregated, a small bucket of whiskey and a tin cup. The men became jovial as they drank.

"Have one, cap!" they clamored.

Waters smiled sadly and pushed the cup away. "Cap'n's oughtn't to drink," he said; "have you forgot?"

The memory of the dead captain brought silence, and Waters left the place, going to his room and locking himself in. He lay awake late, wondering if he should not get up and destroy the liquor. No, he thought, they would go wild if he did, and he knew he could no longer control by fear. He felt that his usurped authority had been swallowed in the gloom. It was no longer a captain against a crew; it was one man against seven, and the growing desperation increased the odds.

Once he raised himself in his bunk, resolved to get up and destroy the liquor, even if he should be killed for it. Then his vow to Hanway checked him. He dropped back again upon his pillow. "No," he mused, "I must live if all the rest die." His vow had become an obsession.

He lay awake listening to the coyotes; for the snow had hardened and they were enabled to run about.

Yi yi yi yi-yoo-o-ow-ow-oo-ow.

It was a heart-broken cry.

"Pore devils!" mused Waters; "pore shiverin' devils! Their bellies is flappin' together, and their feet're achin' in the frost. Still, if I was a coyote for awhile, I'd start south and run—run—run like the wind. God! Wouldn't I run!"

Gradually the yelp and howl of the coyotes grew

dimmer, and he fell asleep, dreaming that he was a coyote leaping wildly over the frozen snow to the south. He felt the keen night-air bite his face as he flew, and saw beside him his moving shadow that the moon cast. He ran—ran—ran, breathlessly, terror-stricken; but the shadow ran beside him.

Then a loud sound as of crashing timbers awakened him. The *Lucas* leaped and trembled. He got up dizzily, and could hardly believe that he was awake. Were the engines working? He could hear their sobbing and groaning. He dressed quickly and went out on deck. No one stirred in the cabin; the men slept heavily with their liquor.

A light came up the aft stairs, from the open door of the engine room. Waters ran down the stairs and entered. The engine had been fired up and the furnace was red hot. The machinery was in motion, and Waters knew what had caused the crashing sound that had awakened him. The side-wheels, buried in the frozen sand, had been shattered.

He rushed to the throttle and shut down the engine. Then he looked at the indicator; it had reached 167 and was rapidly rising, for the valve had been tied down.

"Damn that Hanway!" cried Waters.

He cut the cords that held the valve, and released the steam. When the roar of the escaping steam had died, a sound from the deck attracted Waters' attention. It was as the cry of a coyote, only louder and more hopelessly broken-hearted.

Waters ran up to the deck, and there in the starlight, he beheld Hanway in his night clothes, upon his hands and knees in the snow. His head was thrown back, and his face upturned to the bitter sky. He was answering the lonesome coyotes with their own terrible heart-broken plaint.

Waters' momentary anger suddenly changed to a great pity. He went to the man and touched him gently.

"Come on, Jim," he said. "Come on back to bed now; I'll take care of the engine. You're cold, and you'd better go to bed."

"All right, Waters," said Hanway in a thin, plaintive voice; "I got her fired up, but somehow—somehow—let's see—somehow, I couldn't get the damn throttle open, I guess. Send her through for all she's worth, Waters; but wake me up when we get to St. Louis; 'cause, you know, the boy's been waiting—waiting—waiting—huh?"

He looked searchingly into Waters' face, and began to sob.

Waters took him to bed, where he soon fell into a nervous sleep. All through the night Waters watched by the bunk of the engineer, with a great pity at his heart, like a mother watching a sick child. And at last the pale dawn came wearily over the waste of snow.

V

Mutiny

During the days that followed, a sense of impending calamity grew upon Waters. He no longer removed his clothes at night, and slept restlessly. He had carefully concealed the condition of Hanway from the rest, fearing the effect it might have upon them. His haunting sense of impending danger was increased daily by the growing morbidness of the men. They seldom moved away from the fire, and had ceased to call him captain at those rare intervals when they broke their sullen silence. At meals, when an insufficient supply of fried bacon was meted out by Waters, they no longer ate like men. They devoured like wolves, and after sullenly disposing of every morsel, withdrew from the table grumbling. And Waters constantly wore his revolvers, fearing some sudden violence.

Sustained by his one purpose of fulfilling the vow to Hanway, Waters alone tried to maintain a cheerful spirit in the face of famine. Foreseeing the possible result of the ravenous hunger of the men, he had seized the remaining supply of bacon and hidden it in his room, producing daily enough to keep himself and the men from starvation.

During the latter part of January, the second engineer and a deck hand refused to get up one morning at the sound of the bell. Waters found them lying listless in their bunks, their eyes lustreless under swollen lids. On the third morning their condition had grown decidedly worse. Their tongues were swollen and bleeding, and their dried, mummy-like faces were marked with bruise-like blotches.

Waters summoned all the strength of his weakening spirit to fight the dread that held him in its clutches. He watched by the sick men, caring for them as best he could.

During this time Hanway seemed to struggle out of his gloom. Though feeble, he went about the boat, talking hopefully of the Spring and the continuation of the trip. But the rising spirits of Hanway were not shared by the three who were still able to get about. They quarrelled much among themselves, like peevish children, their anger arising at the most trivial provocation. When their two companions fell sick, their peevishness increased, and they complained childishly to Waters of their food.

At the end of two weeks, the sick men became delirious and sank into lethargy. Their gums had become spongy and oozed blood; their breaths were foul. Waters watched them through the last night, as the lethargy deepened, and their breathing became weaker and weaker. One died in the morning, and the other in the evening.

Waters chopped another hole in the ice, and the loathsome bodies were given to the river. Of the ten who had started south with the *Lucas,* only five remained; and among them all, Waters alone, sustained by a purpose that daily grew upon him, retained his power to struggle against odds.

One evening as Waters was unlocking the door of his room, where the arms and provisions had been hidden, the sullen three approached him.

"Waters," said one, with the whining voice of a sick child, "give us one of the kegs of whiskey, won't you?"

Waters answered kindly, but with a sinking heart, for he felt that the long feared outbreak of frenzy was at hand.

"I can't," he said; "fellers, I can't do it, 'cause I know you'd sure never see Spring."

"But we won't see Spring nohow," the man answered. "God! Waters, won't you let us die easy?"

"You can't have any!" returned Waters firmly. "I'm cap'n of the *Lucas* yet and——"

Waters had failed to place any significance upon the manner of the men's approach. One had come up on either side, and one in front. The man in front had opened the conversation, and Waters was looking at him as he spoke. To his left stood the brutal-faced deck hand, larger and more powerfully built than the rest, with his hands behind his back.

Before Waters had finished his sentence, there was a sudden movement to his left; then there was a dull roar in his head; he felt himself falling, and a heavy darkness closed in about him.

A dull pain cut through the darkness and silence like a knife. Then slowly a little light filtered into Waters' brain, and a faint sound of shouting. He heard his name called repeatedly as from a great distance. Dizzily he opened his eyes, and saw the face of Hanway over him. He blinked wonderingly at the face that whirled about like the ghastly face of a drowned man in a whirlpool. Slowly the whirling ceased, and he recognized the things in his own room.

His head ached. He placed his hand on the side that ached most, and withdrew it covered with blood. Someone had struck him on the head. Then the memory of his talk with the men came back as from some far time. He raised himself upon his elbow and looked about. A lantern was hanging on the wall. Dazedly he searched the place with his eye for something; what was it? Oh, yes, the liquor!

"God, man!" gasped Hanway, supporting Waters with his frail body; "I thought you were dead!"

"Where's the whiskey?" Waters asked, getting unsteadily to his feet, and leaning against the wall for support.

"They've got it all out on deck! They've been turning the night into hell! Listen!"

Snarls and cries as of wolves at bay broke the night stillness. Instinctively Waters felt for his guns—they were no longer in their holsters. He went to the door, threw it open and stepped out onto the deck. On the deck of the *Lucas* he saw the three men. One lay upon his back in the snow among the kegs. A cold moon shed a dull light over the rim of the east, and illumined the sickly scene. The two other men were swaying dizzily about in the snow, locked in brutal combat. They snarled and snapped at each other's faces like infuriated dogs.

Still stunned with the blow he had received, Waters stood staring dazedly at the fight. He saw the two go down, wallowing in the snow, and cursing and snarling. Still he did not move. It seemed like a nightmare over which he had no control. He heard the sound of choking; then he saw the deck-hand with the brutal face get unsteadily to his feet, leaving his adversary lying in the snow.

He saw the man pull two six-shooters from his hip pockets and deliberately empty them into the two prostrate forms. He heard the devilish laughter of the man, and then fear came upon him like a sickness. He tottered into his room again, and shut the door. He took two revolvers from under his bunk, and loaded them. Then he sat down upon the floor, facing the door, with the guns resting on his knees.

Hanway's teeth chattered as he crouched behind Waters. The two sat listening to the cries and laughter of the drunken man outside. When they heard him pass the door, Waters cocked the revolvers, and held them tremblingly upon the door. In a half conscious way he wondered at his cowardice, but he felt no shame; for it seemed that something strong had oozed out of the wound in his head. It was not until the light of morning found him huddled over his arms, that he could feel ashamed.

VI

The Last of the Lucas

It was the third week in February. Waters, Hanway and the deck-hand alone survived of the ten who had started south with the *Lucas* in the Fall. The two victims of the night's debauch had followed their companions into the river. The deck-hand, owing doubtless to his brute constitution, soon recovered from his debauch. What was not drunk of the liquor had been poured out onto the snow, as the kegs had been shattered by the men in their frenzy. There was no further danger from that source.

Waters still wielded the little authority that was needed. He took the dead cook's place, and measured out the day's rations in quantities small enough to make the limited supply of bacon last during the two months that must pass before the ice would break up.

It was a time of silence. The deck-hand had not spoken since the murdering of his companions. He went about sullenly with his head down. The revolvers taken from Waters after he had been knocked down, were worn constantly by the deck hand. Waters also wore a pair belted about the outside of his coat for ready use, and never turned his back upon the other; for though he had seen the revolvers emptied into the victims of that night's debauch, he suspected that the deck hand had found other ammunition. All three now slept without removing their clothes and boots. Each seemed apprehensive of some imminent culmination of an indefinite fear.

During this time Hanway grew weaker and more peevish. When he spoke, his words were trivial and childish. He seemed to have lost all memory of the past. When Waters endeavored to arouse him from his stupor by speaking of Lucien, he stared blankly. Day by day Waters noted the dying of the man's brain. All that which had been strong in the man's face was slowly passing away, leaving upon his pale features the vacuous expression of a sheep. At times he became idiotic, snivelling pitifully, or breaking into an empty titter at the words of his friend. At such times he seemed to have lost the sense of his own identity. Once at a meal, when putting a piece of bacon to his lips, he suddenly discovered the presence of a hand at his mouth. He grasped it with his other hand, cast it upon the table and gave it a sound beating. Then his impotent anger suddenly passed, and he wept bitterly over his bruised hand.

Through the dismal nights Waters kept watch over Hanway. The Winter had reached its climax, and it was bitterly cold. The timbers of the *Lucas* popped and groaned as they contracted in the cold. The coyotes filled the empty world with their cries. The cables that supported the smokestacks sang keenly in the frosty air.

But one day Hanway appeared lucid. His face had taken on a more human expression; he talked much and sensibly concerning the Spring and the trip south. With the exception of a peculiar hesitancy in his speech, he seemed his old self again.

A great load was lifted off Waters' mind. He became cheerful again, and that night he went early to his bunk. Exhausted with loss of sleep, he soon fell into heavy slumber.

He dreamed he felt a soft southwind on his face, gentle and kind as the caress of a woman. He heard the ice pop and roar, and the grumbling of the awakened river. Then the floods arose, and there was a great shouting and groaning, and the dull sound of ice hurled upon ice—the tumult of the elemental battle. The waters rose higher, and he felt the *Lucas* lift and shake herself like a wet dog. Then he felt the vibration of machinery, and heard the snoring of engines. His heart grew light within him. He was going south, to Calhoun and everything that was dear in the world. In his joy he lifted his voice lustily, and the sound of his cry awakened him.

The *Lucas was* vibrating! The engines *were* snoring and wheezing! But there was no booming of ice; no lifting of the Spring flood; only the terrible silence of the Winter.

He rubbed his eyes, yawned and listened. *Chug—chug-swish; chug—chug-swish.* A lonesome coyote hurled its cry like a pang through the night. Then thoroughly awakened, Waters thought of Hanway; he had started the engines again! Waters rushed forthwith out of his room; for he had not undressed. He was shaken with a great anger; his patience was exhausted.

"Damn that——"

He did not finish his sentence.

At that moment there came a sound of roaring and rending. The boat seemed to leap clear of the ice, her strained timbers shrieking as in pain! Waters was thrown violently against the cabin, and rendered momentarily senseless. When he recovered, he saw that the whole after part of the boat had been shattered, and a cloud of steam, hot with tongues of flame, arose from the wreckage! The boilers had blown up.

He stood transfixed, staring at the flames that momentarily leaped higher. Something moved near him. He turned and looked into the face of the deck hand. In that moment it seemed he had never looked upon a dearer face, though he loathed the man from the bottom of his heart. The sense of human companionship in the lonesome waste, now grown doubly desolate, was overpowering.

"Hurry!" cried Waters; "Hanway's blowed her

up! Drag out everything you want to save. We're in for a long trip!"

Blankets, bacon and ammunition were dragged out and piled in the snow. Then these two who hated and feared each other but a day before, huddled together like two frightened boys, and watched their last hope vanishing in flames.

The *Lucas,* dried with the long Winter, burned like tinder. The wild flame, leaping out of the smoke, hurled back the darkness, and built a ghastly, flickering day in the midst of the night. The bluffs loomed up blood-red, and the wolves, lured by the unaccustomed light, gathered about the edge of the miniature day, yelping and whining in wonder.

After hours, the flames died, and the *Lucas* lay a smouldering hulk, wrapped in smoke. There was no moon; the stars in the intense cold glittered sharp as broken glass, and the sky was like frosty steel.

Without a word, the two men huddled together in their blankets, and waited for the dawn. After an eternity of waiting, the east turned dull red, the stars faded and the bleak waste emerged from the shadow. Only in the east was there promise of anything. There a scarlet patch of sky broke the night's stupor as with a shout, and the sun rose round and red like an opened furnace door, mocking the frozen waste.

VII

A Bit of Paper

After eating a hasty and joyless breakfast, the two survivors of the *Lucas* prepared their packs, and started down the frozen river for the south, where Fort Sully lay. When they had walked a half hour, Waters turned and looked back to where the charred remains of the boat made a black scar upon the white valley. A great sadness welled up in his heart as he thought of Hanway. "Pore Jim!" he muttered, and turned hurriedly to follow his companion.

Dazed by the sudden calamity of the preceding night, the two walked all day in silence, stopping only at noon to build a fire and cook bacon for their dinner. In the evening they made a framework of poles in a wooded nook of the bluffs, and over this hung a blanket. In front of this they built their fire. They prepared their supper, ate, and then rolled up in their blankets under the covering that reflected the heat downward upon them. In the morning they arose stiffened, ate in silence, and pushed on down the silent valley toward the south.

Day after day they walked, weary, hungry, dazed,

with the lonesome white spaces about them, glittering in the sun by day and glinting under the stars by night. By day, nothing to break the hush but the monotonous crunching of their feet in the snow; by night, the popping of the fire and the yelping of the coyotes, gathered about to wonder at the strange phenomenon of fire.

As the days passed with straining toil, Waters became much wearier than his companion, as his wooden leg impeded his progress. He forgot the *Lucas,* forgot Hanway, forgot Lucien, forgot the days and nights of terror in the ice-bound steamboat. He even forgot Calhoun and what awaited him there. He felt only hunger, fatigue, and a mad impulse that drove him ever to the south, where, in some mysterious way, the hush would be broken, and the hunger and fatigue would vanish. The other swung sullenly along, his face deep-stamped with the brute that grew ever within him with the strain of the toil and the hush and hunger.

Bearded, their faces whitened with their frozen breaths, they stumbled southward down the white valley, no longer men who knew of love or pity, but rather aching, weary incarnations of the instinct for home.

One evening after the camp had been made, and supper eaten, Waters rolled up in his blankets, leaving the other sitting by the fire with his head resting on his knees. Worn out with the day's toil, Waters soon fell asleep. When he awakened, it was morning; he stared about him and found himself alone. He called, but heard only echoes from the bluffs. The other had not lain down. Waters saw where his trail ran down the valley to the south. Then his heart sank with misgiving. He looked for the bacon and found it gone!

A great rage shook him; he cursed into the frosty silence, his hands clenched nervously with the desire to kill. He was the primitive beast robbed of its food, and he wanted to kill and devour.

Forgetting the hunger that had assailed him when he awoke, he prepared his pack, threw it across his shoulders, and took the fresh trail that wound mockingly ahead of him and disappeared in the glint of sun upon snow. At noon he did not stop, but struggled on down the path of him he wanted to kill. His rage burned big in him, warming and strengthening where hunger would have chilled and weakened. As he went, his quivering lips shaped maledictions, savage cries of hate. He had forgotten everything now; even the yearning for the south had passed, and he was conscious only of a hideous desire to catch, tear, crush, kill.

But anger is swift and transient; hunger slow and tireless. The day waned, and the dusk swallowed the far windings of the trail. Waters felt his hunger coming on him like a mortal sickness, and still the trail of the faithless continued into the deepening dusk.

Reaching the spot where the other had camped

for dinner, he found a log still smouldering, and near it some bacon rinds. He devoured the leavings of the other's meal, with a bitterness lurking like smouldering coals where his rage had flamed. He sat down by the log, exhausted, his courage dead with his anger, until the last spark of the log died, and the night had driven the last glow from the southwest. Then he thought he would rebuild the fire and lie down. If he never got up—well, what did it matter? He gathered some brush and made it ready to kindle. As he drew a match from his pocket, a bit of paper fell before him in the snow.

He picked it up and tried to read what was scrawled upon it in the gloom. He lit a match that he might read. Stunned with hunger and fatigue, and chilled with his sitting in the cold, he slowly spelled it out in the match glow.

L—u—c—i—e—n H—a—n—

The match went out, but a great light had grown up in his brain. Lucien Hanway! The address written by the engineer when he had said: "Swear before your God that if I die you will look after my boy!"

As in a dream, Waters heard the words again; heard his own answer: "I swear that, Jim; I do before God;" heard the overtaxed engine throbbing like a great heart yearning for home; saw the haggard, anxious face of him who ran a futile race with Dread and Death; remembered how this vow had kept him up and made him strong when calamity followed calamity through the terrors of hush and storm, in the face of famine and riot, disease and death.

And as he thought thus, his weakness passed; he chilled no more; he was no longer weary. Even the bitterness of burnt-out anger passed, and as he got to his feet, slung his pack on his shoulders and took the trail, the great still spaces were no longer lonesome. A something strong and kind and calm seemed brooding in the hush that gently chided his former violence.

Through the stillness, under the quiet, scintillant stars, he rushed down the white valley, breathing strength from the infinite calm. Midnight passed, the stars of morning rose and paled and faded in the dawn; and Waters came upon a nook in the bluffs where the trail stopped before a smouldering fire and a sleeping man.

He cautiously approached the sleeper and gazed upon his face whitened with his breath. As he gazed, the light of a great pity suffused his face and softened his eye, bloodshot with the hardship of the trail.

"Pore devil!" he muttered.

He found the bacon hanging upon the framework near the man's head. He took his knife and carefully cut the piece of meat in halves. One he placed in his pack, and hung the other where he had found it. Then he took one of his revolvers from its holster, cocked it and laid it carefully upon the sleeping man's breast. As he started to go away, he saw that the fire had fallen low. He hurriedly replenished it from a small pile of wood lying near by, and then walked rapidly away into the south. When he came to a bend in the river, he turned and looked back. The flame burned with a kindly light in the distance, and the man had not yet gotten up. A thin gray column of smoke mounted from the fire toward the sky where the floating frost sparkled in the dawn, and it seemed to Waters like a finger pointing.

"Better'n killin'," he muttered; then with a heart grown strangely light, he pushed on about the shoulder of the bluff, and toiled onward into the south.

VIII

Bread Upon the Waters

Waters did not stop to rest all that day. As he walked, he cut a strip of bacon and chewed it for his dinner. He felt that he must put as many hours as possible between himself and the other. He could not run the risk of being overtaken asleep, now that he had rediscovered his purpose. He was the father of a dead man's child, and he must not fail. He walked until late at night, then built a fire, prepared his supper, ate, and slept. But notwithstanding his utter weariness, for he had travelled long without rest, his sleep was broken, and long before sunrise, he got up, replenished his fire, cooked his breakfast and pushed on.

But his limbs were stiff and weak and he felt a strange giddiness at times. By sheer will he drove his unwilling body southward. As the day advanced, the giddiness increased. But Waters knew, through his familiarity with the bluffs along the river, that he was now within fifty miles of the Fort. He had been walking thirteen days, but to his dazed mind the period reached far back into ancient time.

"Only fifty years," he muttered deliriously; "miles—no, years—miles—miles—fifty. Get there in fifty years, if I don't give out. But I won't, I can't. Jim's watchin' me—can't give out—can't—can't." The words went on in his head of their own accord, timing their own recurrence to the labored, painful dragging of the feet.

A light snow had fallen during the night, and fitful gusts of wind whirled it in fantastic wraiths ahead of the delirious toiler.

His fancy built images in the fitful maze. Once he saw ahead of him the face of a boy he did not know. It was the face of Hanway translated into youth. "I'm comin', Lucien, I'm comin'," said Waters in a husky whisper, that was meant for a shout. The snow maze cleared and the image passed, and Waters still pushed through the white waste that danced giddily about him like an ocean in a gale. Once a flurry of snow sprang up at his feet, and spun down the stretch ahead, glittering in the sunlight. It took on the form of the Island Girl, with her hair like flame about her body, glowing from the bath at dawn. Waters' weary heart leaped, and he urged his tottering limbs into a trot, vainly trying to reach the vision. He stumbled and fell upon his face in the snow. The earth whirled about him giddily. He tried to get up, muttering, "can't—can't—can't stop"; but the light passed and the whirling ceased, and he was so comfortable there that he fell asleep.

Twinges of pain, as of the pricking of needles in his fingers and toes, aroused him. He opened his eye wearily. He was wrapped in one of his blankets and the other was arranged as a canopy over his head. A rousing fire burned near by. In spite of a strange numbness in his limbs, he raised himself to a sitting posture and looked about. It was night. Dazedly he wondered. Surely the last he had known he was on the trail! How did it happen that he was now in camp beside a warm fire?

He got up and experienced more pain as he stepped on his foot. Yes, he remembered he had fallen, but he didn't remember getting up, much less making camp and going to bed. "Must have frosted my foot and hands," he thought. He looked about him wonderingly, trying to remember when he had done all this. As he looked about, he discovered a half dozen slices of bacon sizzling on a hot stone by the fire. He looked about for his piece of bacon, and found it hanging under the shelter where he had awakened. It was just as he had left it; none had been cut off. He went back to the fire, and his hunger came at sight of the waiting meal. He ate greedily. Then he placed snow on the hot stone, and as it melted, caught the water in his hands and drank. He began to feel stronger, and could think clearly. He sat down by the fire and wondered. As he gazed downward, his glance fell upon the holster that had been empty when he fell. His revolver, that he had left on the breast of the other, was there in its place.

Then it all became clear to Waters. He smiled into the flames. "Better'n killin'," he said. Then he went back to his blankets, and fell into a heavy, peaceful sleep.

He awakened late next morning, and started south. To his surprise, he found a good path ahead of him, as though some one had dragged something to break the trail. A great peace, as of one who has won a victory, filled his heart, though his limbs were dull and heavy, and his foot ached with every step. Toward evening the trail led into a sheltered nook in the bluffs. Waters followed it, and found a heap of wood ready to be lit. Also he found a small log covered with snow, and worn by being dragged on the ice.

The next day his weakness came upon him again. All that day and the next, he struggled southward, with his aching gaze fixed upon the trail. Delirious with exhaustion, he stumbled along with but one thought—that he must fulfil his vow to Hanway. The white waste whirled about him. He staggered, fell, got up and stumbled on, with the one fixed idea goading him like a whip. And then the time came when he could no longer arise when he fell.

For a long while there was only darkness and numbness; then he was aroused by voices and the stamping of horses, coming faintly from afar. Then he was half conscious of a giddy rushing through the air, the sound of dogs' feet, and the hiss of runners in the snow.

When Waters wakened, he was lying in a bunk. He saw a strange face above him, wavering as in the heat of Summer. His temples throbbed, and his whole body was a burning ache.

"Who're you?" said Waters, his own voice sounding dimly to him.

"I'm the major," said the face, smiling kindly, and seeming hazy as though it were at a great distance. "Who are you? The other fellow didn't say."

"I'm—I'm——" His head reeled and throbbed as he searched the bewildering maze of his mind for the elusive answer.

"I'm—uh—I'm—Jim Han—Han-way; ain't I?"

IX

A Notch Deepened

The Summer following Mrs. Sprangs' return to Fort Calhoun was a long, lonesome one. Specks came up from his school in July, only to return again in August. The gossips of the village worked overtime continually, and Mrs. Sprangs found herself isolated with the child June.

"Gracious me!" said Mrs. Griggs puffingly. "They'd ought to get married now and clear out of here! Him sendin' her boy to school like his'n; and his poor little innocent flower of a wife hardly in her grave; and her a-coddlin' his baby like it was her'n, and poor, hard-workin' Mr. Sprangs as slaved his life away in the mines for her, hardly begun to molder in his grave!"

When the Fall came, the gossip of the village was aggravated by the sight of the woman with the child walking out to the river in the sombre, autumnal evenings, where she would stand gazing with quiet eyes up the stretches of the river, fading into the dusk.

Boats appeared and passed, but not the *Island*

Girl. And then at last the Winter came; the river became a winding strip of white, and the woman no longer gazed up the stream, but sat patiently at home with the little girl huddled at her breast, waiting for the Spring.

At Sully, days and weeks passed, of which Waters had no knowledge. He existed in a feverish, phantasmagoric world of snow wastes, burning steamboats, madmen, faces, faces, faces. They boiled and seethed about him—these faces. Now there was wave after wave of brutal faces that leered at him; now it was the face of James Hanway infinitely multiplied—a pitiful, tragic face. Now it was the face of the Island Girl floating in dazzling billows of golden hair—whole riotous sunsets of burning hair. Now again it was a quiet flood of gentle, motherly faces—the face of Mrs. Sprangs, infinitely multiplied.

Like a drowning man, he cried out to these faces, but they gave no answer. Then suddenly it all subsided with a lingering melancholy sound, as when the frothy waves begin to grow quiet after a storm, and the consciousness of day burst upon him—a glad, golden day of Spring.

He still heard a deep sullen roaring. He also heard a step near him, and the face of an elderly man, a quiet, reassuring man, bent over him.

"We've notified her," said the Face. "I'm the surgeon of the Fort, you know. How are you feeling?"

"Who's that?" said Waters dazedly.

"Why, Mrs. Sprangs, of Fort Calhoun. You have been speaking of her a great deal of the time; a near relation, no doubt. So we sent her a letter by stage, telling her of your condition. You seemed about to pass in for a while. But you are getting along finely now. You must be as quiet as possible."

The face withdrew, and Waters lay, too weak to follow it with his gaze, staring at a strange wall, and pondering in bewilderment. They had notified her? Would she come? he wondered. How long had he been there? It seemed only yesterday that he had been struggling through the white waste, so weary, so weary.

What was that sound? That booming and clashing and rending? Ah, the music of it! It was the river breaking its chains; it was the hoarse, glad cry of the Spring! He tried to rise, but he could not.

"I must've been pretty well done up!" he mused. "Been layin' here quite a spell! Ice breakin' up, eh? Got to get well pretty soon, 'cause the *Island Girl* 'll be along after while to get me. Lucien Hanway! Oh, thank God I didn't die! I believe I would've died if it hadn't been for him! I'll go and get him as soon as I get well. Oh, a feller ain't so bad off that has sons give to him ready-made, I guess!

"Mrs. Sprangs knows it! Wonder if she'll come? If she does—if she does——"

He felt very weak and giddy and sleepy, and the world dwindled away again into the realm of faces; only quiet faces now—kind, quiet faces.

Weeks passed; the river cleared itself of ice, and Waters was able at last to stroll about the Fort in the sunlight. He spent many hours at the river, waiting for the first sight of the *Island Girl's* smoke, and dreaming the old dreams over. Would *she* come? Would she come, bringing the old sunrise with her—the one he had toiled so hard to build, only to have it fall into gray clouds under his touch?

One day in May, two boats pulled up at the little settlement of Fort Sully. One was the *Island Girl* from the north, and the other the *Emilie* from the south; the old *Emilie,* from which he had been cast in disgrace upon the island. Yet this time it was not the same *Emilie*—not the *Emilie* of drunkenness and bitter dreams; for it brought Mrs. Sprangs and June.

At sight of her face, Waters felt the dawn in his blood. She had come—for him—because he needed her!

And yet, a something strange seemed to have come between them. Why did she seem so distant? Why did she spoil it all by saying: "I thought you would like to see June again, because they said you were very sick and might die"?

Was that all? Oh, the poor lingering dawn that would not climb!

They embarked on the *Island Girl* for the south.

Sitting together on the deck, Waters recounted to her the adventures of the Winter; told her of Lucien Hanway, and how he had struggled to keep his promise to the dead engineer. And then, when he ceased, she sat in constrained silence—only silence.

Oh, the poor lingering dawn!

In the evening of the second day, the *Island Girl* pulled in at Old Man's Island.

"I want to go and look at the old places again," Waters said to Mrs. Sprangs. "Will you come along?" And they went in silence.

They passed through the woods, looked in at the door of the deserted cabin, gazed upon the spring, and at last climbed to the summit of the bluff and sat beneath the isolated scrub oak.

Many minutes passed in silence. At length Waters spoke in a low, strange voice.

"Mrs. Sprangs," he said, "do you see these nicks in my wooden leg? Three of 'em! Well, right here where she can hear, I want to tell you about 'em. This first one—I cut that the first time I was happy—that was when you was good to me ,when I was bad. I cut that second one when I saw that the poor little butterfly loved me. And this third one I cut for June. It's my whole life, Mrs. Sprangs—all that's good of it. But I can't stand lookin' at 'em as they are. I want to change 'em. Tell me, must I cut the first one clean away? Or must I cut away the second one? Oh, it'd hurt to do either!"

He took out his knife and nervously passed it over and over the three notches.

"Mrs. Sprangs," he said, "you seem like she was in you. I can see her lookin' out of your eyes! I've been tryin' to build me a sunrise for a long spell, and, somehow, it'd tumble back into the dark again. It never got to be noon. You see, God has put a fambly in our way. We'd have Specks and June and Lucien, 'cause I'm goin' south to get him right away.

"Tell me, which nick shall I cut away?"

"Give me the knife," she said quietly, dropping her eyes from the earnest gaze of Waters.

She took the knife, carefully deepened the first notch; then bent her head and kissed it.